I0760439

the NIGHTMARE QUEEN

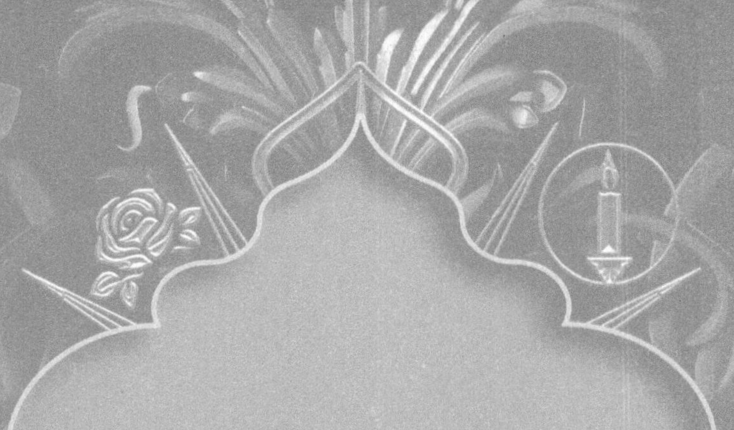

ANASTASIS BLYTHE

the NIGHTMARE QUEEN

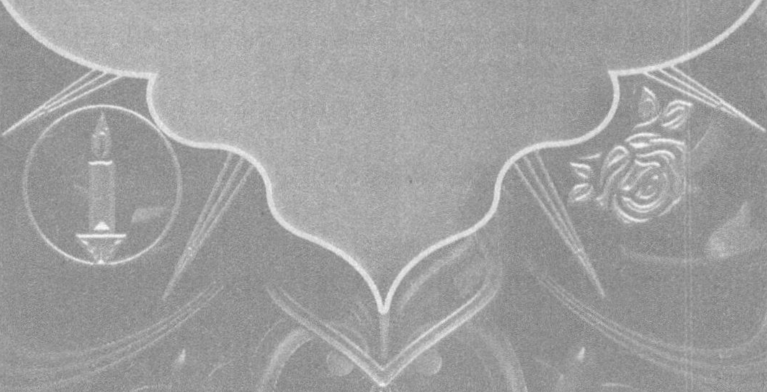

THE NIGHTMARE QUEEN

www.AnastasisBlythe.com

Hardcover ISBN: 978-1-960606-15-0

Jacket Cover design by Saint Jupiter.
Laminate Cover and Interior Design by Dragonpen Designs.

FOR HANNAH

Your friendship is one of my dearest treasures. I like to think that if our fairies Flora and Moonstone ever met, they'd be friends for life too.

CHAPTER 1

NADIRA

THE VISIONS THAT flood my awareness are made of blood.

A groan peels from my dry throat. My body throbs, as though I have been hammered to a pulp. I drag my eyelids open, only to have the bright disc of the sun—low in the sky—nearly blind me. I wince, then force myself to roll up on one elbow.

Smooth, gray stones shift beneath my weight. The rush of water and the rhythm of waves remind of where I am.

Valehaven.

The capital of Faerieland.

My hand goes to my belt for the comfort of a knife, only to find an unfamiliar hilt. One studded with gemstones. The violent images engulf me with fresh clarity.

I see Eshe's limp form in my arms. Her eyes vacant. Half her torso blackened from the searing rage of a fae's magicked blow. The Wolf's crimson mouth flashing in a wild grin as he took the Bridge, clamped this collar around my throat to cut off my magic, locked me in a cage, stole my blood, and began terrorizing Arbasa.

Then I see Kaladen, lying on his back before the High King of the Fae's throne, his throat slit and his blood like a blanket beneath him.

That gets me to my knees. Kaladen isn't dead. I would know if he was.

I wish I could offer myself the same comfort about Eshe.

But no. My heart burns from the weight of that grief.

All of it happened because I let myself be taken in by Raha's attempt on Eshe's life—not realizing it was a trap the entire time. The Wolf beat us all, because I demanded that Kaladen use his strength to revive my dead friend even though both of us knew it was useless.

My stomach twists. I want to grab the previous version of me and strangle her. *You did this because you are a fool!* Now Kaladen and all of Arbasa will suffer because I was too blind, too caught up in the past, to realize the goodness I had right in front of me.

I'm not sure I can ever forgive myself for this mistake. If Kaladen is, indeed, alive, I'm not sure he will forgive me either.

But if there is one person who can take back the Bridge, restore Arbasa, and avenge Eshe's death, it is Kaladen.

Even if he won't take me back, I will do whatever I can to save him. It will likely cost my life, but what was my life ever worth anyway? Perhaps this is why I survived all that Jabir put me through, and why I survived the peril of the Bridge—because I was meant to die saving Kaladen, so he could right the wrongs created by my shortsightedness.

I am going to get my husband back. I swear it on Eshe's death.

A little chirp from my ankles rips my attention back to the present. The sinuous green vine beside me is like a thin snake, except that instead of fangs and beady eyes, its head is a little, folded bud.

She wraps around my ankle and tries to yank me away from the water.

"Badh-o?" I croak, barely remembering she is *Badh-o* and not my nemesis vine, *Badh-a*. I forgot she came with me through the portal. "What are you—"

She lets out a high-pitched *"Squee!"* and points with one of her leaves.

I look up just as something slithers out of the water onto the shore. It is nearly as long as I am tall, thick as my leg around its middle, and covered in scales. Its strange, reptilian mouth is open, showing a row of fangs. I scramble to my feet and back away. My hand goes to the gemstone-studded hilt of the very sorry blade I pilfered from the Wolf's lackeys. My other hand closes around a nearly useless arrow. I let it go, instead mentally reaching into my gut to access the freezing core of my magic.

I find nothing. Just a locked cage I cannot open.

I grit my teeth, skittering further backward as the creature slinks out of the river onto the rocks. If it attacks me, I have little more than my own fists to protect myself.

It has no arms or legs, only a long, wispy fin for a tail. Its mouth never moves, remaining the same gaping maw as its black eyes search along the shore and pass over me. Is it . . . a sea serpent? I remember distant legends of the sort, but I always pictured them much bigger.

The creature slides over the smooth rocks, swinging its head from side to side. It does not come for me, but scoots its way toward the ocean, where it slips beneath the surface once more and disappears.

My breath eases out of my lungs. I wait a moment, then creep forward. If I intend to get to the gleaming white palace in the cliff face, I have to cross the bridge that spans the river emptying into the ocean. Badh-o stays quiet, moving silently at my feet. When I reach the bridge, I peer over the edge into the rushing water.

I suck in a gasp. "Look, Badh-o!"

As I watch, dozens of sea serpents swim through the currents into the ocean. Their scales gleam all different colors that catch the dying sunlight. They're babies, I finally realize. Migrating from their birthplace. I'm glad they aren't interested in a human snack right now. If baby sea serpents had been my end and prevented me from saving Kaladen, I would have never forgiven myself.

Once I'm across the bridge, the vine beside me tugs at my ankle once more.

"What is it?" I whisper, ducking behind the white marble of the staircase before mounting it.

She lets out a series of almost-inaudible clicks.

"I'm not the Neverseen King. I cannot understand your words," I reply.

Her leaves vibrate—an expression of frustration. Then she coils around my sandal, trying to drag it in another direction.

"You know a better way to get into the Valehaven palace?" I guess.

"Squeeeeak!"

I nod once. "Lead the way."

She takes me away from the grand staircase, toward the cliffside. Oceanwater splashes on my sirwal and the scarf I pull low over my face like a hood.

With the sun dipping on the horizon—setting, despite the early hour in my own world—the ocean glitters and foams.

It is beautiful, and I hate it. I hate all of Valehaven, no matter how blindingly lovely the white marble is against the climbing greenery or the pink sky.

We reach the far side of the palace, where the cliff is steep but there are no climbing Valehaven vines with spying eyes made of white blossoms. And certainly no stairs.

Good.

I pull my *jurbah* rope from my belt and fasten its anchor to one end. With a flick, I toss it up the cliffside, aiming for just above a nice ledge. It catches, and I yank to be sure it's firmly lodged.

I hold out my arm to Badh-o. "Need a ride?"

She *meeps* in gratitude and slides up my sleeve. Almost immediately, she draws back sharply, recoiling from the iron collar around my neck.

"I don't like the collar either," I grumble. She slides down my back and curls around my belt, holding on tightly with leaf-fingers. "Get comfortable. This might take a while." To myself, I mutter, "My forearms are going to die."

Then I wrap one end of the rope around my hand, fisting it tightly.

Time to begin the arduous climb.

My forearms are not the only things burning by the time I hoist myself up onto the ledge. It's barely big enough for me to stand on. My fingernails dig into salty dirt around the jutting edge of a rock, holding myself steady as the ocean breeze dries the sweat stinging my eyes. I dare not look down for fear my balance will pitch and I will fall to my death.

Badh-o makes a high-pitched sound from my belt.

"You are *not* allowed to complain," I tell her sternly. "I'm the one doing all the work."

Then I unhook my anchor from the rocks and, bracing myself, fling it higher again. The edge of the ledge I'm standing on crumbles, and I swallow my scream as I throw myself against the cliffside to keep from falling.

Rocks hit the ground far below. I shudder. Badh-o squeaks.

"Don't give me that." Wind whips my hair into my face, and I curse it. "You'd hardly bruise from the fall. I'd be the one to pay the price. So no complaining. I'm being careful."

With that, I will my knees to stop shaking, wrap the rope around my hand once more, and begin the second leg of the climb.

When I finally pull myself onto the top of the cliff, my entire body feels like milk pudding. I crawl away from the edge of the cliff and collapse against long, waving grass. My hand goes to my belt, checking that I didn't lose either of my nearly useless weapons or my vine.

I touch the collar around my throat. My head throbs in memory of the pain that overcomes me when I try to work magic now. Even using a drop of my own blood to break the lock of the cage I was in and open the Valehaven Portal was enough to knock me unconscious for several minutes.

Valehaven is too dangerous for me to risk being unconscious. I assume the High King has wards on this palace like Kaladen had in Arbasa—wards that would alert him when someone entered. I'm going to have to fight hard and work cleverly to ensure I don't get caught while trying to find Kaladen.

I'll either be killed on the spot or tortured for fae sport—or, I will be returned to the Wolf.

The Wolf won't be so careless with me a second time.

The vision of his teeth tearing into a human throat sears across my mind. His laughter when he cut me to fill a vial with my blood haunts my ears. I hate to think that, as long as I am in Valehaven, there is nothing standing between the Wolf and complete, senseless destruction of my people.

But I cannot defeat the Wolf. Only Kaladen can.

So I must be swift.

The first thing I must do is find my husband and discover how badly he is wounded.

I will worry about freeing him after that.

Climbing to my feet, I quickly wind up my rope and tuck it back into my belt as the vine slides down my leg to the ground. "Lead the way, Badh-o."

The sun is only a shallow semicircle on the horizon as Badh-o slides through the long grass, leading me into a thin wood that provides a barrier between the edge of the cliff and the Valehaven palace grounds. Noise hums louder with each step I take. The back of my neck prickles, making me stop and search the area for signs I've been spotted.

But it is the trees themselves, tall and rich with foliage, that seem to watch me. Bending just slightly closer, rustling their leaves as I slink beneath their canopy. A thin branch catches my hair scarf. I disentangle it before it can snag anything else. The next minute, it's like the trees suddenly pull back, keeping their branches out of my reach.

They must also hate my iron collar.

I never imagined this bane might actually be a measure of protection.

The high strains of a flute are the first sounds to greet me as I make my way through the forest. Laughter tells me I'm getting closer. I keep my senses sharp, glad for all the practice I've had stealing through darkness. My nose tingles with the buzz I've come to recognize as magic. It gets stronger the louder the music and ruckus grow. My temples begin pulsating—the warning beats of a drum. Apparently even breathing too much magic into my lungs triggers a reaction from my collar. I hope it doesn't get too much worse than this.

I freeze.

There, not twenty paces from me, is a pair of humanoid fae lying on a blanket beneath one of the trees, twisted in an amorous embrace.

I hope they are too occupied to notice me.

For twelve seconds punctuated by sloppy kisses, I don't move. Then I continue, veering widely to the left to give them berth.

Not even a minute later, I stumble across a blood-soaked body lying in the long grass. It's a female fae, with light pink hair draped over her like a gown—now stained scarlet.

I scan the area for signs of the fae's murderer and find none, then crouch beside the body.

Badh-o prods my calf angrily.

"I'm not wasting time!" I hiss at her. "I'm looking for a better knife!"

The murder weapon is not on her person, to my dismay. I straighten.

Then I hit the ground with a force nearly enough to shatter bones. The air is knocked from my lungs. I try to roll, but something heavy pins me. I twist my neck and throw up my forearm instinctively.

Badh-o shrieks wordlessly and shoots up the next tree.

A female fae, with violet eyes and long fangs, eyes me with eager interest. "Human!"

Her curiosity makes her loosen her hold. I wheel back my arm and punch her straight in the nose as hard as I can. She is quick, but still only manages a partial dodge. Two of my knuckles land—and the shock widening her irises tells me she is personally offended by those two knuckles.

Her long nails come for my face. I grab her wrist and try to force her blow to the side. Pain rakes across my temple. I grit my teeth, throwing my weight. I manage to lock us into a roll, so she isn't *always* on top of me. Spittle flies from her thick lips as she tries to pin me. But I am *done* being used for sport by fae.

I am not a prize, or a slave, or a toy.

Her fist twists into my hair and scarf. She yanks on my head at a painful angle. I knee her in the back of the thigh and send her shooting forward. I try to reach for my knife, but both my hands are far too occupied keeping her from murdering me. We roll again, grappling fiercely. My back hits a knot of tree roots in the ground. My cry transforms into a growl and my strength surges as she goes to snap my neck with her hands. I kick hard, throwing her to the side. She lunges for me. I roll backward and flip to my feet.

Suddenly, a third body is between us. Holding up one boney hand, extended from the folds of a ragged cloak. To my shock, the fae woman immediately stops upon seeing the hunched form.

"Be gone," croaks the creature to the fae.

Her violet eyes slide to mine. Her lips curl upward, and then she saunters off as though nothing just happened.

The moment we are alone, the cloaked bundle of bones creaks, "I knew you would come!" and comes toward me.

I sidestep and whip out my knife. The rubies in the hilt dig into my palm. "Do not come closer, Eye of Baltor."

The creature chuckles—a raspy, ageless sound that seems to come from its long, wart-covered nose. The nose is the only part of the Eye that is not covered in tattered brown cloak.

"I knew you would come," it wheezes. "I saw it. I killed, and I waited for you."

It comes for me once more, ignoring my blade. Relentless as I skip out of its reach. "What do you want?" I demand.

"Bargain with me, Queen Nadira of Arbasa."

Kaladen's warning to never, ever bargain with a fae rings in my mind. "No bargains."

"I know why you're here, sweet assassin. Do you know how many things I could give you that you desire? Your husband's freedom."

So he *is* alive.

"Your lost surname—"

"I know my name." *Nadira Ashrift Felladyr.* I lunge forward and catch the Eye beneath its chin, the tip of my blade poised for blood.

The Eye goes still.

"You might be immortal," I growl, stepping closer and pushing harder on the dull blade. The Eye flinches slightly. "But immortals can feel pain, no? Do not make an enemy of me, or I will cut you to ribbons."

I don't know if I could best the Eye in combat. It probably has a wealth of magic that could overpower me in a blink. But I don't care—I'm not afraid to die. Not anymore.

The Eye seems to smile beneath its hood. Then it steps back, away from me. "I saw this too. Don't you think it's amusing? To test fate and see where it bends and breaks? You will accept one of my bargains someday. I have foreseen it. I am excited to see you crack."

"I will not bargain with you," I reply.

Then I turn heel to put as much distance between me and the Eye as I can.

"You should be thankful for that collar," the Eye calls out. "The iron conceals your human scent."

I almost stop, surprised. It might be a lie, but I have no way of knowing. Badh-o joins me in my flight, and I glare down at her for abandoning me. She squeaks abashedly. I roll my eyes.

We come upon the celebration very suddenly.

I duck behind a tree. It leans away from me and my magicked collar. Badh-o wraps around the arm I have braced against the trunk as I peer out at the scene before me.

Lumiral globes hang from branches and float through the air, though their light is almost unnecessary. The moon is vast above us, hung low and fat and only five days from full.

Only five days until Lulythinar—when the Bridge portals at the Arbasa palace will break open and destroy the human world and others if they are not properly contained. Portals that even Kaladen struggles to keep sealed, and there is not a single person—human, fae, or otherwise—who knows portal magic better than him.

My fingernails curl into tree bark.

Hundreds of fae fill the greens before me. I've been here once before, when Kaladen came to present me to High King Faradir, and I thought this place was rowdy then.

It was nothing like now.

The fae dance in frenzied circles. Drink flows more abundantly than the river that empties into the sea. Color rises into my cheeks at some of the debauchery before me, but the specifics are quickly lost in the storm of merrymaking.

At least they seem too distracted to notice a single human woman creeping along the edges of their party.

I slide from one tree to the next, trying to view from another angle. There is no sign of Kaladen yet. My heart pounds relentlessly, ready to betray me to any fae who wanders too near.

From my new angle, I can see a throne in the center of the greens. A large, golden throne, in which sits a luminous presence.

High King Faradir.

By his side, laughing with his lips twisted in a sneer and drinking from a deep, silver goblet is another beautiful man I hate.

Prince Trenian.

He kidnapped me and tried to force Kaladen into a binding bargain to get me back. Fortunately, I was able to escape.

Hugging close to the shadows, my gaze narrows on the two of them. I watch their mouths move, their body language that communicates thinly veiled dislike of each other. Then Trenian twists his head to one side, his grin widening as he says something to someone. His mouth forms three distinct syllables.

Kaladen.

My heart leaps forward three beats. Grabbing Badh-o in my fist—she squeaks—I scurry to the next tree and the next. Until, at last, I circle silently around the celebration.

I am forced to keep my perimeter wide, and even then I have to carefully dodge fae who have wandered away from the celebration into the forest. One such fae lifts his nose into the air as I pass, sniffing. Then he returns to his wine.

I near the edge of the forest. If I go much further, I will find myself on the palace steps, visible for all to see. I crouch closer to the ground, peering into the greens, looking for—

The breath steals from my lungs.

Before me, in the center of the green, is a broad back, crisscrossed with scars. He is forced to kneel, his wrists bound in chains. His shoulders are pulled wide, his arms pulled taut. He is stripped to the waist, so even the slightest shift in his body is visible in his stretched muscles.

His head is not bowed. His hands fist around the chains holding him captive. Even though I can only see his back, I know exactly what fearsome expression he wears.

"Kaladen," I mouth silently.

There is blood and sweat smeared across his golden skin.

Trenian approaches him, a dark smirk playing across his mouth. He tips his goblet toward Kaladen. "Would you like a drink?"

"I think he'd rather drink your blood," laughs a female who steps into my view. Her green hair is twisted up into a towering updo over a foot tall, punctuated with delicate starfish decorations. Her dress is like watery mother-of-pearl, fluttering around her like gentle waves and catching the light of the moon and *lumiral* globes.

Yirmuth.

The High King watches from his throne, looking bored even though his sapphire eyes—so like Kaladen's—spark.

"Darling," says Yirmuth, sidling up to Kaladen and bending to bring her face close to his. He doesn't react, not even when she takes one long, talon-tipped finger and slides it from his temple to the corded muscles of his throat.

Fire simmers in my gut. I clench my fist around the hilt of my knife.

"Darling," Yirmuth purrs. "Just give them your name and then you will be free. We already know you are an Ashrift. It's one word, Kaladen. Then the High King has agreed to let you go. You will be free, and I will be your new wife. The High King even promised to make you his choicest warrior again. It'll be like the old days. You'll never have to worry about the Wolf or portals ever again."

I stop breathing, straining to hear if he replies.

"I already have a wife," he growls.

"Well, yes, but not for much longer. The Wolf will probably use her up for Lulythinar. And if not, it's easy enough to slit her throat and end the bonding between you."

Kaladen's voice is so low, so dark, yet it carries across the strains of flute and the laughter of the celebrators.

"If anyone—fae, man, or beast—harms my wife, I will loosen the bonds of Crenfyre and smile as it devours every last good thing in this world."

My feet root to the spot. Does this mean . . .? Could it be possible that he doesn't despise me for what I've done?

"There's the Kaladen I know," quips Trenian with a laugh. "Come, Yirmuth, you cannot persuade him. The Wolf will get his name from the mortal girl. Have no fear."

Kaladen's name. *Felladyr.*

Why do they want his name so badly? Kaladen once told me names in the hands of other fae gave them power like a binding bargain. But what can they want from Kaladen that they don't already have?

"I need to find a way to get close to him," I whisper to Badh-o. She nods her little budding head in vigorous agreement.

We retrace our steps. The night only grows darker, despite the brightness of the moon. Fae wandering deeper into the wood force me into further caution and a wider berth to avoid running into them. It must be two hours later by the time I finally near the celebration on the opposite side of the green. The back of High King Faradir's throne looms in my vision.

I find some dense shrubs at the base of a towering oak to hide behind. This close to the High King, and my head throbs from my iron collar. Are Kaladen's chains iron too? They must be. How else could they restrain him?

My calf cramps from all the kneeling I've done, but I don't care—because I can see Kaladen's face now.

His head is lowered, his hair falling in his face. He still grips the chains that fasten his arms wide. As though even the High King cannot snuff out his defiance.

He is wounded. Blood slides down his temple, his cheekbone, his jaw. Bruises line his torso. His knuckles are black and bloody.

He's no longer connected to the healing magic of the Bridge.

Suddenly, his head shoots up. Blazing cerulean eyes pierce mine like a blade.

I freeze.

Kaladen also goes still.

My lungs empty. The raucous sounds around us dim to a dull hum, nearly drowned out by the pulsing beat of our hearts. As if the marriage bond between us snaps back into place, pounding with renewed vigor.

His jaw flexes hard. Something flares bright and hot in his gaze. He gives his head a quick, tiny flick to the left. Telling me to slide out from behind the shrubbery.

I hesitate. I scan the area around us quickly, but no one is watching. Swallowing, I stay in a crouch, but slip sideways. Into his view.

His gaze travels over me swiftly, settling onto my wounded arm from where the Wolf cut me, the small cut on my temple from the fae I just wrestled, and the collar around my throat. His eyes narrow in contained fury. Then his attention returns to my face. He flicks his head back, telling me to return to my hiding spot.

He wanted to make sure I was alright. That was why he had me step out. Here he is, chained and bleeding, surrounded by his enemies, and his concern is first and foremost that I am not hurt.

Kaladen's focus slides away from me to the High King. Trenian seems to have disappeared, though where to I can never hope to guess.

"How long will you keep me here as a spectacle before you return me to my cell?" Kaladen growls.

My lips part. He's getting me information.

"As long as I want," Faradir replies irritably. "You have tried me all these decades. Now I will try you."

"You know you cannot fully sever my connection to the Bridge without my full name," replies Kaladen. "You know you're not going to get it. Not from me, and not from my wife. So I suggest we bargain."

"I don't like making bargains, nephew. The Wolf has promised me that he will have your name from the human woman by Lulythinar."

Kaladen's gaze flicks to mine for a fraction of a second. Something cuts through the fury, the gritted-teeth rage—*pride*. I can almost hear the thought behind that look: *"Will he, now?"*

He returns to Faradir, every last vestige of warmth gone from his face. "Even if you severed my connection to the Bridge by Lulythinar, do you truly think the Wolf can contain it? If you're wrong, you'll pay that price in blood. I am your only hope to control that unstable monster of a Bridge."

"There's a reason we set this Bridge to open into the human world and not into Valehaven. Do you take me for a fool? I am aware of the danger of Lulythinar."

"But are you aware of the danger of the Wolf?" Kaladen says, shifting to one knee and planting a foot firmly on the ground. His chains rattle together. "You have listened to his honeyed words all these years. Do you not think it suspicious that he would take the Bridge now—instead of taking it after Lulythinar, when it's most stable? What makes you so sure, Faradir, that he does not only aspire for my throne, but yours as well?"

From this angle, all I can see of the High King is a hand that grips the armrest of his throne. At Kaladen's words, that grip tightens just a hair, tendons in that beautiful hand standing out.

Trenian once accused Kaladen of forgetting the ways of Valehaven. I'm beginning to think he was utterly and completely wrong.

"The Wolf needed to attack when the Bridge was unstable," replies the High King. "Even he admitted he couldn't take you down matching strength to strength."

The severe line of Kaladen's mouth twists slightly. "A good cover, isn't it?"

Faradir gets to his feet. He lifts a goblet to his lips and waves a hand at Kaladen. "Guards, I've tired of the prisoner's chatter. Take him back to his cell. He's had enough fresh air for the night."

As a dozen seven-foot-tall guards with white, feathered wings hurry to the pillars Kaladen is chained to, he surges forward.

"Are you so afraid of me, O High King, that you only feel safe when I am surrounded by iron in the depths of your palace? Locked away in that deep cave, where you cannot hear my voice of reason?"

Then his gaze shoots to me, a meaningful gleam in his bright eyes. But I already know what I need to do.

Badh-o latches onto my wrist as I bolt out of my hiding place. Running behind the throne, toward the palace. As I do, Kaladen lets out a violent roar. His chains unfastened from the pillars, he surges toward the High King—who flinches backward in surprise.

"Restrain him!" Faradir demands. "There are twelve of you, you imbeciles!"

It's the perfect distraction to allow me to emerge from the shelter of the trees and dart up the marble steps and into the Valehaven palace.

CHAPTER 2

NADIRA

"DEPTHS OF THE palace," I mutter almost silently to myself, hurrying through the vast marble-white hallways. More guards were summoned from their posts inside to restrain Kaladen. It gives me a window of time when no one is here to catch me. They're all outside celebrating. Or trying to subdue my husband.

"Do you know where it is?" I whisper to Badh-o. She shakes her bud. "That doesn't surprise me. I bet you've rarely left the Bridge."

I don't know how to find Kaladen's prison, but I know several things about fae. One, they are very concerned about their image, given the glamours most of them wear. Two, they fear anyone who might ruin their power.

Following my course of logic, I abandon the largest, most open hallways and search for pathways that are big enough to drag a prisoner through but not so prominent that guests would run across such unsavory sights.

This logic takes me away from carved statues, waterfalls, and dazzling arrays of climbing greenery. I avoid the wide, arched hallways and veer down smaller passageways. I cut through one such hallway, only to find myself in a vast open space. *Lumiral* globes and the last faintest glows of dying sunlight turn everything a dark, golden hue. Water rushes in a stream through the center. It fills the air with the gurgle of life. Blood rushing in my ears, I backtrack.

I glance every which way. Pressure builds up inside my chest. Everything is beautiful. Everything is glorious and sparkling. How am I to find a dungeon in a place like this?

"You may think you've got me now, but I will break free and I will flay every inch of skin from your body!" Kaladen's roar echoes through the towering, shadowed ceiling of the palace. Not as far behind me as I hoped.

I curse silently, while simultaneously thanking him for warning me of his progress. Badh-o wraps tightly around my ankle and utters a near-silent peep.

Think, Nadira, think! I demand silently. No matter how fast I move, or what corridors I stick my head down, I cannot find a single door that is anything less than pure artistry. *Locked away in that deep cave,* Kaladen had said.

I'm losing what little time I have.

I cut across hallways again, and end back up in the vast corridor with the stream of water. My hands go to my hair, fisting in the strands and pulling. The water gurgles, happily oblivious to my fear. There must be something—

Deep cave.

Water.

Light scatters the fog in my mind. This water flowing through the palace has a source. A *spring.* The dungeon must be near the spring. So to find the dungeon, all I must do is follow the water upstream.

"Hang on!" I tell my vine, bursting into a sprint. Her cry of surprise is drowned out by the rushing water. This part of the palace is flat and empty, so nothing impedes me as I run silently next to the rushes and colorful grass growing out of the water.

The stream veers to the left, and I follow it. Twice, I am forced to duck into the shadows to avoid tall, winged fae guards.

"You will not imprison me for long!" Kaladen bellows—so close I nearly jump out of my skin. I gasp and run faster.

I skitter to a stop in front of a wooden, engraved door. The water disappears into stone, seeming to bubble up into nowhere. My triumph is swallowed by the din of struggle barely behind me. I try the handle.

Locked.

When I glance back, the cast of light approaches. I have only seconds—and it's too late to retrace my steps. I've got to get through this door, or else I'm dead.

"Can you pick the lock?" I hiss at Badh-o. She replies in a series of quiet squeaks—a long enough answer that it cannot be a simple yes or no. So somewhere in the middle.

I wish Eshe was here.

Whipping out the arrow from my belt, I shove the tip into the lock, trying to find the tumblers. I get two into place, but the tip isn't long enough to reach the rest. "Can you finish?" I plead desperately to Badh-o as the sound of Kaladen struggling with his army of guards comes even closer.

She shimmies up my leg and side to my wrist. She sticks out her tail, wedging it into the lock. Reaching farther than I can manage.

I glance back at the turn of the hallway just as bright light rounds the corner.

This must be the right place, I tell myself to ease the frantic pounding of my blood.

The lock clicks.

I keep my gasp firmly clenched behind my teeth, push open the door, and stick my arrow back in my belt. Then I glance at

Badh-o. "Stay outside," I hiss, setting her on the ground before shutting and locking the door. The last thing I see of her is her bud tilted in confusion.

Then I turn around.

"Sands," I curse again. It's a wide, windowless room with only one single *lumiral* globe to illuminate the dark stone flooring and thick wood beams holding up the ceiling. Various torture implements hang from the walls. Embers glow in the fireplace, different sized pokers lined up beside it.

If anyone tortures Kaladen, I *will* destroy them.

Even if it's the High King himself.

"Definitely in the right place," I whisper.

There are five doors. I don't have time to explore all of them. I pray there isn't an army of fae warriors on the other side, waiting to rip me to pieces. The globe hangs near the first door, and as I approach it, something stirs inside my gut. If my magic weren't locked so tightly, I would think it was my ice.

Then, as the sound of Kaladen's shouting reaches just outside, I grab the handle. It's locked. I don't have time to pick it, so I move to the next one. It gives.

I say a prayer and plunge inside.

The stone beneath my feet isn't carefully laid flooring, sealed together with grout, but raw and natural. And *wet*.

"The spring," I whisper. From the way my voice carries, it is a large, cavernous space. Hopefully empty. It is too dark to tell otherwise.

I hesitate. My hand finds the slick side of the cave. I blink, letting my eyes adjust to the dimness. A subtle glow carries from ahead. I blink again. Is that a pool? With something glowing at the bottom?

The utter silence seems to confirm that no one else is here.

Noise erupts from behind me, like a door slamming against its hinges. A sound like crashing iron pokers sends my spine stiffening.

I dart to the side, nearly slipping on the slick surface. I catch my balance by grabbing a wet stonelike pillar. My vision continues to adjust to the darkness, until I can make out what seems to be a high ledge big enough to support me.

Kaladen's wordless roar warns me as they reach the door.

Voices coming from behind me. Bursting shouts from Kaladen.

I grab whatever handholds I can find and pull myself up the side of the cave wall. My core clenches with effort, my arms screaming from the abuse after scaling that cliff. I slip and nearly fall straight to the bottom. I grab hold of something solid with one hand, and with the other, I yank out my rope, loop it with my teeth, and throw it. It doesn't catch. I readjust my grip before I fall and throw again. This time it catches. I haul myself up to what seems to be the ledge and ease onto my belly, my knife in my hand, as I watch the door.

I really hope the Eye was right about my collar covering my human scent. If not, I'm just sitting here asking to be slaughtered.

A guard's foot kicks the door open. "Stop fighting us!"

"I may be a prisoner," Kaladen snarls over the clang of chains, "but I will never be an easy captive."

Eight guards hold the chains binding his wrists, dragging him through the doorway. The rest of the guards take up the rear, pressing the tips of their massive spears into Kaladen's back and trying to prod him forward. Still, he resists. Every step down into the cave is a battle. Even when they splash into water, barks of pain and grunts of effort continue rising to my hiding place.

My mouth twists despite myself. I know what he's doing.

He's keeping them occupied so that if I made it in, they wouldn't notice me.

Splashes and more grunts sound as two loud *clicks* snap into place. I keep my head ducked low, so I cannot confirm, but it seems like they just fastened Kaladen's chains. The guards sigh in relief, sloshing out of the pool. One slips and curses.

Suddenly, Kaladen roars, surging forward in his chains.

The sound is so loud even I flinch, my heart leaping straight to my throat. One of the guards lets out a girlish scream.

"He's fastened," one calls. "He can't get loose. Keep your heads, men."

They hurry up the raw, wet stones to the door. It slams with a firm click. Then a thud—a thrown bolt. They've locked me in here too.

I wait, counting in my head.

One, two, three, four, five.

Not a single sound comes from below. I wait until I reach sixty before I lift my head.

Kaladen is chained with his arms above his head, waist-deep in the pool. The dim blue glow reflects off the harsh lines of his face, the streaks of blood dripping down his toned torso. His shoulder-length hair falls about his jaw and drips beads of water that land with delicate little *plops* in the pool.

He is staring right at me.

My breath catches. Did he know I was here the entire time? Does the marriage bond between us enable him to find me so easily when others had no suspicion of my presence?

I loop my rope around a rock jutting out of the cave's wall and silently lower myself down to the ground. I land in a crouch. Kaladen's eyes are fixed intently on me, watching me move, watching me wind up my rope and tuck it back into my belt, watching my progress toward him.

I kneel at the edge of the pool. His mouth curls into a smirk.

"You should be called the Wraith instead of the Mourner," he says. "I ought to rebuke you for risking so much to come after me."

Tears gather on my lower lashes. "I was so afraid you were dead."

His gaze softens. "I am hard to kill, little assassin."

I plunge into the pool. It's shockingly warm, but I don't care. Clear water swirls around my calves, my thighs, my waist as I close the distance between me and my husband. My arms go around his neck, and his chains rattle as he bends to meet me. His mouth captures mine. Ferocious and wild and tender all at once. I long for his arms around me. I long for his crushing embraces. I long to feel his bruising strength consuming me.

His arms strain against his bonds, trying to get as close to me as he can. His lips shift to my jaw, ducking his head to drag warm kisses along my neck. A sound I don't recognize emerges from deep in my throat, and I cling to him even tighter so there isn't a fragment of air between us. He nuzzles aside my scarf to kiss my ear.

"I love you," I gasp. "I love you, and I'm so sorry. When I realized you were gone, I was so afraid I wouldn't get to tell you either of those things. And Kaladen—"

He nuzzles against my temple softly. "Shh. You did nothing wrong."

The words come out in a broken sob. "I shouldn't have asked you to heal Eshe. I knew you couldn't bring her back, but I just couldn't accept her loss, and now—"

"Hush, assassin." He says it like one might say *darling* or *beloved*. "It wasn't your fault. I am sorry I couldn't make it in time to save her."

"It wasn't you. It was the Wolf. It's his fault she died." The tears come in earnest now as I hold tight to him, drinking in his strength. "I will see his death. We will find a way to get you out of here. And then we will kill him."

"We will, indeed," he murmurs.

Breath shudders in and out of my lungs, mingling with the *thump, thump* of his heartbeat.

"I'm afraid to go back," I whisper quietly. "I'm afraid to kill the Wolf and to reclaim the Bridge. I'm afraid that if we survive Lulythinar and go back to *normal life*—whatever that is—that I will only realize just how empty it is without Eshe. Sometimes I know I'm going to be alright, that no matter how heavy the burden of grief may get, I will survive it. But other times, I'm not so sure. What if the grief never goes away? What if it becomes my new captor? What if this loss finds victory over me?"

Kaladen tilts his head, pressing his forehead against mine. "Your grief will never fully go away, but that doesn't mean it will have victory over you. You will cry for your friend a thousand times, and each one is sacred."

I'm shaking against him. "Sometimes I still think it's all a dream. That I will go back to Arbasa and find her waiting for me. I know when I return—*if* I return—I will look for her." Even one glimpse of her sun-bleached hair would make me so joyous I could shout. "I will try to find her voice in the wind. I will find remnants of her. Her clothes, the dresses you had made for her that she loved so much. I just don't know how I will believe that she's gone."

"You loved her, and you always will." He presses a gentle kiss to my hairline. "Some days you will think of her and cry, and other days you will think of her and smile."

I look up at him until tears make him blurry. A flood of compassion and empathy fills my core where I used to feel my ice magic. "I'm so sorry that you lost Liliana. I'm so sorry for the grief you carried all these years."

He smiles down at me—*smiles*, while he's chained in a cave dungeon in the bowels of Valehaven palace—and only bends to brush his nose against mine. Then he kisses me deeply. Warm and slow and breathtaking. "We are going to get through this, Nadira. *All* of this. Valehaven, the Wolf, Lulythinar, Eshe's loss. We will get through it."

It is an impossible vow. He cannot promise such things to me. We both know it. I search his eyes, and I find the truth there. Hiding in the depths of his cerulean gaze.

We won't survive this. He does not believe we will. He only says so to ease my fears.

But whether it is the High King, the Wolf, or the Bridge that destroys us remains to be seen.

"We will," I say firmly, wiping my cheeks with my damp sleeve and pretending the cold certainty of my own death did not just settle into my gut. Pretending I did not read the truth behind his lie. "And the first step is getting you out of this dungeon."

Kaladen nods his head toward my throat, his gaze darkening, his voice dropping in pitch. "You need to get that collar off. The Wolf did that to you, didn't he?"

I cut him off before he can mutter some violent threat of retribution. "How am I supposed to get it off? I assumed you could get it off once you were free."

"I can." He rotates his wrists in his chains, flexing his fingers. "It's a polluting spell—you'll need something with enough magical strength and prowess to absorb that pollution. Like the High King or Prince Trenian. Or the Wolf, since he cast it. I could bargain with Trenian, perhaps, to—" His head whips to the door. "Someone is coming! Hide! No—don't get out of the pool. You'll leave wet footsteps. Hide there."

He gestures sharply with his head, pointing to the edge of the pool to the right, where it's deeper. "Swim underneath. There's an air pocket where you can breathe. Hurry!"

I don't ask any of the questions I want to—like how in the Great Desert he knows about the air pocket—and dive under the water. I swim as Kaladen taught me, though I move faster when I get my feet on the rocky bottom and push myself forward. The water moves around me, warm and silky, until I duck under the stone. I use my hands to run along the underside of the overhang until I find the air pocket Kaladen described.

It's far smaller than I expect. I arch my neck back and only have enough room to get my mouth and nose and one ear out of the water. Tight fire rises in my chest, urging me to gasp for air and get out of this claustrophobic space. But I force my breath to even, my lungs to loosen. I stay where I am.

Kaladen begins struggling and splashing water. To hide any remnants of me. He stops just before the door opens very softly. No loud guard footsteps stomp down the slippery stones. Instead, I'd guess a phantom had opened the door.

"Yirmuth," Kaladen hums in a low snarl. "To what do I owe the displeasure of this visit?"

"I come bearing terrible news," she replies in that liquid voice of hers. A very subtle shift in the water makes me strain my one ear. She has stepped into the water and approaches my husband.

I am going to murder every single one of these Valehaven fae.

"Tell me your news from the shore," Kaladen growls. "Or don't tell me at all. I've had enough terrible news as of late."

She tsks quietly, and I can almost imagine her trailing her finger down the side of his face again. I force myself not to seethe, because I need more air to seethe, and this air pocket is already starting to taste stale.

"It's about your human wife." Her pout is audible.

I stiffen. Kaladen makes no reply.

"The Wolf caught her. It's a tragedy those who were there at the Bridge have been whispering of. How she nearly evaded him, but how he was too skilled for her. He made her his prisoner. He put her in a cage. *Your wife*, Kaladen—he locked her in a cage. He sliced her open for her blood. They are saying the Wolf declared he intended to take her to his bed and torture her to get your name. She is in tremendous danger. You must spare her. I've heard humans are fragile little things."

I want to laugh and bare my teeth at this fae. I'd like to show her just how *fragile* I am. I'd like to show her just how much of the Wolf's prisoner I am.

My mouth twists at the thought of Kaladen's reaction, even though I'm sure he hides his thoughts well.

"How can I spare her?" Kaladen asks at last. "I am Faradir's prisoner. Chained here in his dungeon. Thanks, in part, to your aid of the Wolf."

The water swishes, as if she comes even closer to him. "Give me your name, Kaladen. If you do, I shall personally go to the Bridge and rescue her from the clutches of the Wolf. You won't have to endure more of the High King's torture. Your human wife will be spared a cruel, witless demise. Bargain with me."

Torture? I gulp a large lungful of air and end up taking a bit of water into my mouth. It should have been obvious, and yet I'd hoped that his lack of significant wounds indicated that he had been spared so far.

Maybe we *should* give them Kaladen's name. It'll sever his connection to the Bridge, and he will be free of that burden forever. He and I could run away together. I would never have to go back to the Arbasa palace and see all the things that remind me of Eshe. I could start over, and it would be like none of this had ever happened.

Then several faces flash before my eyes. Zara, the orphan girl, and Abbi, the big-eared boy who'd tried to weave Kaladen's hair into a basket. Tariq, the faithful city guard who nearly gave his life to save Eshe's. I think of the faces of the people who had accepted me as their queen. The foreign dignitaries who I brokered trade deals with.

My *home*.

My *people*.

I cannot abandon them. Not to the Wolf. Not to destruction during Lulythinar. Not to fall into neglect and anarchy.

No. I won't allow it. Just like I won't allow the High King to destroy my husband.

I hear Kaladen's voice from the Valehaven celebration: *"I am your only hope to control that unstable monster of a Bridge."*

And then the High King's calloused reply: *"There's a reason we set this Bridge to open into the human world and not into Valehaven."*

These fae may think of my people, my *world* as disposable.

But we are not so *fragile* as they believe.

"Yirmuth," Kaladen says, in a tone of almost exasperated exhaustion, "you and I both know our goals will never align. Why do you plague me with bargains as though you think I am foolish enough to take them?"

Her cadence turns angry, losing its veneer of sweetness. "You will destroy yourself. You will destroy your human wife. You will destroy the Bridge. You will destroy *me*. All for what?"

"Go marry Trenian, if you want power. Go marry the Wolf. Stop pretending to care about me, the Bridge, or my wife."

"Kaladen, really! How can you be so dense? I know you care about that human girl. So let me help you. Let me help her."

“Enough!” Kaladen roars loud enough the water surges, nearly cutting off my air hole completely. “Leave me this instant!”

It’s so startling, so frightening, that I’m not surprised when the water sloshes and the careless sounds of Yirmuth’s wet footsteps scurry up the path. When she’s safely at the door, she shrieks back at him: “You will regret not taking my help when you watch me tear out the throat of that girl you claim to care about!”

“I will never regret refusing a snake like you!” Kaladen roars, hurling the words like javelins.

They have their desired effect: the door slams shut.

CHAPTER 3

NADIRA

"YOU CAN COME out," Kaladen says after several long minutes of silence.

I draw in a deep breath, close my eyes, and duck under the water. The cave feels darker when I come up again and wipe the water from my eyes. I sputter for a second, letting the last residual tightness from my hiding spot unwind from my neck.

Then I find Kaladen's gaze heavy on me. He looks at me with a sort of grimness that is only emphasized by the chains he hangs from.

"They've been torturing you?" I whisper.

Steel enters his gaze. "Nothing I cannot handle."

If this blasted collar didn't cut off my magic, a flood of ice would have filled my belly. "Kaladen—"

"Please," he breathes. "I do not know how much time we have left. We need to spend it discussing other things. You need to get out of here without being caught. I *refuse* to let them get their hands on you. If they have you, they have me."

"Kaladen," I protest. "You know you cannot—"

"No, Nadira," he shoots back. His eyes blaze, twin bursts of fire so strong they could set the entire world ablaze. "The second you are taken captive, I will give them my name to spare you."

The air steals from my lungs. He glares at me, as though daring me to argue with him.

A small fissure in my heart heals. I look away. The rocks at the bottom of the pool shift beneath my weight. "Why do they want your name so badly? I know they can use it to break the connection between you and the Bridge, but why do they care?"

"They cannot have rogue Neverseen Kings. Someone without the duty of the Bridge but the ability to wield it is the High King's greatest threat."

I tilt my head to one side. "Why doesn't the High King just . . . kill you?"

"He cannot. It would break a law of Faerie for him to cut off an integrated part of his own magic. The Throne of Faerie cannot go against itself."

I nod once. "So the only way to neutralize the threat of your existence is to harness your name to break the connection between you and the Bridge."

His mouth quirks slightly. "There's my clever pupil. Now listen. I don't know how long we have until the Wolf lets a portal at the Bridge open into Risya—intentionally or otherwise. I'll know when it happens. I'm most worried about Crenfyre. The Wolf doesn't have the means to seal it. If he cannot seal it, it can devour the entire human world before it moves on to the rest of the portals."

A loud bang from beyond the dungeon door makes me flinch. We both go quiet, listening. His ears are sharper than mine, so when he shakes his head and says, "No one is coming," I ask the question I've been wondering for ages.

"How do you seal Crenfyre?" When he doesn't answer right away, I add, "We cannot enter it to seal it the normal way—though I don't understand how we cannot enter it in the dream realm like the others. So . . . how?"

He sighs. "The dream realm only protects you if the portal doesn't open into the dream realm. Crenfyre always opens into both dimensions—and probably others, if they exist. To seal it, I have used the method of the previous Neverseen King. Ages ago, someone put over a dozen humans under the influence of faerie fruit for the sole purpose of entering Crenfyre and stealing mist from near its anchor. No one knows how they did it exactly, except that there was enough time between Crenfyre pollution and death that each human could take the bottled mist and pass it to the next person, and so on, until they were all dead, and we had enough bottled mist to seal the portal."

My mind trips over itself, guessing what his next words are even before he speaks them.

"I always kept a small vial of that mist on my belt, so I could reseal Crenfyre as quickly as possible. When I woke after I lost consciousness at the Bridge, I was chained here in this dungeon—only broken shards left on my belt of the vial I carried."

"So there's no way to seal Crenfyre," I say, trying to keep my voice from turning shrill. I remember what that lethal mist did to the Arbasa palace, to two of the other women competing for Kaladen's hand—Mahja and Gaya.

"There's another vial."

I lift my head. Behind him, along the wall of the cavern, the eerie green light seems to pulse slightly. "What?"

"I split the mist between two vials, in case of a situation like this. The other one is in the rainforest portal, in the treehouse. With the souls of the portals we collected."

At once, I remember the glowing rainbow auras of those egg-shaped portal souls, all nested neatly in rows in an otherwise nondescript, regular cabinet. "So . . . should I go back to Arbasa and give this vial to the Wolf?"

Kaladen gives a humorless snort. "I suppose that would be one option." His attention shifts back to me, eyeing my face and torso up and down before saying, "You need to rest. You look like you haven't slept in days."

"Pretty close," I admit. "But I can't sleep. Not with—"

He flicks his eyes up to the narrow ledge where I hid earlier. "Sleep up there. I'll wake you if anyone comes."

"No, no, there's too much we need to discuss. How to get my collar off. How to get you free. What to do about Crenfyre—"

His leg swings in the water, coming to wrap around the backs of my knees, pulling me against his chest in the only way he can. I catch myself with my hands against him, and when I look up, he strains against his chains to kiss me.

In that moment, I forget things such as curses and portals and High Kings. My existence is only the warmth of his lips, his solid frame against mine, and the fact that neither of us are broken just yet.

"Please rest," he murmurs, running his lips over my nose. "The High King will not summon me for hours yet. We have time."

I sigh. "Fine."

He smiles. I stand on my tiptoes to kiss the corner of that smile. Then I trudge out of the pool, my clothes soaked and clinging. Now that the prospect of sleep is at hand, my limbs decide they are made of butter, and it's a feat of extra care to climb the side of the cave to the ledge where I have enough room to lie down.

The last thing I see is Kaladen flipping between watching me and the door.

It feels like I wake only seconds later—to the sound of Kaladen's roughened, "*Nadira*, wake *up*!"

I shoot upright. Nothing has changed in my surroundings of a cave lined with glowworms, and the pool Kaladen stands in. Nothing, except his face wreathed in panic.

"They're coming!" he hisses. "And . . . and . . ." He bites back the words as if he isn't sure he should tell me whatever he was starting to say.

"And what?" I hiss back, making sure I'm tucked out of sight, and pulling my knife from my belt. "What else is wrong? Have they come to torture you?"

"The goblin portal opened almost an hour ago," he says, and by now I can hear the footsteps of the guards coming toward the door. "It hasn't been sealed."

I swallow my horror just as Kaladen whips his attention away from me. Guards throw open the door and come marching into the small space. There are more of them this time. They approach cautiously.

"We can keep this civil," says one of the guards, stepping closer to Kaladen.

Hair falls into Kaladen's eyes as he smirks.

The moment they unfasten the chains he hangs from, he lunges. Several of the guards curse. Kaladen manages to land a fierce kick and slings his shackles like a whip. It lands with a sickening *crack* as a guard cries out in pain. Then it's all twenty guards piled on top of Kaladen, who roars and thrashes as they grab his chains and regain control of him.

His grunt of pain makes me squeeze my eyes shut. *He can handle this,* I tell myself, wishing I could strangle him for sacrificing himself like this to ensure the guards don't notice me.

There's so much shouting, so much grunting, punctuated only by splashes and the clang of shackles. Then, at last, they succeed in dragging Kaladen out of the pool and up the wet steps toward the door.

The High King is going to torture him.

I want to vomit.

Kaladen lets himself be taken quickly out of the chamber. The door thuds behind him, leaving me in echoing dimness. I press my forehead against stone, squeezing my eyes shut.

He can handle himself. Pain and torture and destruction—he can take it. As much as I want to rescue him from this, there is something else I need to do first.

I wait long enough for Kaladen and his guards to be long gone. Then I lower myself from the ledge. The door is locked, but that doesn't slow me down. Every guard in the vicinity was called to restrain Kaladen, so no one stops me as I slip back into the dark room. I creep to the door and make a soft *squee*, mimicking Badh-o's favorite noise. Only a moment later, she replies. Telling me the coast is clear.

I slip through the large door into the dawn light of the Valehaven palace.

"Pretend you're an assassin plotting murder," I whisper to Badh-o as she slides up to my belt, rubbing a leaf along my arm as though she missed me. "We've got a plan to make. And someone to corner."

"Squee!" she replies.

CHAPTER 4

KALADEN

I DON'T MAKE it easy for them to chain me to that table.

"It's truly pointless to struggle," drawls Trenian from across the room. He leans against the wall, ankles crossed, buffing his fingernails.

Not pointless. No effort expended, no wound incurred, no shame suffered is pointless when my wife's life is on the line.

I wish Faradir hadn't called me so soon. I wish Nadira and I hadn't been separated so suddenly, before we could form a plan. The open goblin portal tugs relentlessly at my mind. I try to dismiss it, but every second it rips my attention back to it. Back to the danger Arbasa is in at this very moment. And knowing goblins, they won't settle for just terrorizing the human world. They will eat away at all the other portals in the palace.

The High King comes to my side, light on his feet and so radiantly golden in this dimly lit room with its low ceiling and shelves of poison lining the walls. He looks down his elegant nose to where I lie, strapped down by chains of iron that burn into my skin.

I glare back at him.

"All we want is your name," says Faradir without a flicker of emotion on his face.

"*We?*" laughs Trenian. "Speak for yourself, Father. I'd prefer you didn't bring me into your nasty little torture sessions. They do awful things for my complexion."

Faradir's mask is gone in a second. He whirls like a snake to strike at the prince. "Not another word out of your mouth or so help me I will put *you* on this table!"

Trenian grins and mimes sealing his lips shut.

But the moment the High King turns back to me, he's speaking again. "Kaladen, do me a favor and just give my father your name so I can go back to my wine and my games. These sessions are endlessly boring for me."

Faradir turns and blasts a bolt of white-hot magic. It smashes into the wall above Trenian's head and rains plaster on the floor. Trenian, not flinching even slightly, only lifts his eyes from his fingernails. "Does that mean I can go?"

The longer these chains wrap around me, the deeper the burn. I don't care about the drama between the two of them, but in this moment, I might hate them both more than they hate each other.

"Cheers, Kaladen!" cries Trenian, saluting me as he saunters out of the room with a kick of his booted heel against the doorframe.

When the door shuts behind him, the room goes so deathly quiet, the only sounds in my ears are the gentle swish of the High King's robes and the fluttering of dry pages spread across a desk. And the rattle of my chains when I breathe.

Faradir has pulled himself back to his composure and regards me with glittering cobalt eyes. Eyes that match my own.

"Would your sister be glad to see us like this?" I say, my mouth twisting slightly as I fortify myself for what is about to come. I cannot remember the last time I spoke of my mother, nor did I think I would mention her now in front of the High King. It's the closest I'll ever come to preying on any scraps of his compassion. Because we both know he doesn't have any.

He doesn't react to my statement. Only sniffs delicately and places his cool hands on my bare abdomen. I resist the urge to contract my core and brace hard.

"I'm sure she would understand the circumstances," he replies.

Then my senses flare sharply.

The scent of dried parchment and ink—normally pleasant—become so overpowering I nearly choke. The scent mingles with sulfur and rotten egg from the bottled poisons. The High King's own smell, of biting, tangy magic and suffocating perfume wash over me like a tidal wave.

My skin explodes in sensitivity. The iron chains digging into my flesh feel like dozens of brands, sinking all the way through my body to the painfully cold table beneath me. Every bead of sweat becomes agony, like the pass of air over severely burned flesh. Each hair follicle on my body turns to overwhelming pain.

The beat of my own heart drives a head-pounding rhythm. Every sound in the room, from my breathing to Faradir's, to the slightest crush of his robes and the flicker of paper from the desk, to the shift of dust on the top shelves becomes so loud, so pulsating, it drowns out all thought. I fight to keep my mouth closed, to not allow a single sound of pain to escape my lips and add to the eardrum-splitting cacophony around me, but even the rattle of my teeth is unbearable.

My blood turns to lava inside my veins, flooding every inch of my body with heat so searing it becomes like ice. Even my mouth becomes drowned with taste—copper, from biting down on my tongue too hard—so augmented it is unbearable.

There is no room for thought as the terrorizing of my senses turns to full-bodied torment. Every movement only magnifies the pain. When a tight grunt finally escapes me, it is like an explosion to my ears.

So I exist in the torture and bear it with one singular thought:
They don't have Nadira. They don't have Nadira.
They will not get her.
They will not hurt her.
And I will *never* give him my name.

CHAPTER 5

NADIRA

MY FEET BRACE on either side of the wall, my hands plastered against the beam above the hallway's opening. I paste myself against the ceiling's shadows, waiting. Watching. Counting in my head.

Then, finally, he comes.

I hold my breath as he walks beneath me. He whistles like he hasn't a care in the world, his hands in his pockets, a spring in his step.

I drop to the ground silently. My hand fists around the hilt of my knife. I'm glad for my height, because if I were any shorter, this would be impossible.

I slide my knife against Trenian's throat. His whistle stutters to a stop as he goes still. My voice is low and dark, like a slithering snake's. "Do exactly what I say or you'll never smile again."

He smiles, as though to prove me wrong. "Do my ears deceive me, or is that the voice of Queen Nadira—come all the way from the human lands? You know, Kaladen will have a heart attack if he finds out you're here."

I press the blade tighter against his throat. "Walk."

He doesn't move. "What if I don't want to?"

My gaze shoots to his hands, resting at his side. I've seen the magic bolts he can summon in a split second. *Like the bolt that killed Eshe.* Resolve hardens my voice as I bring my mouth close to the prince's ear. "Then you will find out exactly how good I am with a knife."

He chuckles, but he walks. I guide him the short distance to his own quarters.

"You *are* good," he says when we reach his door. "Last time I said I wouldn't make the mistake of underestimating you again, but I'm afraid you continue to surprise me. Do you have the entire layout of this palace in that pretty head of yours?"

I narrow my eyes and growl, "Open the door and dismiss your servants except the youngest, who I want available. And no tricks. I know you fae move fast, but all I need is a fraction of a second."

"Noted, Queen Nadira," he replies as he steps over the threshold into his quarters. "Edvear! Take the staff elsewhere. I have an assassin threatening my life if you stay. But she bids me keep my youngest staff member, so please send in Mofla."

"I beg your pardon—Master!" cries a voice from the dining room.

"At once, my excellent steward."

I don't get a good look at the steward, but I hear the clomp of hooves as he leaves and immediately my mind returns to Eldreth of the Star City. I kick the door shut behind me and prod Trenian forward into his reception room. Among the comfortable couches and end tables are a pair of dark wood, vine-threaded chairs. I force him to sit in one.

Badh-o, who has been hiding in the ankle of my sirwal, slips free and takes my *jurbah* rope from my belt. I keep my knife against the prince's jugular, sparing a thought for how much I long for Separator as Badh-o makes quick work of binding the prince's hands and ankles to the chair.

Trenian flexes his hands, noting the bindings. They're not the best knots, but they will do exactly what I need them to do: keep him from any fast moves.

"Impressive work," says the prince, without even a hint of fear in his voice. He nods at the rope, the vine that slinks to my belt, my knife. "Though I would have thought you'd have a better knife than that."

"The quality of my knife only affects how painful death is for you," I reply, dancing the tip over his throat as he once did to me.

He looks at me—really looks at me, with one eyebrow cocked and golden-flecked eyes running over my face. His face melts into a grin. "I think I like you. Now that you have me trussed up like a damsel in distress, what can I do for you?"

"I need information."

"I'll bargain with you for anything you want to know."

I smirk and press my blade harder against his neck.

"Or," he says, as a drop of bright blue blood slides and pools in the hollow between his collarbones, "I will give you what you want to know in exchange for you not killing me."

"Such a smart prince," I say.

He lifts both eyebrows. "Make that face more often, and you might make it into my nightmares."

Just then, a small girl with long pointy ears and white hair down to her knees enters the room and bows herself low to the ground. Her voice doesn't shake. "You summoned me, master."

"Yes, thank you, Mofla," says Trenian, as though he isn't held at knife point or tied to his own chair. "Queen Nadira has use of you."

"Just make yourself comfortable, where I can see you," I say, gesturing to one of the couches nearby. She quickly does as she's told and does not look upon her master's situation as if it is at all unusual.

The gears seem to be turning in Trenian's mind as he glances between me and his servant, but there is no spark of understanding in his irises until I begin speaking again.

"Where is the High King torturing Kaladen?"

"Oh!" cries Trenian with a laugh. "How did I not see it immediately? You are too clever!"

I step closer, angling my knife so it's painful. "Answer the question."

"She's your lie detector. Mountains of Ildrid, I *do* like you and all your surprises!"

"Trenian."

"They're in my father's poison chamber. He likes doing various diabolical things up there. I think the poisons inspire him."

"Tell me where it is."

I prod him until his answer is sufficient for my mental map to have a clear designation for the room. Then I move on. "How long will they be there?"

"Some hours, likely."

"Give me your best estimate. Three hours? Eight? Seventy-two?"

"Four."

"Where will he be taken then?"

"Back to his prison cell."

The way he says it makes my scalp prickle. I need to word my questions more carefully. "Where will he be taken *immediately* after the High King is finished torturing him?"

Trenian smirks. This is all a game to him, isn't it? "To the throne room. Faradir likes to show off his captive enemies at their weakest."

I grit my teeth. "And immediately after that?"

"He will be taken to Yirmuth's rooms."

"What?" I demand, my anger rising in a sharp spike. "Why?"

He shrugs. "To see if kindness is his weakness."

"Yirmuth isn't kind."

"From your vantage point, perhaps. She's not too terrible as far as fae go. She seems to have some genuine care for my cousin, which is unusual."

"He doesn't think so."

"No, he doesn't. But I know her better than he does. Kaladen has made his preference for humans over fae very clear, so it doesn't surprise me that he would misread her."

Enough talk of Yirmuth. I lift my chin slightly. "And where do they take him immediately after that?"

"Back to his cell—or out to the palace greens, if night has fallen by then."

"And how long is he usually kept on the palace greens at night?"

"It depends on my father's mood."

I glance at the girl, who has not made a single sound. She just sits cross-legged on the nearby couch with large black eyes studying the two of us. I return to my questions. "Are you going to tell the High King I'm here?"

"No."

The girl bursts into a fit of furious coughing. *A lie.*

"My apologies, dearie," says Trenian with a slightly soured grin toward the girl.

I drag my knife down the sinews of his throat. "Don't make me ask again."

"Well, you see, I know you're going to give me some vicious threat if I say I'm going to tell the High King you're here. I don't *intend* to tell him you're here—unless he makes me. Which is very possible. I'm not going to die for your secrets."

I let my glare talk for me.

He nods once. "I see you wish for me to die for your secrets. Listen, may I be frank with you, O one who wields a knife against me?"

My hesitancy must be written across my face, because he chuckles. Then he surges forward, heedless of the way my blade cuts into him before I pull it back to avoid *actually* killing him. It catches me even more off-guard when the prince's tone isn't at all cavalier, but dark and urgent.

"You stand on *very* precarious ground. If you're caught here in Valehaven, it will spell the end for Kaladen."

I force him back into the chair, fury burning like a furnace in my chest as I press my blade harder against him. "Isn't that what you want, O prince who speaks lies? You helped orchestrate my husband's downfall."

Trenian's teeth flash. "I have done *nothing* of my own volition to weaken Kaladen's position as the Neverseen King."

I wait for the girl to start coughing, but she remains silent. He's not lying.

"I want Kaladen to be the Neverseen King," he says, and the girl gives no reaction again.

My lips pull back in a snarl. "Then why did you kidnap me? Why did you attempt to bind him to your will?"

"Because your life isn't the only one at stake here. Mine also hangs in a precarious balance. My father hates me—which, the feeling is mutual—and he has set his heart on my death. I need collateral. I need someone on my side who has power that can stand against the High King."

"Then why not just ask Kaladen?" I demand. "Why make an enemy out of him by endangering me?"

"In a world as treasonous as Valehaven, you need more than goodwill to secure something. You need something binding, and few fae will allow the risk of a bargain unless something they want is at stake."

"Every time I come to Valehaven, I think worse of the fae," I mutter.

Trenian laughs at that, the spark returning to his eye. "You'd fit in well here."

"That is not a compliment."

"Sure it is." His gaze drops to my collar. "That's a nasty piece of spellwork you've got around your neck. Someone trying to cut off your claws? A pity."

"I heard you could get it off."

He chews on his lip, studying the collar. "I can, yes."

"Then do it."

He winces. "I'm afraid that's not how this works."

I wait for him to explain, blowing a hair out of my face, even though I know exactly what he will say.

"We can make a bargain in which you convince Kaladen to offer me his favor in exchange for me removing your collar."

"Or," I say, "you could consider removing my collar as an investment in your future collateral. You help me now, which will help Kaladen regain his throne, which will put him in a position where he could help you."

Still, he shakes his head. "It's bargains, darling. We work in bargains, or we don't work at all. I told you: we're an untrusting lot here in Valehaven."

I come closer to him, pressing the blade so hard into his flesh it bleeds. "Or perhaps you help me, and I don't kill you."

He smiles up at me at that—a roguish, smirking twist of his lips, as if he knows a dozen secrets I don't. I expect him to slap some retort back in my face, something about how he could easily escape my bonds if he tried. But he doesn't. He sits there in silence.

Calling my bluff.

Of course I'm not going to kill him. He's the closest thing I have to an ally. We both want Kaladen back on his throne. We both want the destruction of the Wolf and the High King. Despite how much I might despise the prince, he might be the only person within a ten-mile radius that has interests aligning with mine.

I step back, withdrawing my knife.

"What?" asks Trenian, chuckling. "You aren't going to bargain with me?"

I snap my fingers, and Badh-o hurries to undo his bonds. She looks so odd, like a centipede with all her little stems and leaves busy unwinding her knots at once. "Good girl," I say to her once she's done and slides back to my ankle. I wrap my rope around my fist before fastening it to my belt.

Trenian stays seated, rubbing his wrists, watching Badh-o and then me in turns. "Kaladen told you not to bargain with us, didn't he?"

"Wasn't he right to?" I ask by way of reply.

He opens his mouth, then glances at the girl sitting silently and watching us. His gaze slides back to me, amusement twisting his lips. "Maybe he hasn't forgotten the ways of Valehaven."

"You didn't answer that question."

He cracks his knuckles, then springs to his feet. "And since you don't have a knife to my throat anymore, I don't have to. Come. Would you like some refreshments while you're here? My cooks are very good at preparing human food."

I intend to decline, but my stomach takes that moment to remind me with a violent wave of hunger that I haven't eaten in . . . I don't even know how long. "Is it poisoned?"

Trenian throws back his head and laughs. "I am not going to poison you. It is a valid concern, but I think we both understand that we are not enemies."

"At this point."

"At this point," he agrees.

The girl on the couch doesn't make a sound, so I count Trenian's words as truthful and satiate my gnawing hunger on the bountiful spread his steward brings out. When I'm finished and preparing to leave, Trenian says, "I could give you directions to Yirmuth's room."

My gaze shoots to his. He looks at me with a veil of innocence, but his eyes glitter a little too brightly. "I thought you said you weren't going to help me unless I bargained with you."

He checks his fingernails, leaning against the wall of his dining room as I head toward the door of his quarters. "I'm not helping. I'm *facilitating*. Possibly your own death, if you're not careful around Yirmuth. But as I can tell that you intend to invade Kaladen's itinerary for the day, my honest opinion is that you would have the highest chance of success against Yirmuth."

His young servant has remained with us throughout the remainder of our conversation, despite the prince having every opportunity to dismiss her. He has a look about him that says he's got some trick up his sleeve, but at this point, I'm not sure what other option I have but to trust him.

"Then tell me," I say.

After discussing the plan, he follows me outside his quarters as I leave. He looks as though he has something to say. I pause. "What is it?"

"His chains. You might have already gathered this, but you can release him from those chains with a drop of your blood on each lock."

I stare at him. It's that simple? So I could have freed him earlier if I had put the pieces together? I curse myself for not reasoning that out. Of course, if my blood unlocked doors, it would also unlock chains. Why didn't I realize this? "Thank you."

"Don't thank me," he says with a grin that is both dazzling and rueful. "Not yet, at least."

CHAPTER 6

NADIRA

MY FIRST TASK is to locate Yirmuth, which Trenian *facilitates*. She's in the throne room, evidently waiting for the High King to finish Kaladen's torture and drag him there. I barely keep my blood from boiling over every time I think of what my husband might be enduring. I cannot lose my head—not even for a moment.

My second task, after confirming that Yirmuth isn't in her chambers, is breaking in.

It'll just be like old times, I tell myself, my mind returning to all those assassination jobs I hated so much. The daylight does me no favors, forcing me to hunker down into hiding places anytime someone comes by as I make my way to the part of the palace where Yirmuth's quarters reside.

Per Trenian's information, this is one of the guest wings, so all the doors are polished oak and otherwise nondescript. He warned me not to try a window as that would alert the wards she would have erected. So I wait until the hallway is empty, and then approach the single door to Yirmuth's domain.

As expected, it is locked, though not with a usual means. There is no keyhole in sight.

If I use my blood to unlock this door, the force from my collar will knock me unconscious. I cannot risk being so vulnerable—especially now that my safety affects more than my own life.

"Badh-o," I whisper.

Her body is wrapped around my ankle, and at my voice, she tilts one flower bud up to me, her leaves floating silently in the air. "Brrp!"

"If I give you my blood, can you use it to unlock the door?"

"Grrrraw!"

I take that to be a *maybe*, which is better than a *no*. I rake my finger over my scabbed thumb and smear the stinging wound across her proffered leaf. She unwinds from my ankle, slides across the floor to the door, and rises like a snake before its charmer to press the leaf against the lock.

It clicks.

I grin despite myself. "Excellent job. Now see if you can open the door for me so Yirmuth doesn't smell my humanity when she comes."

Badh-o wraps around the handle and pulls. She pulls so hard that a little, *"Squeak!"* emits from her blossom.

"It's fine," I say, covering my hand with my scarf—as if that will help—and opening the door. Maybe my iron collar will protect my scent.

The chamber before me is open and clean. A vast window overlooks the sea, salty air blowing past ribbons of seafoam silk that function as gauzy curtains. The window Trenian warned me away from. Pillars of coral rise in decoration throughout the room. Enormous shells are arranged about the room, their edges carved in intricate waves, soft kelp-woven cushions placed on their shiny abalone surfaces. *Chairs*, my brain processes distantly as I scan the room for sign of occupancy.

It is empty, so far as eyes can tell. Badh-o and I split up. She takes one hallway and disappears, while I take the opposite. I find two more doors. One is a bedroom, but I hardly recognize it as such, for instead of a bed, there is a shallow stone basin framed in bleached driftwood and full of waving seaweed, sand, and even swimming multicolored fish. The other room is a bathing chamber, more normal as far as those go.

Both rooms are completely empty.

I return to the main room and inspect the window. I dare not stick my head out of it for fear of activating any wards, but from what I can tell, it is a sheer drop straight to the ocean below. If I were to attempt an escape, I'd have to anchor my rope here, inside this room, which would leave it exposed to the quick blades of my enemies.

Badh-o chirps as she comes from the other hallway, indicating no one is present there either. I say a prayer of thanks and find a hiding spot behind a coral pillar, facing the doorway, my back to the window.

And here, with Badh-o tangled around my ankle, I wait.

I listen carefully for any sign of approach. For a long time, I strain for even the faintest trace of footsteps. It finally occurs to me that the room might be spelled to keep sound out. *Just lovely.*

Abruptly the door swings open, confirming my suspicions.

I duck behind the pillar and refuse to breathe.

There's Kaladen.

He's chained. His head sags forward slightly, and he doesn't fight as his guards drag him into the room. They hook his chains to grooves in the floor among the seashell chairs, forcing him to kneel and giving him so little slack he cannot stand. His legs shake slightly, his chest moving with each breath.

I expect his head to shoot up, his gaze to find where I'm hiding.

He never does.

Keep your anger under control, I tell myself when my limbs nearly combust into flames at the sight of him like this. At the thought of what he just endured.

If he's here, it means he didn't break. Which means I cannot afford to be the one to break.

Yirmuth enters after the guards. She stands in front of Kaladen, in a long, partially translucent gown of sea green, looking down at him as though upon a pitiful creature. She doesn't pay heed to the guards as they close the door, leaving her and Kaladen seemingly alone.

"Kaladen," she says softly, and that tone could almost convince me she cared.

My mind is hard at work. All I need to do is subdue Yirmuth. I can break Kaladen out of his chains with my blood—I can even give the blood to Badh-o to avoid suffering the intense consequences of applying the blood myself.

That tall, willowy fae woman is the one thing standing between me and having my husband back. Once Kaladen is free, he can save Arbasa and the Bridge from the Wolf.

My hand trembles from the energy rising inside me.

Yirmuth tilts her head to one side. Her pearl-woven hair falls over one elegant shoulder. "Are you alright?"

He finally lifts his gaze from the floor. His eyelids drag open, his attention fixing wordlessly on her.

"Oh don't look at me like that. You know it is your own fault that you keep getting tortured. It is just a name, Kaladen. Have you forgotten what I offered you about your human bride? You claimed to care about her, and now you are letting her suffer in the hands of the Wolf. You know what he is. Have you any doubt in your mind of what he will do to her? Why do you insist upon clinging to the Bridge when you know as well as I that it is a curse? Let the High King free you of that burden. Let me help you spare what is left of your wife."

Kaladen gives no answer.

Badh-o leans slightly around the pillar, watching, her leaves sagging. I gently touch her beneath her wilted blossom, in solidarity of what she feels. She isn't expecting it, and startles. Her reaction is almost soundless, just a leaping of leaves, and if we were in the human world, it wouldn't be enough to give us away.

But Yirmuth's voice sharpens. "What just made you flinch?"

Kaladen says nothing, breathing hard, his eyes glued to hers. But I feel the weight of his attention burning into me. He's trying so hard to not give us away. If he hadn't just been tortured, he would have managed it.

Yirmuth whirls. My heart surges. I brace behind the column, flexing my fingers on the hilt of my knife. Badh-o dives for cover.

Faster than a snake, Yirmuth is at my side. Her taloned fingers come for my throat. I fly backward, ramming into the wall to avoid her grip.

Kaladen surges in his chains. "Don't you *dare* touch her!"

Yirmuth's eyes glitter like the ocean at sunset as she corners me. "So this is why you wouldn't give away your name. Your little wife was here all along."

My lips pull back from my teeth. I don't give her a chance to brace herself before I attack.

CHAPTER 7

KALADEN

NADIRA SHOOTS LIKE a star from the corner of the room, hurtling toward Yirmuth. At the last second, instead of aiming at the fae's heart, she tucks herself low and slashes her knife toward her thigh. Yirmuth slides to the side. Barely enough to dodge the worst of the blade, and even then the knife slices through fluttering dress.

Yirmuth's hand is already flying. She clips Nadira's shoulder, throwing her off-balance. Nadira rolls and springs back to her feet. But Yirmuth is already there again. She grabs Nadira's wrist, the one with the knife, and yanks her toward the wide open window—as though to throw her over the cliff's edge.

"If you hurt her, I will destroy you!" I bellow. I send every ounce of my waning strength into trying to physically pull my chains from their grooves in the floor. They clang and screech and sear my flesh in agony, but they do not give. I pull harder. My voice rises to a fever pitch. "Yirmuth!"

The fae woman pays me no heed. Nadira's feet hit the side of the wall, sweat breaking out on her forehead as she exerts her strength against the wall, leaning into the ground to avoid giving Yirmuth the leverage she needs to hurl her out the window.

This is far more torturous than anything I endured at Faradir's hand.

"Give me his name!" Yirmuth demands of Nadira.

Nadira's only reply is a guttural battle cry of rage.

Yirmuth tries to pry the knife from Nadira's grip with far stronger hands, and yet somehow Nadira manages to maintain her hold. She falls flat against the ground and sends her feet over her head, kicking them forcefully into Yirmuth's knees. A slight grunt of pain emits from the fae woman, and she drops her hold.

Nadira takes her chance to put distance between them. She darts toward me—to my great relief. If Yirmuth comes close enough, within the short reach of my chains, I might be able to hurt her. Not that Yirmuth would be so foolish. But if I can be a buttress between her and my wife, I could spare Nadira.

For how long?

Only minutes, if that. All Yirmuth must do is call the guards. They will overpower Nadira in a second. There is no escape from this chamber. And if Faradir gets his hands on her—

Yirmuth doesn't let Nadira get to me. In a bounding leap, she has an iron grip on the back of Nadira's tunic and tosses her to the ground like a ragdoll.

"Yirmuth!" I scream. "Bargain with me!"

She casts me one fiery look and then pounces upon Nadira, who isn't fast enough to roll away after smashing into a shell chair. An invisible knife drives between my ribs when Yirmuth gets Nadira pinned on a bed of glasslike abalone. If only her magic wasn't locked, she could kill Yirmuth as if it were nothing!

"Bargain with me!" I cry desperately, as Yirmuth slams her fist down on Nadira's wrist to break her grip on the knife she keeps driving at the fae woman's throat. Nadira cries out in pain, and the sound cuts me in half.

"Yirmuth!"

"Give me his name!" Yirmuth snarls into Nadira's face, her teeth coming so near her vulnerable throat. "Give me his name!"

Nadira twists and shoots up, slamming her collar into Yirmuth's cheek. The fae screams in agony and draws back. It gives Nadira just the barest advantage to plunge her knife toward Yirmuth's ribs. But Yirmuth explodes in a rage.

Her glamours disappear in a moment, her skin sinking into a boggy green, her eyes becoming animal black, her mouth rearranging into multi rows of fangs, large blue webbing sprouting from her ears like bat wings. Gills flare along her sides, venomous spines erupting from her back. Her shriek is like a call of the wild ocean depths.

"You will give me his name!" she screams in that ear-splitting pitch.

"I will not!" Nadira screams back.

"Let her go!" I roar frantically.

Then, suddenly, as though he materialized out of thin air, Trenian is beside me. Just as Yirmuth strikes—slashing her claws across Nadira's face. I surge in my chains as blood flies in every direction and Nadira screams in pain. Yirmuth doesn't let up, demanding my name, knocking the knife from Nadira's hand so it skitters across the floor. She has Nadira by the hair, but my wife has gone limp. As though she has fainted.

"Prince Trenian! Stop this!" I roar into the grim face of the prince. "Stop this immediately!"

Trenian's face is icy.

Not triumphant, or smug, or cavalier. Just cold and merciless. "Bargain with me. Give me your favor, to be redeemed by me at any time and any place and for anything, and in return, I will kill Yirmuth."

I hesitate for a split second. I didn't truly consider Yirmuth my enemy. Not until now, when she yanks on Nadira's hair, her claws precisely angled at her jugular while avoiding the collar.

"Deal," I spit.

Trenian is across the room the next moment. He grabs Yirmuth by the back of the neck and rips her off Nadira, who rolls to safety, gasping and shoving up on her hands, her scarf falling in her face.

Trenian moves so swiftly, Yirmuth has only a second for her eyes to widen before he takes Nadira's own fallen knife and slices it across her throat. He lets go, and she falls motionless to the ground—black eyes still open and unseeing, her blood staining the pale floor.

Nadira breathes hard, still on her hands and knees, barely conscious. She looks between me and Trenian. Three bloody stripes cut across the right side of her face. One of them missed her eye by less than an inch. My blood boils in my veins.

My mind still rings with the bargain I've made, my skin stinging from my chains and where the tattoo appeared. Though I should chastise myself for allowing a situation where I would indebt myself to the future High King this much, I cannot regret it. Not as Nadira's dark brown eyes meet mine and burn with emotion.

My relief that she is still alive cascades through me.

Trenian flips her knife in the air, its jeweled hilt flashing with each rotation before he catches it again. "Tell anyone who asks that *you* were the one who killed Yirmuth. You humans are so prone to lying, so lie well, my lovely Queen Nadira."

He tosses her knife. It lands with frightening precision beside her knee, tip embedded in the floor.

Nadira surges to unsteady feet just before he slips out the door. "You can't leave! We need to get Kaladen out of here. We both need this."

Trenian's eyes crinkle in a mirthless smile. "Don't you remember? Your life isn't the only one at stake. I've got a father who wants me dead, so I must be careful. This"—he gestures at the scene of Yirmuth's death and my imprisonment—"is far out of step with his interests.

So I have to be a good little son now. But I'd judge that you have five to ten more minutes before the guards descend upon you and realize what has happened. So long!"

He's gone before Nadira can stop him. She releases a wordless growl and then kneels beside me. "Badh-o! Come here quickly!"

The vine slithers from her hiding spot behind a pillar. Nadira takes several drops of blood from her face and smears them across Badh-o's leaves. Though her entire body must hurt, not a sign of it shows across her features. She is nothing but gritty determination. Her hands find my face, then trail down my shoulders, my collarbones, my chest—checking for injury. She won't find one. That is not how the High King tortures.

"You need to get out of here!" I hiss.

Badh-o slides toward me and presses one leaf against the shackles on my ankle.

"Badh-o, no!" I cry, but it's too late.

The little vine's burst of pain cuts me as she shrinks back.

"Badh-o!" Nadira scoops up the vine. "What is wrong? Kaladen—why didn't it work?"

"She cannot touch iron any more than I can!"

Grimness passes over her blood-streaked face. "I'll try to be fast, but this will knock me unconscious for a few—"

"Stop!" I command, drawing back from the crimson fingers she brings to my chains. I finally understand what she is trying to do. "Your blood cannot unlock these chains! Iron isn't like other locks—it suppresses magic. Even the magic of human blood."

She stares at me. Almost in disbelief. "No, no, they must. Trenian—" She stops herself. Scarlet flares like a red tide across her cheeks. Her words come out in a violent spit. "He lied to me."

A force rises inside me, subdued only by these cursed chains. "He told you that your blood would unlock my chains."

"We stepped out of his rooms." She rakes a hand through her wild hair, clenching it into a fist. "My lie detector wasn't there. I knew it sounded too simple. If my blood could unlock iron locks, I could have already gotten my collar off. How could I have forgotten that? How could I have believed him?"

Cold clarity comes over me. "You thought you had a way to get me free. That is why you came." My recent gratitude at Trenian for saving her poisons in my gut. When I am free, I will rip him limb from limb. "You've got to get out of here. *Now*—while you still can!"

"How can I get you out of this?" Her hands are running over my sweat-streaked chest and shoulders, dodging the iron chains, but inspecting them all the same. "There must be a way. Kaladen, you're shaking! What did the High King do to you?"

"Nadira," I growl, "get out of here at once. The guards will be here any second, and you cannot be caught. There is no way to get me out of these chains. Not without the guard keys."

"This is my chance to get you out."

"Then how are you going to get me out of these chains, little assassin? Can your teeth cut through iron? Can you rip this anchor from the earth with your bare strength?"

Tears fill her eyes. "I cannot let you be taken again. I need to think. I will think of something. There must be a way. There *must* be."

She runs to the window, leaning out of it to survey the options. Suddenly, her head jerks to one side. When she turns around, her dark eyes are sparking. She runs back to me. I cannot help how my gut clenches at the blood drying on her face. "There are guards posted outside—with crossbows! They were prepared for you to try to escape. Which means there *must* be a way for you to escape. There must be *something* that they were worried about you discovering."

"It's a precaution. They are likely there in case I broke free while they untethered my chains."

"No, there *must* be something." Her gaze scans the entire room, her focus sharp and the tension in her body like a tightly coiled spring.

I lift my voice and snarl frantically: "*Nadira,* you must leave *this instant*!"

"I will *not*!" she shoots back furiously. "And I *cannot*. I can see the shadows of at least one person standing outside that door. There is no escape without you."

"Then you must hide! This room is soundproof, and we won't get warning when the guards return!"

Badh-o lets out a series of frantic squeaks from where she has slithered near the door. They reform in my mind: *Guards! Guards! Fast here!*

Nadira doesn't need to understand her words to understand her meaning. Our gazes snag together, silent communication buzzing between us as we both turn toward Yirmuth's body—too far away from me to have killed her, and surrounded in a pool of blood that cannot be cleaned in the span of a heartbeat.

I curse under my breath furiously. *"Hide,"* I mouth at her, even though I know it's useless.

She purses her lips, staring at me grimly.

"You are not *dying for me,"* I mouth, surging upright and yanking at my chains, ignoring the burn of iron on my wrists as I throw every ounce of strength I have into a futile attempt to rip my shackles from their posts in the ground. *"I won't let Faradir get his hands on you!"*

She doesn't do what I say, but instead searches the area with a sharp gaze. Quickly, she scoops up several chunks of smashed pillar and seashell chair, and drives them like wedges beneath the door, sticking her tongue out in concentration as she sets them just right.

Then, satisfied, she rushes to Yirmuth's body and searches it for weapons. Her growl of frustration is inaudible when she finds nothing.

Badh-o shrieks and dives for Nadira's ankle.

They're here.

The panicked pulse of my blood is far more painful than anything else I've endured. But begging Nadira to hide clearly isn't working. Instead, I jerk my chin toward the hallway I'm closest to. "Check her bedroom for weapons!"

She leaps over Yirmuth's body and disappears beyond a door. She emerges a second later with a bow and a quiver of arrows. The grin she shoots me is far too bright for the situation we're in.

I note the number of arrows. *Ten*. So few.

The latch on the door turns. The door swings half an inch, and sticks.

Nadira takes her spot in the washroom, kneeling behind the crack she left open in the door, her arrow nocked and aimed at the main door. I drag my eyes away from her, toward the door just as her makeshift lock breaks, and the door bursts open and guards rush in at once.

"What—?" one of the guards blurts, taking in me thoroughly chained as I ought to be, and Yirmuth's body lying on the opposite side of the room.

"Someone else is here!" says the second guard.

That's when an arrow suddenly sprouts from his neck. He falls.

Several guards are already at my side, armed with gloved hands as they bend to check my shackles. But the next second, one of them falls, and all pandemonium erupts. I pull on my chains as hard as I can, and a roar bursts from the depths of my gut. I've got to do whatever I can to keep them distracted from Nadira as she picks the guards off one by one.

Six are down in a matter of seconds.

Steel clashes against stone as a dropped sword skitters across the floor. A guard slips in the pool of Yirmuth's blood and crashes into one of the only intact seashell chairs, shattering it on impact. Something crashes behind me—did Nadira miss? No—another guard hits the ground, gurgling.

They seem to realize where the arrows are coming from, despite the way I clash my chains together and roar as though I am free and breaking away from every restraint.

The arrows stop. Ten guards are down. She's run out.

Guards charge into the bathing chamber as more rush to restrain me. A whirl of silk, the flash of a blade, and two more guards hit the ground.

"It's the human!" someone cries.

I throw my strength into another wild burst for freedom, but this time flowing from my desperation to keep Faradir's hands off my wife.

A searing blast of magic shoots into the bathing chamber.

"You cannot hurt her!" I scream, my voice breaking in half. "Faradir wants her alive! You cannot kill her!"

But the second after sheer horror cuts through me, I realize the bond between Nadira and me is still strong. She isn't dead. That blast wasn't to kill her, only to disorient her.

The bathing chamber is such a small space. Three guards push inside, followed by the sound of tight grunts and hard blows. She's cornered, and there are so many more guards pouring through the doors.

There's no way she can fight them all. With her magic, she would have had a chance. But with that collar . . .

I watch, helpless and defeated and aching, as three guards drag her from the bathing chamber. She sports a new, thin cut along one collarbone, blood dripping onto her tunic as they bind her wrists behind her.

She meets my eye. My previous words pass between us.

If they have you, they have me.

"Take them both to the High King. He'll be glad at this development," says one of the guards.

CHAPTER 8

NADIRA

I CONSERVE MY energy, refusing to wear myself out when there's no way I'm escaping the small army of guards that escort us to the High King. Not *yet*.

But these bonds, stars be blessed, are *rope*, and not chains. I don't recognize the knot, but I've gotten out of plenty of knots I didn't know. It is the one thing that keeps me calm and focused, instead of crazy with panic that because of Trenian's one lie, all of Arbasa may be destroyed.

I must bide my time.

Badh-o stays hidden in my sirwal, ready to come to my aid the moment I call. She is thin and warm against my skin. A soft comfort that I value more with each passing minute. She could have stayed hidden so the guards didn't drag her into this, but she chose to stay with me.

Behind me, Kaladen breathes hard. His eyes burn into the back of my head. Once, I try to turn around, only for a guard's steely hand to grip my neck and force me to look forward. I keep my teeth from grinding too loudly.

We enter the river hallway I discovered yesterday and used to find Kaladen's cell. It is brightly lit now with white sunlight that brings out the sparkling life of the marble. I listen to the peaceful whisper of the flowing water while my mind spins to form some semblance of a plan. *Anything* that will give us a chance to escape.

Cursed, wretched Prince Trenian. I will hate him until I die—which will likely be today.

Suddenly, metal screeches and a body goes flying. The sound is jarring enough that I can partially whirl, my guards' grips on my arms relaxing slightly, and watch as one of Kaladen's guards falls into the stream with a surprised cry. Kaladen releases an ear-piercing roar. He slams his shoulder into his other guard, though this time with less success. At once, it seems as though a hundred guards fall upon him.

I seize the distraction, recognizing his attempt to offer me escape. I duck under one's arm to twist free of his grip. But the guards seem prepared for such a maneuver. More surround me and shove me to the ground, practically smothering my body with their crushing weight as I nearly scream for air.

Quickly, I go still. This is not a battle I can win. Kaladen's bellows go on for another minute, the sound of struggle pained and violent behind me. I take the small sips of air I can manage and chant repeatedly in my head: *You will find a way out of this. Kaladen will be spared. Arbasa will be protected. This isn't the end.*

At last, the suffocating pressure is removed, and I'm dragged to my feet. My head swims. I demand it to clear, clenching my jaw and blinking hard as I lean heavier on one of my guards. There is no hope to chance a look back at my husband.

We continue onward, through the river hallway, to the even grander one still. I cannot help tracing my mental map until we reach a pair of doors thrice as tall as a man. A great tree is carved into it, with roots more expansive than the branches. It looks so like the tree that acts as a portal to Valehaven from the Bridge.

The throne room.

"We'll take him in first and then bring the human in after," says one guard.

Kaladen shoots me a wild look as they drag him past me. I nod back once, trying to tell him with my eyes not to worry about me. As if that is possible.

The door closes behind them, separating us, swallowing my husband whole.

I'm not going to let the High King get Kaladen's name. No matter what, I won't let that happen. I'll kill myself before I let that happen. It will be hard in my current situation, with my knife and even my arrow gone. But I can do it with rope.

I might not have been able to take my life in the Arbasa belltower, but I can do it now. There is something inside me so much stronger than my fear of pain. The cry for revenge on Eshe's death. The need to protect my homeland from these wicked creatures who would sacrifice it on the altar of their politics. And a burning love for my husband.

The fae so often like to speak of how *delicate* we humans are. Perhaps they will forget my weakness, and torture me just a little too much. I could easily die that way.

I am the only way the High King can gain control of Kaladen.

He might have me right this moment, but I will find a way. I will *not* let him take my husband's name from my lips. No matter what it costs me. No matter how much pain I must endure.

"Queen Nadira," rasps a cold voice from behind me.

I would whirl, but the guards' hands grip me firmly in place. Instead, puffing hair out of my face, I turn my head enough to catch a glimpse of a long, hooked nose protruding from a tattered hood. I face forward again. "Come to rescue me, Eye?"

"I have come to claim your husband's name from you."

The attention of the guards on either side of me seems to sharpen, their icy expressions shifting to interest.

I scoff. My mind is occupied plotting how to successfully kill myself in the throne room, should it come to that. Rope takes too long. Someone would stop me. "Shall you extract it from my mind?"

"I will bargain with you for it."

"No bargains."

"I can bargain with you for Kaladen Ashrift's freedom, and for your own, too."

Freedom. How alluring. These fae and their trickery. Freedom won't mean much if Kaladen has no power over the Bridge and cannot defeat the Wolf. Freedom won't mean much if all Arbasa is to be devoured by the power of Lulythinar in only a few days. I've almost worked my bonds loose by now. If I were to bargain with the Eye, I would need something *very* specific and *very* tangible that I can ask for in return. There are a host of things I need right now—Kaladen's chains off, my collar removed, the Wolf destroyed, Lulythinar stalled, the High King and his guards killed. There exists a hundred different ways to word each request, and a great many of the foolish—

I blink.

Kaladen told me never to bargain with the fae. After dealing with Trenian, I understand why.

But . . .

But could I trick them at their own game?

My mind dives ahead, running so fast I can barely keep up with it. The words are out before I can stop them. "You would give me anything I wanted if I told you the name Kaladen bid me not to use? The name I called him by; the name that none of you fae know? That name?"

The guards' grip on my elbows tightens. I carefully finagle the last of my bonds, but keep my hands still clasped behind me as if I remain bound. The Eye tilts its head toward me eagerly, and I can almost catch the glimpse of one large, lidless eye in the shadows of its cloak.

"Yes," it croaks. "That name."

"Then will you accept my bargain, Eye of Baltor, and give me your favor, to be used at any time or place of my choosing, to give me whatever I ask, in exchange for that name, belonging to Kaladen Ashrift, that I have called him by and he bid me not to use?" My lips tingle with the words. I might have to call in the Eye's bargain *immediately*, but I need a few extra moments to think about exactly how to phrase my order. If I do it poorly, I could land us in an even worse situation than we're in now.

"I accept your bargain, Queen Nadira, on the condition that you tell me Kaladen's name at once," says the Eye. It lifts one boney arm toward me. "May it be so."

I fight to hide my satisfied smile. "May it be so."

The familiar burning of a bargain tattoo blazes just beneath my left collarbone. My tongue begins itching, the name I swore to give bubbling behind my teeth.

"Give me his name," demands the Eye.

The doors swing open, and a cry emerges: "Bring in the human!"

I shove aside Kaladen's name briefly to blurt to the Eye, "Give me something to call you with! To redeem my favor!"

The Eye reaches out a knobby hand and shoves a single strand of hair into the pocket of my sirwal. "Now give me the name, girl!"

"Sultan," I whisper to the Eye, as they drag me into the High King's throne room.

CHAPTER 9

NADIRA

I HAVE THE name!" cries the Eye. "I have Kaladen Ashrift's name! The human girl has given it to me!"

The throne room is dazzling beauty, with the High King seated on a throne at its center—a small, radiant sun shining above the stream encircling him. I barely register the beauty, for my focus goes immediately to Kaladen's stiffening shoulders, his great form forced to kneel before Faradir. Prince Trenian lounges against a pillar at the foot of the dais, a cold smirk twisting his beautiful mouth as his gold-flecked gaze finds me. That look seems to say, *"What did you expect from me, my dear?"* I would lunge forward to strangle him, throwing aside the appearance of being bound. Except there is one more figure present. A figure rippling with lean muscle, thick with hair.

The Wolf.

He stands at the High King's left hand and flashes a feral, long-fanged smile at me. My blood runs cold as his eyes run lasciviously over me.

He's here. He's found me.

"There's my lovely human bride," says the Wolf. "I've missed you so, my dear Queen Nadira."

"*My dear Queen Nadira*," Prince Trenian mimics, tossing his tone high, as if he thinks the sight of me and Kaladen bound and forced to our knees before the High King is a tableau created specifically for his amusement.

"You have the name?" demands Faradir, his golden aura of attention snapping between the Eye and me. "Give it to me at once."

The Eye holds up one bony finger. "A vision of your future for the name, O wondrous High King, my liege."

Faradir waves one perfectly proportioned hand. "Very well. Take your vision quickly and hand over the name."

Kaladen and I trade glances. I dare not reveal anything on my face, so when I pull my gaze forward once more, I have not a clue what he thinks I have given the Eye.

The Eye stands before the High King, tilting its head back, and opening its hands toward the throne. Faradir stares at the ceiling in irritation, his jaw resting on one finger, waiting for the Eye to be finished.

I see no sign of vision being transferred. No bright light or pulsating aura. It is just one minute of us all standing there silently, waiting.

Then the Eye takes a step back. "Ah. What a delight to see another vision."

"Anything that concerns me?" Faradir asks in bored tones.

"Oh indeed, my liege. Some day you shall be overthrown."

Faradir's fist slams down on the armrest of his throne. "How dare you poison the ears of my court by speaking such lies!"

"You should know better than to spout such troublesome prophecies," says Trenian with a wink at me. He keeps his body language languid and easy, but I don't miss the way his gaze darkens as his attention returns to his father.

"Give me the name and be gone immediately, Eye," barks Faradir. "Before I decide the ghosts are better recipients of your prophecies."

"The name given to me, my liege, is Sultan."

And with that, the Eye turns to leave the throne room. Panic sears throughout my entire body. If the Eye leaves, I may not be able to call in my bargain.

"Wait!" I cry, trying to get to my feet. The guard at my right immediately shoves me back down to my knees. Kaladen's gaze burns into the side of my face, but I cannot look at him right now. "The Eye must—"

"Gag her immediately," says Faradir. "Do not let her call in any bargains!"

The fae's hand that clamps down over mine is cold like marble and just as white. I bite as hard as I can, and blood fills my mouth. I let go of my bonds, slam my elbow between the ribs of the nearest guard. I yank hard, pulling my head to one side, opening my mouth to scream the favor at the Eye, but a wad of cloth is stuffed between my teeth, my arms restrained once more. I nearly choke on how much fabric forces my jaws apart and pins my tongue. I thrash, but it's no use. In but a minute, three guards have me face down on the ground, their weight nearly driving me into the icelike floor.

"Nadira!" cries Kaladen, his voice threaded with fear and fury.

"I'm afraid I made the same mistake," says Trenian with a laugh. "Rope doesn't work on this one. She's too clever for all that."

I cannot see anything of the High King except a pair of luminescent, golden feet. They are braced wide for action as he calls, "Bind her with chains! Mountains of Ildrid, she's one human girl! Why must it take so many of you to restrain her?"

I breathe hard, panting through my nose as shackles clamp down on my wrists. Footsteps come toward me—hairy feet with long, sharp nails like talons. The Wolf. He squats down beside me, bringing his angular face into my field of vision and grinning at me. He reaches toward me, grabbing my jaw and forcing me to look up at him. My collar seems to dull the connection between Kaladen and me, but I can still feel his pulsating rage as the Wolf caresses a hand over my face, touches my hair.

"I'm so happy to have you back, human wife," says the Wolf.

"I'm not your wife," I try to snarl back, but cannot.

The High King's voice echoes through the throne room. "Kaladen Ashrift Sultan, I hereby command—" He cuts off suddenly and curses violently. The Wolf releases my face in surprise. I can barely arch to see the fury painted across Faradir's beautiful face. "That human *minx* tricked us! Sultan isn't his name!"

Trenian's chuckle is like a fly around sour pudding. "I think Sultan might be one of those human titles. She must have worded her bargain with the Eye well indeed."

I still cannot turn enough to see Kaladen, but I can feel his radiating shock and . . . maybe just a tinge of awe. It's a moment I wish I could glory in, a victory I never expected to claim.

But the next moment, something invisible but oh so tangible grabs me by the throat. I choke. It tightens. Stars erupt across my vision as I fail to drag in air through my clogged mouth. A gargled sound emerges from my throat. I fight frantically to rip my chains free so I can find some way to breathe, but the force around my throat doesn't relent, and neither do my chains.

"Stop!" Kaladen roars. "We need her for the Bridge! *Stop this right now!* Curse it, Faradir! Let her go!"

"Your name," the High King growls to him as my vision turns black, as my lungs collapse on themselves.

"I will not give you my name if you kill her! Release her now, or you will *never* be able to sever my connection to the Bridge!"

The pressure around my throat vanishes. I gasp, and nearly choke again on my gag, almost passing out because I cannot breathe through my nose fast enough.

"And fix her gag!" Kaladen demands. His voice is powerful, but it shakes just slightly. Enough for me to know exactly how terrified he is.

The guards yank me to my knees and rip out the bundle of cloth they shoved in my mouth. I breathe desperately. Then it's shoved back in again, but not nearly so far. I continue breathing, tears of relief pricking my eyes.

"I will give you my name—"

"No!" I try to cry, but it comes out muffled. Kaladen looks at me, and it's like his very heart gleams in his eyes.

You must let me do this, he says with those eyes. *You must let me spare you.*

I shake my head violently, begging him. Pleading with him. There has to be some other way. If I could only call in my favor with the Eye right now! If only I was bound by rope and not chain, maybe I could bolt for the doors and escape before they could catch me. If only the Wolf wasn't a mere foot away from me, eyeing me hungrily as though he barely holds himself back from ripping out my throat like I've seen him do to others.

"—in exchange for Queen Nadira being returned to her time in Arbasa immediately, alive, unharmed, and unfettered to the Wolf's bondage. For that, and that only, will I give you the name you have so long sought."

"*Your* name," Faradir interjects.

"My name. My full name."

I am still shaking my head, still screaming through my bonds for Kaladen to not do this—even though I know he has no choice except let me die.

"You always had a weakness for human women," says Faradir, as if Kaladen was a monster like Eldreth of the Star City, who killed Eshe. "Very well. Let it be so."

Kaladen's gaze finds mine and holds it. "Let it be so."

My people will burn. My world will burn. The Wolf will destroy us all, piece by piece, and when Lulythinar comes, it will devour everything that is left.

We will be nothing.

I will have nothing.

Kaladen will be lost to me forever.

My husband gets to his feet, and the guards don't stop him. As if they see the end of Kaladen Ashrift's reign as the Neverseen King of this age. As if they know there is nothing he can do to fight now.

He stands firmly, feet braced wide, shoulders broad and strong, his chin lifted, as he faces the throne and declares: "My name is Kaladen Ashrift Felladyr."

The Wolf lifts his hungry gaze from me to his rival. He slavers at the jaw, the energy of thrill radiating from him. His body seems to flicker slightly between man and beast. One minute I see a sinewy body of tight muscles, and the next fangs and claws and a dripping maw.

"Kaladen Ashrift Felladyr," says the High King with a slow, satisfied smile. Even I can sense the power billowing from him when he says those words. My collar reacts to the magnitude of magic, sending spikes of pain into my temples so strong I am forced to squeeze my eyes shut. "From now until the dawn after Lulythinar, you shall serve the Wolf as aid at the Bridge. You shall do whatever he commands. And then, once Lulythinar is done and gone, you shall return to me and await your next bidding."

What?

I stare blankly at the scene before me.

It's like my mind can't even comprehend what the High King has just said. The High King was supposed to sever the connection between Kaladen and the Bridge. He was supposed to strip Kaladen of all his powers. But instead . . .

Kaladen is looking at me with such tremendous horror, and I can almost hear the vicious grin coming from the Wolf only a pace away from us.

We are truly doomed.

Faradir's voice rings out again across the room: "Take the human girl and return her to her world. I have no further use for her."

Strong hands grab me, yanking me to my feet. I try to scream for Kaladen, but the gag prevents all but a muffled grunt from escaping me.

They drag me away. Everything happens so fast. I don't know what to do.

He should have let them kill me, I think to myself. *He should have let them kill me.*

The last thing I see before the throne room doors close is the Wolf, his glowing eyes fixed on me. His visage flickers between man and beast, his fangs dripping, and his hands shifting into talons.

CHAPTER 10

KALADEN

I STAND AT attention in the throne room in Arbasa. In the throne where I once saw Nadira sitting in a blood-red gown and crowned in diadems, facing her people, now sits the Wolf, his long bony legs crossed, one over the other, as he grips the armrests of her throne.

Broken portals pluck at my awareness, nearly killing me with the need to seal them. Harder to ignore now that I am here at the Bridge. Every part of me rebels; every fiber of my being wants to rip the Wolf limb from limb. I want to tear into him with my bare hands. But I cannot, because he possesses my name.

"Kaladen Ashrift Felladyr," says the Wolf, and then he chuckles. The sound grates down my spine. He has a stain of dry blood spreading from the corner of his mouth down to his chin. "I am honored to have your aid as we approach Lulythinar." He grins, as though from an esoteric joke. "You will do as I say, and together, we will keep Arbasa, this human land, and all the rest of the Fae lands intact. Does that sound like a good plan?"

I do not reply. I stand still and resist the urge to clench my hands into fists. I keep my gaze level, never shifting my eyes from his, and I wait.

I wait and I wait. I'm not going to rush his orders, because somewhere, Nadira is here in this city or in this palace, and if she has an ounce of sense in her, she'll run away as far and as fast as she can. Any moment of delay could be the difference between her life and death.

I am not surprised when the Wolf reveals what his first order for me is. "Kaladen Ashrift Felladyr," he says again, seeming to enjoy the way my name buzzes in the air, giving him so much power. "I want you to find the assassin, the human girl, and bring her to me. You have until nightfall. Understand?"

The weight of the order falls like a chain around my neck, tightening, threatening to choke off my air and strangle me bit by bit.

"Oh, and do not remove her collar. Now, tell me that you shall do it and give the proper reverence due your sovereign."

The words immediately fight to leave my body, but I refuse to let them go without a measure of struggle, as I clamp my jaw shut with every scrap of strength I have. The Wolf forgot one crucial thing.

He hasn't ordered me not to kill him.

I will do as he says, and I will watch for the moment he lets his guard down. I only have one chance to kill him before he realizes his mistake.

At last, the words emerge: "I shall do as you bid, my liege."

CHAPTER 11

NADIRA

MY HEAD THROBS with splitting pain as I am thrown through the Valehaven Portal. My hands land on the ground, my chest heaving as I try to breathe through the pain. Badh-o, emerging from clinging to my ankle beneath my sirwal, strokes a leaf over my cheek while I breathe until, finally, the pounding recedes enough for me to get up and stagger to the doorway.

Kaladen is a prisoner. A prisoner of the Wolf.

I don't know how much time I have before the Wolf comes for more of my blood. He didn't look inclined to let me go when I was in the throne room.

"He doesn't have me now," I growl into the darkness.

But the moment I climb out of the window into the rising dawn beyond, the sight before me is like yet another punch to the gut.

Inky blue goblins fill the courtyard. They hang from windows, run across the courtyard, and swim in the fountain. I can only imagine how bad it is in the city.

"Sands," I curse. Badh-o squeaks in horror, then ducks beneath the safe folds of my sirwal again. This is so much worse than I expected.

I need to close the portal, I tell myself, even though my first instinct is to run into the city to try to fight the goblins. More pour out of a window on the first floor of the palace. There is no use trying to fight the stream without closing the portal. I'm just going to have to trust that the city guard can handle the goblins until I get there.

I break into a sprint and then almost stop dead in my tracks. Without Kaladen, I can't enter the dream realm. And if I can't enter the dream realm, then I won't be protected when I'm closing the portal. I'll be vulnerable to any injury, even death.

I grit my teeth firmly, resolutely. I will seal this portal, and it will not kill me.

Then I run.

I hurry through the hallways. The window that the goblins are pouring out of is so full I can't break through the stream without being injured more than necessary. So I take the hallway instead—stopping in elation when I discover the lone scimitar of a fallen city guard. I pick it up, and its weight is a heavy comfort in my hand.

I expect to find the Wolf waiting for me at any moment, attempting to seal the portal, or maybe this was a trap to keep me from running as far away from him as I can get. Maybe he knew the only thing that would bring me back was hurting my people.

But he is not waiting when I enter the Golden Hall.

The goblins pay me no heed as they rush unhindered from their portal. Their blue bodies are so dark in the dawn that they almost seem black, their fangs shining in the light of the portal. Their hammers are ready to destroy anything they encounter. The light of excitement gleams in their yellow eyes, their pleasure matchless at having unfettered access to the human world.

I hesitate, facing that stream. I have sealed this portal myself in the dream realm, but I had my magic then. This time, I don't. It's just me and this scimitar.

"Here goes nothing," I mutter to myself.

Then it suddenly hits me. The first time this portal opened, we sealed it without entering. We sealed it with the goblins' own blood because they were near the anchor of their own portal. I give a dry little snort. If I can just kill them fast enough to get enough blood, maybe I can seal the portal with a mix of their blood and mine.

If I can just figure out how to do it without injuring myself too grievously . . .

I come up behind the portal, keeping my footsteps quiet, though it isn't really necessary with how loud the goblins are, shrieking and screaming over the portal and out the window. I don't know how there are so many. It seems like an endless fountain of them, as though they are being birthed from the very depths of their world itself. But I pull myself together.

I sneak around the edge of the portal and start slicing with my scimitar. My blade meets resistance; it is so dulled that it takes extra force to pierce the leathery skin of the goblins. I hate how it feels in my fist, the way it's like trying to cut through something gruesome that refuses to be severed.

The goblins notice me.

They pick up their axes and turn to attack. I retreat with my blade, avoiding being quickly swarmed and watch their blood drip onto the floor. *Not nearly enough.*

I remember that first day, the competition for the Neverseen King's hand in marriage. There was so much carnage before we could close the portal. Firming my resolve, I stab a goblin in the back of the throat, yank its hammer free, and begin smashing everything in sight.

Liquid splashes on my face, but if I slow down, if I start to doubt myself, the shrieks of the goblins will turn into the screams of the people in the city—the orphans in the streets, the innocents who do not deserve to die a violent death at the hands of these monsters.

"This is so gross," I mutter as I slit the throat of one goblin and fling it into the portal. The portal shakes, the effect of the goblin's own blood weakening its hold. My arms ache as I continue to stab and throw. The creatures are heavy, and I almost drop one when a hammer lands with bone-crushing force against my foot. I scream, but it's enough—the portal snaps shut. As fast as I can, I cut my thumb open and smear my blood along with the goblins' to seal the portal completely.

It blinks closed like an eye.

The goblins in the room—*dozens*—suddenly turn to me, horror filling their wide-moon eyes.

Then, they attack as one.

"Sands," I curse.

A searing blast of light comes crashing close to my face. I fling up a hand to cover my eyes as they burn. Urgency demands I keep moving, knowing that the goblins are coming for me, but when I peel open my lids, I see nothing but giant spots across my vision for several excruciating seconds. Seconds where I haven't a clue what direction to run.

Finally, the spots clear, and there is Kaladen.

His upraised hand lowers slowly, giving me time to process that the goblins are all dead. Eradicated with his bolt of magic. He stands in the entrance of the Golden Hall, the doors flung wide on either side of his broad frame. He is properly clothed now, in black, with a long, sweeping cloak that catches the draft from the open window. His sapphire eyes are brighter than stars in the darkness of the unlit room.

His voice is lethal as he strides toward me. "Run while you still can."

My stomach bottoms out. I dive to one side and sprint through the doorway.

I dash down the corridor, limping on my injured foot as I go, until I make it to the banister on the first floor, panting hard. My hand lands on the wooden railing. It is cold as frost to the touch. Its distant voice that emerges in my mind is small and frightened.

Danger, it whispers. *Sorry.*

"I'll fix the danger, I promise," I tell it, glancing around wildly for any sign that Kaladen has followed me. "I need to get to the city. Badh-o, are you alright?"

She *meeps* in reply, still clinging to my leg. She scooted up toward my knee in the fight. I don't blame her.

A creak above me yanks my attention up the stairs. A shadow spills against the railing and wall—a shadow of a giant, lurching animal on four legs, its maw agape with fanged teeth the size of my forearms.

"Is that you, little bride?" the Wolf calls.

I curse internally, ignore the throbbing pain of my foot, and dive out the doors into the abandoned courtyard.

There are fewer goblins here, and none of them notice me. I breathe a prayer of relief as I embrace the covering of gray, overcast skies and run toward the gate.

Kaladen always knew when I left, so I assume the Wolf will know too. But luckily for me, the last of the maniacal goblin horde rushes through the gates, which have been torn open. Who knew yet another curse could turn into a blessing?

I slip out alongside the goblins and hurry into the city of Risya.

I have killed over a dozen goblins by the time I finally reach the city. It is overrun, far worse than I could have imagined. Goblins climb up every structure. They swing through open windows, eliciting screams. The streets are full of city guards, struggling to fight back the monstrous onslaught.

I leave them to their work and instead rush into an alleyway. There are fewer goblins here, so it's easy enough to sneak up and cut down the ones I find. But the shrieking tells me they are everywhere. When the goblin shrieks turn into childlike screams, I burst into a sprint.

It's like the *beechka* outbreak when hordes of flying creatures assaulted the city and swarmed the most unsuspecting victims. But this is so much worse. These small creatures are vicious and deadly. By the time I track down a group of orphans, several of the children bleed from places where the goblins' hammers found them. A loud cry rips from deep inside me as I cut down every last one of the goblins until I'm soaked in my own sweat and thick blue blood slides down my skin. The pain of my foot grows harder to ignore, but I ignore it anyway as I turn to the children.

There are six of them that look like they were separated from the rest of their group. They all hold makeshift weapons and are a little bit older than the last group Eshe and I helped. A mixture of awe and fear shine in their dark eyes.

One particular pair immediately catches my attention.

"Zara!" I cry. "What are you doing? Where is Tariq? Aren't you supposed to be with him?"

Her black eyes burn above the scratches and smears of dirt along her young face. "I need to get more of my friends away from the attack. There's a safe house. Tariq guards it."

Safe house. A great, whooshing sigh of relief escapes me. "Tell me where it is. I'll help you get there."

The safe house, as it turns out, is the city guard headquarters. Tariq stands, filthy, ragged, but still strong and handsome, at the entrance, cutting down anything that comes within reach of his scimitar. He has guards stationed in a semicircle around the headquarters, creating a line of defense that none of the goblins can get through.

"There you are!" Tariq shouts at Zara the moment she ushers the children she found up to the threshold. "No more sneaking out of this guardhouse or I'll have your hide! You could have been killed!"

"Tariq!" I cry, so relieved to see his familiar face that I stumble on my bad foot.

His head whips to follow the sound of my voice. "Nadira! We've been so worried about you! Get inside!"

I hobble toward him, only for one guard to hold up his scimitar in front of me. I stop.

"She's the Mourner!" he shouts to Tariq.

My blood runs cold.

"Let her pass," Tariq demands. "She is our ally."

The guard hesitates, dragging his gaze over my torn and dirty clothes, the weapon in my hand. Then a goblin hurls toward him, and he whirls to attack. He jerks his head my way, bidding me to pass. For just one instant, a dark thought clouds my focus, telling me that I *am* the Mourner, and the Mourner does not belong with others.

No. I am not the Mourner any longer. I am no longer a slave forced to kill those who do not deserve it. I am my own person. Nadira Ashrift Felladyr.

I hurry forward as fast as I can on my injured foot. Tariq opens the door, drags me inside, and then slams it shut. He's breathing terribly hard, and so am I.

"Come upstairs with me." He glances at my foot, bruised purple in my worn sandal, then scoops an arm under my shoulder. "Lean your weight on me."

I could weep from how good it is to be with someone I trust, someone who is good. Together, we hobble up the rickety staircase in dimness. Not a single lantern has been lit in the entire place, and if not for the creak of wood above me, I would think the complex completely abandoned. Zara has already herded her friends up the stairs. Their voices mingle with others, young with a hushed brightness. When we reach the next floor, a door is open, and when I peer inside, there are over two dozen children filling it. Most of them quietly eat flatbread, but one I recognize attempts a handstand—his food hanging from his mouth. His too large ears stick out on either side of his head. *Abbi.* I smile at him, waving, and he flops to the ground, turning right side up and yanking his flatbread out of his mouth to wave back.

Just before Zara peels off to go to those rooms, Tariq stops her with a hand on her thin shoulder.

"I'm serious, Zara. Please take me or one of my men with you next time if you're going to venture into the city during a disaster like this. Once we get through this, I promise to train you well enough that you can go by yourself."

She nods, rolling her eyes like any girl on the cusp of womanhood would do to her older brother. Tariq exchanges a few words with the children, calling them each by name.

They see me in the doorway and a few recognize me, crying happily, "Hello Nadira!"

I wave back. A wave of sadness makes it hard to smile. These children were everything to Eshe. She would have been so glad to see them so well taken care of and protected. Badh-o slips free of my ankle and slithers into the room to say a quick hello. Abbi cries happily at the sight of her, and her flower bursts into bloom in reply. She always loved the children.

A distinct sense of pleasure radiates from her erect blossom as she returns to me.

When Tariq shuts the door and motions for me to follow him toward another room, I say, "You seem a lot closer to the children than I remember."

"Being cooped up in this guardhouse with them for four days will do that."

I freeze on the threshold of the next room—an armory—as he grabs a crossbow off the wall and tosses it to me. I catch it by instinct. "Four days?" My voice comes out in a croak.

His dark eyes catch mine, reading the shock there. "We were all separated four days ago. None of us knew where you were and when I tried to get back into the palace to find you and the Neverseen King, it was overrun with strange creatures. I was forced to retreat."

I catch my balance on the doorframe. *Four days*. I've lost three days because the portal didn't put me back exactly where I left. That leaves only two days until Lulythinar. My breathing comes faster with the sheer weight of what is before us.

We needed more time, and now I've lost *three entire days.*

And, I think with a crumbling heart, *I've lost Kaladen.*

"Are you alright?" asks Tariq, studying me and taking a step away from his wall of weapons. His eyes land on the collar around my neck. A thousand questions seem to bubble to his lips, but he only speaks the one.

I close my eyes briefly. I didn't go through the hell of Valehaven to give up hope now. Kaladen's imprisonment won't be for nothing.

Eshe didn't die in vain. I won't allow it.

I push off the wall, shifting the crossbow to my right hand and hobbling to the wall next to Tariq, grabbing a quiver of arrows while I try to ignore the pain shooting up my leg. "There's much I need to discuss with you. And . . ." My voice falters slightly, but I need to know. "What happened to Eshe's body?"

He is busy taking his own crossbow and arrows from the wall. At my question, his brow softens. "I've kept her safe. The children and I perfumed and wrapped her body. She's on the top floor of this guardhouse, resting in a bed we carried up the stairs."

Fresh tears well up, clouding my vision. I reach out and catch his arm. The words are barely audible when they leave my mouth: "Thank you."

He swallows and looks away. "She was a special woman. I didn't know her long, but it didn't take much to see that. We all intend to give her a proper burial as befits one so noble." He gestures with his chin at the rest of the wall before me. "Take whatever you need. They probably aren't as good as what you are used to, but they're better than nothing."

I squeeze his arm and let go, not trusting myself to speak. I quickly arm myself with an abundance of knives and trade my scimitar for a better one, in addition to the crossbow I already carry. Tariq grabs two more quivers of arrows and leads the way up another flight of stairs. His boots stomp loudly as we go—completely at odds with the silent way I instinctively move.

"If we need to talk, we might as well be productive," he says with a half-smile as he shoves open a door and points to the windows facing three directions. "We called this the eagle's nest. It's the best archer position in the entire guardhouse. Let me know if you run out of arrows. Sit down and get your weight off that foot."

Badh-o slides onto one of the windowsills, lets out a sighing squeak of relief, and winds herself into a circle. A second later, a quiet humming begins. I cover my mouth as I smile. How adorable—she's snoring! The poor thing must be utterly spent. Like I am.

I take up my post at the window opposite Tariq's. I load the crossbow, squint into the street below. There are so many inky blue targets running around that it's almost hard to pick one. I narrow in on a goblin trying to bang through the ripped shutters of a house, aim, and fire. The goblin falls.

"Keep track of how many you kill," says Tariq, already on his third shot. "There will be a prize later."

I cannot help my laugh and begin shooting in earnest. "Challenge accepted."

It's quiet for several minutes, except the twang of our arrows. My thoughts fill to the brim, and I'm not even sure where to begin. I'm grateful that Tariq doesn't rush me.

"The night Eshe died," I say at last, "one of Kaladen's enemies came through one of the portals—the one that leads to Valehaven, where Kaladen and the fae like him are from. This enemy is called the Wolf, and he captured me and Kaladen. He intended to claim the position of Neverseen King." I stop, suddenly wondering if Tariq understands anything I'm saying.

"He explained everything to me," says Tariq, not even looking up from his crossbow.

"You are adept at reading minds."

"No, I just pay attention."

I give a soft snort just before I pull the trigger and kill another goblin off the roof of someone's home. "The Wolf apparently thought I came along with the position of Neverseen King. He's the one who put the collar on me. It blocks my magic completely. I cannot even directly use my blood to seal or open portals without losing consciousness."

"What attempts have you made at removing it?"

"Kaladen says it has to be removed by someone with enough power to absorb the *pollution* of the spell." My hand goes to the pocket of my sirwal where the Eye's hair rests. I have the power to remove it right now, yet I cannot bring myself to use it. There are *so many things* I need, so many wrongs I need to right, that I'm terrified the second I call in my favor, I'll realize how I should have used it on something else. The removal of my collar feels so tremendously small a need in comparison to Kaladen's lost throne and the looming threat of Lulythinar.

I could ask for Kaladen to have his throne restored, but while in possession of Kaladen's name, the High King could simply order him to hand the throne over again. Ordering the Wolf's death could temporarily fix things—until the High King found some other horrible candidate for Kaladen's throne. If I asked for the disaster of Lulythinar to be thwarted, my people spared, or mine and Kaladen's life spared, any of those things could be granted in a way that only forestalls disaster a single day.

I shoot away the thought by picking off another goblin in the streets below. Already, the streets are far less overrun. We would be fighting a losing battle if I hadn't closed that portal. "After I escaped the Wolf, I went to Valehaven." I quickly summarize what happened, ending on the grim note of, "And now the Wolf and Kaladen are back here in Arbasa. When I closed the goblin portal, I saw Kaladen. He . . . told me to run away as fast as I could. So I came here."

Tariq loads his crossbow and shoots with fluid precision. "So we must count Kaladen our enemy for now."

"Not an enemy to kill," I say quickly.

"But an enemy to flee from."

My hollow stomach turns over on itself. I shoot another goblin.

"It's been dangerous here too," Tariq says. "This new ruler, the Wolf—"

"Citizens of the human lands!" cries a voice from the streets below us.

Tariq yanks his crossbow out of the window and hisses, "Get down!"

I've already flattened to the floor, my heart pounding at that harsh, grating voice. My gaze seizes with Tariq's as we stay below the windows. "I need to leave. The Wolf has come for me. I cannot let him hurt the children. I have to keep him away."

His face is flint. "Not yet."

"I am your new Neverseen King!" bellows the Wolf from below. "I decree that a living human be brought to the palace every morning at dawn—or I shall come get two instead."

Visions flash through my mind of the things I've seen him do to vulnerable humans. Tariq and I don't break eye contact, our common fear binding us together as the Wolf continues. He's right below us now. I hope our defending guards have taken shelter.

"I am looking for my wife: the Mourner, Queen Nadira. If you have seen her, hand her over at once!"

Tariq's jaw hardens. Then his attention snags over my head. I turn to follow his gaze and find the figure of a woman, wearing an overlarge cloak, crouched on the nearby roof. She watches the street, keeping her head low so she isn't spotted.

Why does she seem familiar somehow?

As we watch, she scurries further away from us, following the Wolf's progression down the street. His back is to us now, so I brave a glance out the window—only to discover that Kaladen, not wearing a stitch of shadow to cover his clean, fine garments or his face, follows a step behind the shadow-cloaked Wolf. From here, Kaladen looks terrifying, with his massive height and breadth and the purposeful way he strides down the street. As though he is not a prisoner at the Wolf's very whims.

I clench my teeth. I will get my husband back.

Movement draws my attention from the street back to the rooftop. The woman has moved several houses down from us and now balances a crossbow on her left arm as she takes aim. When she does, a portion of her hood blows aside, revealing a glimpse of her profile.

My eyes widen.

Kanza.

The last surviving woman from the competitions, besides me and the first girl I never met. It strikes me in that moment—the fact that twelve of us stood before Kaladen's steward, Emin, the first day we were brought to the House, and now nearly all of us are dead. Even Emin himself is gone. Only Kanza, Kaladen, the first girl, and I of that group still breathe.

It feels like another world. Another age entirely. If I'd known what awaited me and the way my life would irrevocably change, I might not have had the courage to face this path. I might have gone back to Jabir.

My hands, braced on the floor, slowly curl into fists. I would never have experienced love like I know now. Love that can rip you apart even as it heals you. Love that . . . *changes* you.

Kanza fires her crossbow.

At the Wolf, I realize belatedly when a bellowing scream echoes from below. She slides off the roof just as a bolt of magic blasts where she had been only a second before. When I peer over the edge of the window, I see that it's Kaladen with an upraised fist, his face a stony mask. The Wolf snarls beside him, his glamoured shadows faltering where the arrow pierced his shoulder. But now he's connected to the Bridge's healing magic, and he only has to yank out the arrow before the wound will begin stitching itself back up.

My heart clenches painfully. I duck back to safety as Kanza disappears into the city.

"She hit him," I whisper quickly to Tariq, who braces his forearms on the floor. "One weakness of the Neverseen Kings is that using healing magic drains their strength. If we can all shoot him at once—if maybe six or seven of us could make the shot—we might have a chance at killing him."

"He's been marching through the city every morning and evening, saying the same thing," says Tariq, getting up and moving to the window. "We can plan an ambush for tonight. I've lost three men already to the creature's appetite."

I follow the path where Kanza disappeared. "You get your men on board. I'll go get us another ally."

CHAPTER 12

KALADEN

"STAND STILL AND do not interfere," was the Wolf's order before he ripped a married couple from their home and slaughtered them. So I stand still, not interfering, as everything inside me seethes and revolts. The other order he gave me before he called me from my pursuit of Nadira to march with him through Risya was: "Protect me." It was not *"Destroy all who lift a finger against me,"* which gave me exactly the room I needed to purposefully miss Kanza when I fired at her on the rooftop. The Wolf must have restored her memories too, not just Raha's.

I keep catching whiffs of Nadira's scent—though it is still muted because of her collar—and I grow more relieved when the further we march into the city, the lesser her scent becomes until it finally disappears altogether. I don't want to know where she is.

Still, the marriage bond between us remains strong. It will not take long at all for me to find her when I finally am forced to hunt her down before sundown.

For this moment, however, I can delay my pursuit.

She ought to be running away, fleeing to some distant kingdom to prevent me from catching her. She isn't, however. She's still in the city, and I doubt she has any intention to leave it.

My ribcage aches from the tension building inside it.

I have only until this evening to kill the Wolf before he does something horrible to Nadira. Every step through the city was a step where I debated whether I could move fast enough to kill him right then. But even though he cried aloud to the people of Risya, paralyzing them with terror, his focus seemed anchored to me.

I couldn't risk it.

I wasn't even sure if the magic would let me, given his order to protect him.

Even now, as he buries his face in his meal, he seems more aware of me than ever. I cannot wait forever for him to forget about me. I curse him silently in my mind.

Suddenly, he lifts his maw, gore streaking down the matted fur of his chin and neck. He gives me a wolfish grin. "I realize I have forgotten an important order."

My stomach bottoms out.

"Do not kill me—or try to kill me. Or weaken or harm me in any way."

An empty chasm yawns before me. One of true hopelessness. If I cannot kill him, and if Nadira cannot escape me, then what will happen to her? What will he do to her? Will he kill her like he killed these two innocents and drain her blood for his use? Or will it be worse?

I give a singular nod, keeping my voice level. "Understood."

The Wolf's grin widens. "Oh, I've ordered you just in time! You were looking for an opportunity, you backstabber!"

I restrain the cutting reply on my tongue. "There are open portals, my liege. Do you want me to tend to them?"

The Wolf picks up part of his meal—the gnawed off arm of one of his victims—and waves it around, pointing the crimson fingers at me. "So noble of you to be concerned with the portals! What do these trifling ones matter when compared to Crenfyre? Just let the Bridge's defenses deal with what comes out of those portals. If you are always sealing them, the defenses will never be activated, and you will have to do so much more work than necessary. And if you're so worried about the city, they have warriors to handle these things. Not that their warriors are worth much, but they're enough for the humans."

He returns to his meal, leaving me stunned where I stand. I knew the Wolf would spell disaster for the Bridge, but this level of sheer *ignorance* is more than I thought him capable of. He talks as if Crenfyre is the only portal of true danger. As if the Neverseen King's one task is containing Crenfyre alone. Does he not realize that protecting the human world is not the only reason we seal these portals? There are *hundreds* of worlds, all protected in their own pocket of space. The wrong creature getting into another world could spell the utter end of that entire world. And with Lulythinar on the horizon, dozens of portals could open at once. If we are not even *trying* to keep them closed—

A dark, bitter part of me thinks that Faradir will be sorry for siding with the Wolf when dracoli from Roltwart burn his beautiful Valehaven palace and turn his exquisite Maltun Sea into a boiling bed of lava.

I do not think the Wolf is *only* lazy, careless, and interested in nothing but my demise. He truly seems to be ignorant of the threat looming before us.

But part of me wonders if there is something else at play here.

"Lulythinar—" I start.

The Wolf spins on his heel, snapping his dripping jaw at me. "Enough from you! I will give you orders, and you will obey them. You will no longer pester me with your petty concerns. There is only one thing on my mind now. Fetch me my bride, Kaladen Ashrift Felladyr."

CHAPTER 13

NADIRA

I CLIMB OUT of the eagle's nest, careful to avoid putting too much weight on my bruised foot. I use my rope to swing to the roof of the next building, and then I'm off after Kanza.

My progress is agonizingly slow compared to my usual pace. Kanza is little more than a flash of cloak ahead of me, leaping lightly between rooftops. But I grit my teeth and press onward. Even one ally can make the difference.

I slip on my bad foot, dislodging a weak stone from a house's upper parapet. It crashes to the ground loudly. Kanza's head whips toward me.

Not knowing what else to do, I wave.

She seems to freeze slightly. Then she turns on her tail and picks up her pace.

"Kanza!" I shout desperately, my throat going hoarse.

She doesn't stop, and a second later, she vanishes completely.

I curse bitterly. I keep moving forward in hope of catching sight of her again—even just an inch of shadow—but my pace flags. I cannot catch up to her in my current state.

Cursing again, I finally give up and use my rope to swing down to the alleyway.

My spine prickles the moment I'm on the ground. I know this feeling. This feeling of being watched.

Weighing my options, I decide to take a gamble. I bend down to survey my aching foot. Mottled blue and purple skin meets my gaze. I give a slight press and wince at the shooting pain. That stupid goblin hammer probably fractured a bone or two.

Cool steel slides against my throat above my collar.

"Hello, Kanza," I say.

"Don't move. Put your hands on the ground where I can see them."

The girl I met in the competition never spoke with this iron-hard voice. Kanza was always timid, one of the sweeter ones, and refused to say an unkind word about the Neverseen King.

I place my hands flat on the dusty ground and go still. I don't speak either.

"Why are you following me, Nadira? Or should I say, *Mourner*?"

Apparently, news traveled fast of my identity when it was revealed. "Because I want to kill the Wolf too."

A small stone crunches under her foot. "You will have to lie a little more convincingly to get me to trust you. You work for the Neverseen King, who serves that monster."

"The Neverseen King is a prisoner of the Wolf."

"He shot me."

"He missed."

The quiet after those words gives me a sliver of hope. I continue, pressing my scrap of advantage.

"You know he didn't have to miss."

She doesn't reply.

"You must have heard the Wolf bellowing in the streets too. Asking the city to turn me over to him. If that does not convince you of where my loyalties lie, I do not know what will."

The silence that follows suddenly strikes me differently. As though my last statement raised her hackles. Does she wonder if the Wolf only called that into the streets to make my position as his spy less conspicuous? Does she think I am his plant, here to make the city fall from the inside?

I'm losing her. She will remove her knife from my neck and flee, knowing that with my injury, I am too slow to catch up to her.

My voice drops to a whisper. "I saved your life, Kanza."

This startles a blurted, "What?" from her lips.

"I found you in that maze after Raha stabbed you. I bound up your wound to keep you from bleeding out and called the Neverseen King. He took you out and healed you, before returning you to your home."

"I didn't do anything to Raha." Kanza's statement is almost defensive, hurt.

"I know," I reply softly. "She thought you were me."

The knife leaves my throat. I stay where I am, ears prickling for the silent rush of her retreat.

Instead, she circles to face me. Her sirwal is torn, the fine color covered in layers of grime. Her tunic is the same, and she sports bruises on the lean, bronzed arms that flash beneath her dark cloak. When my gaze travels up to her face, I find more of the softness I remember of her flashing across her pupils, fighting to hide beneath this harsher persona.

"So—me and you, against two beings of such power?" she asks.

I shrug, my lip lifting in a small smile. "We've got the city guard too."

When we get back to the guardhouse, the city is unusually quiet after the screeching fury of the goblins. Blue bodies lay scattered about the sandy streets. It seems as though the whole city holds its breath for what new terror will come from the Neverseen King's palace next.

Tariq ushers us inside quickly, no less on edge than when they were under attack. Exhaustion lines his handsome face, but he offers a nod to Kanza, who gives a short little wave.

"Kanza, this is Tariq, captain of the guard," I say. "Tariq, this is Kanza, our newest sharpshooter."

Kanza's face flushes slightly at the praise. Now that she is out of danger, she glances around uncertainly, her eyes wide like I remembered them.

"An honor," Tariq replies. "My men will finish their rounds soon and regroup. We will discuss killing the Wolf then. For now, are either of you hungry? There is food. We should eat while we have the chance."

At the mention of food, my whole body goes weak with hunger. "Yes," I say, with a desperate laugh. "Please!"

Kanza nods eagerly, and the three of us take the stairs—Tariq aiding me again to avoid straining my foot more than necessary.

Tariq settles us on the floor in a room separate from the small children, a pile of dates, flatbread, and hummus between us. It is a relief to be seated, not pressing weight on my foot, with a spread of food before me. We all eat greedily, as though none of us have eaten in days. Only Tariq seems to keep a measured pace as he eats, and it reminds me to do the same.

"Kanza," I say, tearing off a piece of my flatbread and scooping up a heap of hummus with it, "if you don't mind me asking, why were you raised as an assassin?"

"Assassin is a bit of a strong word," she replies with a small chuckle. "The leaders of the city knew the legend, that the Neverseen King comes for a bride every hundred years. According to the records they kept through the generations, no bride had been taken for nearly two hundred years. They did not think they would be spared a second time. Many of those men raised their daughters in preparation."

"Preparation for what?" Tariq asks. "To kill the Neverseen King?"

She shrugs. "Different men had different motives. Some hated the Neverseen King, and raised their daughters in hopes they would be strong enough to kill him. My father intended for me to be able to protect myself, if I was taken."

"From Kaladen?" I ask, surprised, thinking back to how positively she always spoke of him.

"Kaladen?"

"The Neverseen King," I correct.

"Oh, no! My family has always been loyal to him. No, it was in case others tried to hurt me if I were queen."

"That must have been tremendous pressure for a young girl to carry," Tariq says.

Kanza looks up at him, her eyebrows going high. Her shoulders relax just slightly, and she turns back to the food spread between us, tucking a lock of her dark hair behind her ear. "Actually, yes. Yes, it was. And the whole ordeal at the palace was much more than I was prepared for. I didn't remember it at first—I simply woke up in my bed one day and felt strangely bewildered, though I hadn't a clue why I should feel that way." A shiver goes through her. "It wasn't until a strange man found me and scared me half to death by sneaking up behind me, that I . . ."

I peel open a date, remove the pit, and stick the date in my mouth. "The Wolf returned your memories."

"I didn't know he was the Wolf." She shivers again. "He was there and gone so fast, and when all the memories came back, I just sat there in shock and anger. Raha almost *killed* me, and I'd done nothing to her."

Tariq's face remains impassive, yet his deliberate inhale and exhale communicate his sense of violated justice.

"No one was prepared for what we faced in the Neverseen King's palace," I say.

Kanza's voice is bitter. "No one, except Safya and Raha."

"It is a sad thing to be prepared for horrors," Tariq mutters quietly.

Kanza looks at him again with that surprise, then, with a blink and a swallow, turns to me. "What about you? You weren't like the women I knew who tried to prepare to be taken. You came from somewhere else."

I pause, another bite of flatbread halting on its way to my mouth. I've never told anyone my story, except for Eshe and Kaladen. During the competition, I had to fight to keep my identity as the Mourner a secret, lest I be caught and executed for my crimes. Even now, if Tariq weren't my ally, it could still happen.

To my shock, I find I want to tell Kanza and Tariq. I . . . *trust* them.

I set down my food. "I was also prepared to be the bride of the Neverseen King, though I did not know it at the time."

I tell them of Jabir, of his fae heritage, how he was able to scent out my magic, how he decided to use me to get revenge on Kaladen. I tell of the way he slaughtered my parents, took me captive, and trained me in the ways of bloodshed. I tell of how he forced me to kill, to become the Mourner.

They listen quietly, neither saying a word, until I finish. Even then, they remain silent. Tariq doesn't look at me, and only his measured breaths indicate his mounting anger.

"All this time," Kanza whispers, and I could swear tears glisten in the gaze she does not lift to mine, "the Mourner was a young girl forced to kill."

Strangely, instead of my own howling winds of rage blowing through me, or the cavernous pull of despair, I feel only a muted sadness. "It is what it is."

The prickle of attention makes me look up. Tariq's dark eyes are fixed on me. His low voice is little but a murmur. "I'm sorry you went through that."

A stronger sense of peace settles into my heart. "If it prepared me to save Kaladen from the Wolf and get Arbasa back, it will have been worth it."

Tromping footsteps up the stairs signals the end of our conversation. We all turn as guards file into the room, weary and spattered with blue blood. Tariq gets to his feet at once, and bids the men to eat their fill of the meal.

He draws his shoulders straight, ever the regal captain of the guard. Kanza, suddenly shy in the presence of so many strangers, scoots with me to the back of the room, but her attention does not shift from Tariq.

His voice rings with command as he declares: "Tonight, we kill the Wolf."

CHAPTER 14

NADIRA

I OFFER TO be part of the group of shooters poised on rooftops for the Wolf's return to the city, but after discussing things with Tariq, we decide on a different task for me.

Since the Wolf clearly has no interest in sealing the portals himself and we have had several ominously quiet hours, it is decided that I will return to the palace to close what portals might open. If another onslaught of foreign creatures from another world descends upon the city, the guards will be far too busy fighting to have a chance to attack the Wolf.

I must give them whatever chance they have to succeed. If we can successfully kill the Wolf and reinstate Kaladen as the Neverseen King, we can use my favor from the Eye to fix one of the other impending disasters.

"Please be careful," Tariq tells me, gripping my shoulder with his broad hand.

I smile. "You, too."

Then I head out of the guardhouse into the hazy afternoon. Kanza wrapped my foot to ease some of the pain, and it helps me work my way faster through the maze of alleyways, toward the palace.

Halfway there, ice runs down my spine.

I know this feeling. It is more than the prickle of eyes on me. It sends cold to my toes, very unlike the sense of Kanza's eyes when she circled back to catch me off my guard.

No, this takes me back to the dark shadows of Lord Kishon's mansion. My last assassination, the night the Neverseen King stole me as his captive. This is a deep certainty that fills my bones. It is the assurance that a hunter has marked me as his prey.

My mouth goes dry.

It must be Kaladen.

I turn on my heel and make a mad dash in the opposite direction, leaping over fallen crates and using a barrel to launch myself high enough to grab a roof's edge and pull myself onto it. My foot screams from the ill use, but I hardly notice it.

In my periphery, I catch a glimpse of a large, cloaked figure dashing toward me.

Definitely Kaladen.

He wears no shadows, and he does not slip into the dream realm, but he's swift and nimble, and he gains ground fast.

I clench my fists and take off once more. I race across the flat rooftop, reaching the parapet. My plan was to leap across the distance to the next roof, but it's too far. I skitter to a stop and swing over the waist-high bricks and drop myself to the ground below. I try not to jar my foot on my landing with a roll, but it immediately gives out when I put weight on it.

Dead blue goblins lie in the street like splatters of thick ink on a page.

Reminding me what is at stake.

I'm not going back to the Wolf.

My teeth grind and I force myself forward. I grab hold of a wall and limp as fast as I can, cutting a zigzag, roundabout path through the alleys, trying anything I can to lose Kaladen. But when I look back, I'm leaving a trail of dusty footprints.

I need to get to the roofs again.

I keep moving, one hand braced along the stone wall of someone's house as I drag my useless foot behind me. There's no way I can get up to the roof, but I move as fast as I can and watch for anything easy to climb. If I were running from anyone else, hiding would be my best option.

But not Kaladen. Not my own husband, whose blood is bonded with mine.

I'm not going back to the Wolf. It becomes a chant that propels me through the pain and makes me work faster. *I'm not going back to the Wolf.*

I turn left into a darker alleyway. When I glance back, a long, terrible shadow stretches in the dimness. My heart leaps to my throat, and I break into an agonizing run. I dodge around empty crates, duck under an empty clothesline, and nearly trip in a wheel rut.

Then I wheel to a sudden stop.

At the end of this alleyway is a three-story building. It's a dead end.

My lungs fill in a silent gasp.

No windows with ledges to easily scale. Even the brick face is smooth, leaving little for handholds or footholds. I whip out my rope. If I can just anchor it somewhere on top—

A hand grabs my wrist.

My blade is out the next instant.

I find myself flattened against the wall, my wrist pinned over my head, my scimitar poised against Kaladen's throat as his powerful gaze slices into me.

The part of me that loves him more than my own life wants to crumble to pieces, to just toss myself into his arms and pray somehow he won't turn me over to the Wolf. That his love for me will be greater than the compulsion that binds his will.

But the rational part of me knows that if I give in now, I'm giving up for all Arbasa. I'm giving up hope of saving Kaladen. Of saving all of us from the Wolf and the High King of Faerie and the ravages of Lulythinar. If I trust him now, I may destroy Tariq's chance of killing the Wolf.

I harden myself against him.

"I don't want to hurt you," I snarl, "but I will if you try to drag me before the Wolf."

Kaladen's cerulean eyes snap. Then his hands are on either side of my face, his weight leaning into me as he pulls me into a violent kiss. My blade falters, my grip weakening, as his kiss sweeps through me. It rips past my guard, past every rational thought, until I can do nothing but kiss him back, matching his fevered desperation. My blade is still between us, flattened, and when I release it, it clatters to the ground.

Kaladen's arms are around me, pressing me to his chest, holding me so hard I cannot draw a breath. For this one moment, I let myself soften completely into him, into his strength, into the hope that somehow everything will be alright.

"I told you to get out of here," he growls savagely into my neck. "You must leave. You must get out of Risya—right now!"

But still he holds me.

"I can't go, Kaladen! Not while—"

His reply is almost violent. "*You must go!* The Wolf has ordered me to bring you to him. I have until sundown. You must get as far away from here as you can! Find a horse, find something. You must be selfish this once, my wife. Get out of here before I am forced to hurt you."

"But the portals—the city—*you*!"

"None of those will matter if he gets his hands on you. I cannot watch you die. I watched Liliana die. I cannot—" His voice shatters. "Nadira, you are all I have left. Spare me, I beg of you. Run away where I will never find you. Don't let me ever see you again."

His broken pleas nearly wrench the tears from my eyes, the thought of never seeing him again too cruel and sharp to bear. "Kaladen, please!"

"Let me see your foot." He scoops me up and sits down against the wall, cradling me in his lap. I soak up the feeling of his bigness surrounding me like a shield. His hand wraps gently around my ankle, bringing it closer and peeling off the bandage. The swelling has only increased, the skin a horrible, mottled color, and at his touch, I flinch. Oh so carefully, as though he handles the thinnest glass, he cups the arch of my foot. I go rigid, breathing through the pain, as he sends his healing magic into my flesh. "You cannot run away well with this foot."

I shake my head once, then lean on his broad shoulder. I close my eyes, fall into his warmth, and in the darkness behind my lids, certainty grows inside me.

I cannot leave Risya. Tariq and Kanza and I—we have a plan. A plan that just might work. Even if it all burns to the ground and the entire city is slaughtered, I cannot give up. We still have a chance at this. A chance to fix this. If I run away, we will lose every hope. I could never live with myself if I didn't even *try*.

But I cannot tell Kaladen. I cannot tell him anything. As long as he is enslaved to the Wolf, I must lie to him. I must be strong enough on my own.

It is strange to feel the icy determination grow in my gut, and yet not have my magic respond to me. It is as though one of my limbs has been cut off, despite feeling its phantom remnants.

The pain leaves my foot like the resolving note of a chord, and I sag in relief. "Thank you."

He holds me close for one more minute, his arms about me, his big hand cupping the back of my head, his legs supporting me. I breathe in his warm scent.

Then he pushes me away, and his beautiful, hardened face twists in anguish. "Get out of here, Nadira."

Tears prickling my lids, I scoop up my fallen scimitar, turn on my heel, and run.

CHAPTER 15

NADIRA

KALADEN DOES NOT pursue me—yet—and I first run as fast as I can to the guardhouse stables, so that if he tracks me, he will think I took a horse and fled the city. Badh-o takes my hair scarf and we split directions, in hopes that she might fool Kaladen with my scent if the horse diversion doesn't. Then I take a roundabout way to the palace.

It is strangely quiet when I arrive. An eerie sort of stillness. My spine prickles, a certainty growing in my gut. Two strings pluck at my awareness, consistent and nagging.

Kaladen once said my connection with the Bridge would grow. Now, I can only take these insistent tugs to mean that two portals are open. Immediately, my blood spikes. Only three portals need to open before the House's defenses activate—and a third could open at any moment.

Even now, as I stand in the open hallway near the Emerald Hall, I think there might be another thread just beyond my awareness. It's asking me to notice it, begging me to realize it, too, wants to open.

No monsters run amok *yet,* but if I leave these two open portals unchecked, the House will activate its defenses—and I'll be completely crippled in my ability to seal anything. I curse the fact that I can't enter the dream realm without Kaladen, and then I rush into action.

I follow one of the threads to a door I've seen before. It's open. I peer inside and hear the mournful plucking of a stringed instrument.

The room—the world—is green.

Not the color of leaves or grass, but the heavy, saturated green of a forest caught in a dream—lush and endless. The walls melt into mossy boughs, and the ceiling vanishes into a leafy canopy. Vines curl from the corners, unmoving and dead in contrast to the vibrant life of Badh-o. Ferns spill from the cracks between the stones beneath my feet, though no dirt anchors them, no sunlight feeds them.

It should feel radiant, like the rainforest portal. But it doesn't.

There are no shadows.

That is what sets my teeth on edge. Despite the thick foliage, the world is flooded with even, source-less light—flat and uncanny. Nothing hides, but nothing lives either. It's as if the room is pretending to be a forest, mimicking nature without understanding it. The air is hushed, and there's no birdsong, no wind, no rustle.

Only a harp.

It stands in the center, tall and golden, shining with a luster that doesn't belong to this world. Strings shimmer faintly as they pluck themselves, over and over again, playing the same three notes. A soft, endless lament.

The sound seems to pierce straight into my ribs.

I hesitate at the threshold, half-expecting something to leap from the illusion of underbrush. But the harp is the only thing that stirs. Its strings tremble faintly with motion I cannot see, and its sorrowing song refuses to stop.

I remember this portal. It was open once, one of the first days I was here—when Kaladen brought me for the competition. He didn't seem worried about it then. I won't be worried now.

I move into action. Piled around the edge of the harp are an abundance of smooth blue pebbles. I pick one up, heart racing, waiting again for something to rush forward and meet the edge of the knife I clutch. But nothing happens. So I take the pebble and rush out of the room. I seal the portal quickly. My breath comes a little easier.

But already, another very subtle plucking on my awareness has grown into an insistent nagging. That third portal has opened.

I must move quickly.

I hurry to the next portal—it's close. The door is cracked, so I push it open the rest of the way. I can't see the seals, not being in the dream realm, but there are teeth marks along the door and on many others. I remember what Kaladen once told me, that goblins chew on magic, and I wonder with cold dread how many portal seals they've damaged.

Inside this portal is a mountain of books. They're strewn every which way—some upside down, spines cracked, pages flying loose, piled higher than I am tall. At the very center, reaching up toward a domed ceiling, is a single, enormous book. It is the size of ten humans.

I don't have time to waste. With my knife drawn, I clamber up the mountain of books, dislodging them as I go, not sparing a thought for the disrespect toward all these words on paper. At the top, the massive book lies open. I notice that someone has been peeling small pieces off the corner—almost as if a rodent has been chewing at this page.

This must be how Kaladen sealed it once—by tearing off a piece of the paper.

I reach out and touch the book. The moment my fingers land on the page, vibrant reds, greens, and blues swirl across its vast expanse. Shapes rise—tall, crowned figures with long, pointed ears and beautiful faces. They're strapped with weapons, and somehow, I know without knowing: these are the Great Kings Kaladen has spoken of.

I watch as they make war against creatures of all kinds, corralling them into their own worlds. I watch them lock each one behind a door. And then the words slip from my mouth: "They're creating the Bridge. All those doors—it's the Bridge."

The final door is split in half, as though lightning had struck it in a jagged line down the center. Mist curls out of it.

Crenfyre.

Why is it . . . broken?

I have no idea how long I stare at the page, watching the images morph, twist, and reassemble—until I see a strange silhouette. A young woman with a scarf over her hair and knives in her hands. She sneaks up behind someone at a desk and slices his throat open.

I jerk back. The colors vanish, leaving the page blank. My heart pounds. My face had only been inches from the page, as if I were being . . . drawn in.

A shiver races down my spine.

I look down and see a torn scrap of paper in my hand.

The one I need.

Nausea churns in my belly. I turn on my heel and scramble out of the portal room. There's a certainty like in a dream—the certainty of death. The story almost . . . *ate* me, almost pulled me inside and imprisoned me forever.

I rush to seal the portal. I scrape open my finger, bleed across the seal, and press the scrap of paper to it. I can't see the seal come to life—but the door stays closed.

Now, on to the third one.

I still don't know where the Wolf is. With any luck, Kaladen thinks I've escaped and will follow Badh-o's trail out of the city. But I can't believe he won't figure out very quickly exactly where I've gone.

I glance at the light streaming through the clear glass ceiling above. It's almost evening. It won't be long before Kaladen brings me before the Wolf, whether he wants to or not. Not long before the Wolf makes his parade through the city—giving Tariq and his guards and Kanza a chance to kill him.

I hurry toward the third portal.

Even before I reach it, a strange ashy cry echoes down the hall, and the scent of sulfur and smoke hits me hard.

My mind won't speak the name, but I know which portal this is. I've never been inside it before. Kaladen never let me near this one.

As I turn the corner, angry red smoke billows from beneath the door. Screeches and the beat of wings emanate beyond that smoke. How long until they realize our world is open to them, and flood Arbasa?

If I can't get this sealed—fast—it will ruin all chance Tariq and Kanza have of killing the Wolf.

"There's nothing to it," I mutter, and plunge into the smoke.

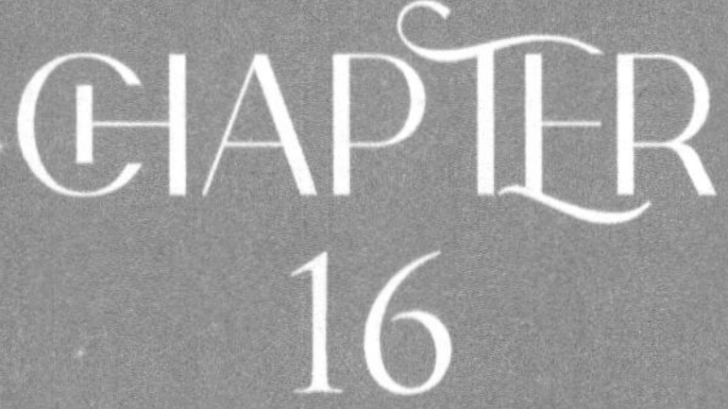

CHAPTER 16

KALADEN

I WISH I was fooled by little Badh-o, but the moment I reached the guardhouse stables, I knew what Nadira had done. She hadn't escaped.

She'd gone to the palace.

I want to strangle her. She won't let me protect her. She is bound and determined to ruin me. Still, I admire her courage. I think back to the first night she stayed at the palace, how terrified she was, how much she struggled deciding if she should throw herself in danger and leave her room when she feared Eshe was hurt.

There is no hesitation in her now. Where she was once shackled completely by fear, she is now motivated by something much stronger.

I hate her even as I love her for it.

I'm almost to the palace when I feel the resolving chord of threads in my chest. One portal, and not long later, the second one closes.

Portals that have been bothering me since I returned, that the Wolf refused to allow me to close.

My first thought is of relief, that the portals are being sealed. My second, quick on the heels of the first, is the horrible realization that Nadira is *in the palace right now* with the Wolf, and I'm not there to protect her—as if my presence would be any protection.

My third thought is stitched of pure dread.

Another portal opens.

Roltwart.

Nadira is going to try to seal it. The portal that killed Liliana.

My blood turns to white-hot fear. She is not strong enough to close that portal—not without the protection of the dream realm.

The words rip from my chest in a terrible cry. "Great Kings!"

I slip into the dream realm and rush to the palace as fast as I can. I cannot be too late. I cannot. If she dies, if Roltwart takes her—

The seal is blackened, chewed to bits by goblins, and the door hangs listlessly on its hinges when I arrive. A creature of charred black coals crawls out of the open door, its reptilian mouth snarling in rows of fangs, smoke pouring from its bulbous nostrils. Its claws scrape the floor, its thick belly dragging, its long tail whipping behind it.

I slaughter the dracoli with a blade through its skull before it can make its way to the city. Then I plunge into the burning red light of Roltwart. "Nadira!" I bellow into the thick, searing smoke. It burns my throat. "Nadira!"

The rocky terrain of Roltwart is unforgiving, the only light coming from magma pouring over the edge of a deep, deep chasm. One like the one Liliana fell into.

"Nadira!" I scream.

Dracoli hiss and crawl across the ground, intrigued by the waning daylight of the open portal into the human world. I kill all within reach, running across the cracked ground toward the anchor.

She's not dead, I tell myself over and over again, clinging to the pulsing link of her heartbeat. I can feel her. She is alive. She is here.

But when the smoke clears, and I reach the mound of hardened, black lava chips surrounding the glowing anchor, there is no sign of her. I cup both hands around my mouth and scream as loud as I can until my voice breaks: *"Nadira!"*

Where is that woman? Oh, why didn't she do as I told her to?

And she's not protected by the dream realm, just like Liliana wasn't when she died—because souls cannot be gathered in the dream realm. It is my nightmare all over again. Where could she be? She's not by the anchor, and she was not between the anchor and the door. So where—

That is when I hear it.

It is like distant thunder, rumbling and rhythmic. The ground shivers from the force of it.

I know exactly where Nadira is.

My blood turns to ice colder than her magic. My voice is raw, shredded. "Nadira, you fool!"

CHAPTER 17

NADIRA

I DID NOT recognize the pulsing beat of Roltwart's heart for the first few minutes inside the portal. I pulled my tunic to cover my nostrils, my eyes burning from the smoke, my lungs on fire. It sounded so far away at first, like a distant storm.

It was not until I touched the blackened charcoal surrounding the anchor that I realized just how . . . *rhythmic* that pulse was.

Because it *was* a pulse.

Kaladen told me the Roltwart heart moves around the portal and only rarely comes near the anchor. It is the only time that a piece of its heart can be taken to be made into a soul.

Immediately, everything inside me returned to the rainforest portal and that cabinet of glowing portal souls. Only two were missing. Two: Roltwart and Crenfyre. If they could be acquired, all of this

Bridge instability, all of this Lulythinar madness could be stopped. Risya and Arbasa could be saved. Tariq, Kanza, the children Eshe died protecting, Kaladen. They could be spared.

And Kaladen isn't here to stop me.

It doesn't matter that he thinks it is impossible to get Crenfyre's soul. We will find a way. Previous Neverseen Kings managed to get that mist to seal Crenfyre—the mist that is also in the rainforest portal. So there must be a way to get a piece of Crenfyre's heart.

Once we have the Roltwart soul and the Wolf is defeated, we can pour all of our energy into solving the problem of Crenfyre.

Right now, I must get a piece of Roltwart's heart.

Not that I have a clue how to do that. Kaladen never told me, of course.

I'll just figure it out.

The first, seemingly obvious step, is to find the place where the heartbeat is loudest.

Five steps toward it, and several more of those dragonlike salamander creatures come zigzagging toward me. I dodge backward, slicing with my scimitar, and my foot catches a ledge. I wheel my arms, my lungs leaping straight into my throat, as I regain my balance and glance behind me.

A deep, dark cut in the red rock, big enough for me to fall into, sends me skittering forward toward the salamanders, hacking blindly with my blade. That chasm wasn't there a moment ago. Is the ground always . . . shifting? Are new chasms constantly opening?

"She fell," Kaladen told me once, *"I've never known a moment more dreadful than when I screamed her name into that canyon. Counting the seconds while I still felt the raging rhythm of her heartbeat, knowing she was alive, alive, alive. And then, abruptly, it stopped."*

I gulp and get around the salamanders—did Kaladen call them dracoli?—before they bite off the foot he just healed. "I'm not going to fall," I growl, more to convince myself than anything. I pretend I don't notice how unsteady my legs feel, or how the blades in my hands quiver.

I hurry toward the *thump, thump, thump* of the thunderous heartbeat. I start at a fast jog, only to wheel to a stop when the ground splits directly in front of me. A geyser of smoke belches from that chasm. At the bottom, red, molten lava flows in a ceaseless stream.

I jog alongside it until I reach a narrow enough stretch for me to leap across. The pulse grows louder and louder. My eyes stream burning tears, and my lungs fill with acrid smoke. Heat sinks through the leather soles of my sandals, blistering my skin. Sweat pours down my skin in near-boiling rivulets.

I stop when the distant thunder has become a loud pounding of the ground beneath my feet. The heart is here. It must be here. I can hardly keep my balance from the way the ground rocks with each beat.

In the red dimness, a crack comes rushing toward me, cutting the red rock clean in half. I fling my body to the side, catching myself against the searing rock with my knuckles. A cry of pain escapes my clenched teeth. I roll to my feet, refusing to even look at my hands as my perspiration-soaked clothes smoke.

The new chasm seems to stretch as far as I can see in both directions, cutting off my escape toward the door. In a sudden, searing moment of terror, I wonder how I will cross it to get back to my world—and if I do cross it, how am I to even find my way out of here? What if I get lost, and die in this dark, red world of blistering heat and smoke?

Don't think about those things, I tell myself, finally admitting the fear-induced weakness spreading through my limbs. *You will make it out. You will save Kaladen, Tariq will kill the Wolf, Lulythinar will be forestalled, and Eshe will not have died in vain.*

Setting my jaw firmly, I approach the edge of the chasm. Since it split, the roar of its pulse is even louder than before, and when I peer into the darkness below me, a light shines.

It is not red like lava. It is a pure, white light. It bathes my face, relief flooding my entire body like a cool wind. I nearly sag to my knees, and only barely remember to squat instead. The glow is about three feet down the side of the chasm, only partially protruding from the rock. It throbs with each beat, and tiny white veins disappear from the heart into the ground.

I don't know how long I have until the chasms change again and the heart is buried once more. Still, premonition washes down my back. If I don't do this right, if I fall, if I am inside the chasm when it snaps shut—

"Nadira!" the choked cry sears across my awareness.

My head whips up. "Kaladen?"

He stands on the opposite side of the chasm, his legs braced wide, his hands outstretched toward me, his face white with panic. "Nadira!"

"I've almost got it!" I shout back. I'm already unwinding my rope, searching for a place to anchor it. I hope it is strong enough to not burn away from the heat. If any rope can handle it, it's my *jurbah* rope. But even so . . .

"Get away from the edge!"

I lift my determined gaze to him. I cannot explain it to him. He won't understand.

"You're going to die!" he screams.

I want to harden my heart to him. If I had my ice magic, I could. Instead, his desperation pierces me. It is like this chasm is my chest, cleaned open, my heart beating into the open air. I force myself to keep moving, to secure the rope around a jagged hold, testing my weight against it.

"Nadira, stop! Please!"

"Don't ask me to stop!" I shout across the distance between us, real tears streaming down my raw cheeks. "You know I must do this!"

"Let me do it—please!"

But he cannot do it. He is on the wrong side of the chasm. It grows harder to breathe by the moment, and I don't know how much longer I can survive in this world, and the heart won't come so close to the portal again before Lulythinar. This is our one chance. And if I die—

I lock my whimper behind my teeth, tugging once more on the rope secured around my waist. Just to make sure. I step to the edge of the drop, the red rock serrated like knives.

Kaladen is on his knees, his hand gripping his edge, ignoring the burns. "Nadira!"

I don't look at him as I lower myself over the edge.

CHAPTER 18

KALADEN

NADIRA SWINGS FROM her rope, one leg anchored against the side of the chasm, the other scrambling in midair. Her hands grip the rope, and for one terrible minute, she just hangs there, clinging and suspended above certain death.

Great Kings, I cannot watch this! It will tear me in two!

I shove away from the ledge, raking my burned palms through my hair, my breath ragged and painful in my chest. My entire body feels ready to explode with panic. If only I could get to her, if only I could get to that other side! I could make sure she doesn't fall. I could drag her up over that ledge and go down myself. Anything to make her stop.

Anything to not—

I hurry back, unable to not know what is happening.

And I am just in time to watch her swing wildly at the end of the rope, and one of her knives—the knife she was using to pierce the heart—goes flying into the abyss below. Her name screams in my head, over and over again. I dare not allow a single sound to escape me, lest she be distracted and die.

The vision keeps reappearing, of Nadira's rope breaking, of her falling, of her disappearing beyond view. One minute, it's her dark head I see, and the next, dirty yellow curls.

I never should have told her about the souls! I should have lied to her. I should have done *anything* but plant this idea in her head.

Her knife drives into the pulsing, white heart. It jolts, and the thunderous beat skips over itself. She braces both feet on the cliff edge, dangling from her rope. She uses her left hand to work her knife, while the other grips her rope.

For one instant, a blossom of hope, as bright and clear as the white heart Nadira cuts, shines into me. Maybe, just maybe, she can do it. Maybe she won't die.

Then the chasm shudders.

It's about to snap shut.

"It's going to close!" I shout into the smoky haze. "Get to the top!"

Can she even hear me? She lets go of the rope, not looking at me, and a tiny glowing white piece falls into her open palm. She pockets it, sheathes her knife, and grabs hold of the rope with both hands.

I cannot think. I cannot breathe. "Get to the top!"

She pulls herself toward the top. The chasm gives another shudder. Rocks crumble on the edge, falling the unfathomable distance to the bottom. I shove away again, fisting my hands in my hair, my chest burning. I cannot watch this.

I can't do anything. I can't do anything. I cannot help her. I cannot protect her.

A scream makes me whirl.

Nadira is almost to the top—and I am just in time to watch the shifting of the chasm snap her anchor.

She falls.

Everything inside me falls with her.

Horror stitches into the very fabric of my being. "*Nadira!*"

But she stops falling.

Somehow, she clings to the burning cliff. With her bare hands. Her legs swing wildly. More of the rockface falls into the abyss.

Then I remember that Liliana didn't fall immediately either—but she still fell. She still died.

I would leap into the chasm if it meant I could save her.

I would die a thousand times over to spare her.

But all I can do is watch, as I've done before, as my wife dies.

Nadira screams again. The sound wrenches me open. She gets a foothold and shoves up, putting an elbow on the ledge.

This hope is a violent, shredding curse.

She gets another elbow up, an ugly yell ripping from her throat. And then her feet are loose once more, wheeling in midair.

This is the moment, I realize, sick with dread. This is the moment she falls.

And then, with an unearthly roar and inhuman strength, Nadira pulls herself up to the ledge all the way to her hips. She rolls forward and scrambles—

She makes it. She pulls her body to safety and collapses on the boiling red rock.

Just as the chasm snaps shut.

I race across the distance between us and sink to my knees beside her. She is scored with burns, her hands and arms the worst, her skin blackened and her hair smoking just before it catches fire. I scoop her up, cradling her limp body to my chest as I run as fast as I can to the door of the portal.

CHAPTER 19

NADIRA

WHEN I COME to, I don't feel nearly so terrible as I expected to. In fact, when I peel open my eyelids and am met with the golden glow just before the sun sets, I can hardly believe how whole and strong I feel.

I realize I am leaning against a hard chest, one arm hanging loosely around my waist. Two long legs stretch out on either side of me on the floor. I lift my head.

Kaladen's lashes flutter briefly. He is slouched against the wall outside of the Roltwart Portal. When our eyes meet, a slanted V forms between his brows, and his weak arm tightens around me, pulling me to him and ducking his head against mine.

If he had much strength left after healing me, he would scold me soundly.

"I'm sorry I scared you," I whisper, curling up against him. "Thank you for healing me. And for getting me out of there."

"I am going to strangle you," he slurs with effort, and strokes the tips of my hair with his thumb.

"It would be well deserved."

His reply is a pained moan. "Don't joke with me right now."

I purse my lips, running my eyes along his big frame, so drained and exhausted. My heart goes out to him, breaking for what I made him endure. I bury my face in his neck and kiss his dirty skin. "I'm sorry, Kaladen."

His other hand lifts, slowly. I twist to look. In his palm, he holds a small egg, glowing a violent red.

"The Roltwart soul!" I cry, taking it reverently as he slides it into my waiting hands. "You've already . . . done whatever you do? To take the piece of heart and condense it?" I frown. "I don't remember what you said you do with it."

"I did, you idiot," he growls. "But you are *not* going inside Crenfyre to get that last soul. I will find a way myself. I cannot—please don't do that to me again."

I nod. There is no part of me that regrets what I did, and I would do it all over again in a heartbeat . . . but I could *almost* regret it, looking at him now.

Despite this, the smallest smile tugs at my lips. "There isn't even one teeny part of you that is glad for what I did?"

"Glad? No."

Part of me falls a little lower at that.

"Begrudgingly impressed? Yes, I will admit that." His words immediately warm me, and when I look up, he shakes his head, his mouth quirking ruefully. He reaches up and pinches my cheek before letting his heavy hand fall away. "I knew I was right to pick you."

I smile in earnest then. It quickly drops as I notice the shadows lengthening around us.

I have until sundown.

He cannot chase me like this, weakened as he is. Though I long to stay here, curled up against him in the illusion of safety, I will ruin everything if I do.

Kaladen seems to watch the hardness come over my face and he nods. "Go. While you still can."

I hate this. I hate it with every fiber of my being.

But I disentangle myself from his arms and get up. His touch slips away. I cast one last glance at him, propped against the wall, so weak. It kills me to walk away from him and leave him so vulnerable.

Then I turn and run as fast as I can.

I make it seem like I'm escaping the palace—even though he is likely not fooled. One thread plucks at my awareness, a portal threatening to break open. I don't know which one it is, but I've got to reseal it quickly. The Wolf will be marching through Risya any minute. I'm almost finished with my job of keeping the portals closed until then.

After that, I can focus on escaping Kaladen.

The thread takes me to one of the far doors on the second floor. The closer I get to it, the more the dread inside me mounts. *Please be one of the doors next to it. Please let it be any other—*

No. The thread grows more insistent until I stop in front of that massive door of crumbling gray wood. Above it is that ominous placard of mist swirling among skeletons.

Crenfyre is breaking down.

I don't know how long I have to reseal it. If it breaks open tonight . . .

A groan escapes me. I drag a hand over my face. Kaladen will kill me. *Again.* But what else am I to do? Stand here, knowing the deadliest portal is about to open? I've seen what Crenfyre can do. I remember what it did to Mahja and Gaya. I remember what it did to the palace courtyard, stealing the life even from the stones.

I wish Badh-o was here to tell me if she sensed the Wolf's presence. I hope he is already out in Risya, exposing himself without Kaladen's protection to the arrows of Tariq's men.

I run as silently as I can down the long hallway to the banister. I quickly place my hand on it, sense its cold trembling. *Is the Wolf in the palace? Yes, or no?*

Yes, it replies.

Does he know I am here?

Yes.

Cold washes through me. *Does he know where I am?*

No.

I breathe a tiny bit easier. I've got a chance. I just need to get to the rainforest portal and get the last bottle of Crenfyre mist. The spare one Kaladen told me about. Inside my pocket, the glowing soul of Roltwart hums, reminding me that I need to put it safely with its brethren.

Where is the Wolf? I ask the banister, giving it a dozen rooms where he could be.

The banister answers, *The throne room.*

I nod swiftly. *Thank you, friend.*

I won't let him sand you, it says fiercely just before I withdraw my hand.

My smile is brief. Then I'm in motion again, heading as fast as I can to the rainforest portal.

***

The rainforest is eerily quiet when I enter. The waterfalls still roar in the distance, but there is something subdued about the sound.

"Not you, too," I grumble, ducking under the rich green foliage. Still, I enjoy the smell of mist and damp earth. It instantly soothes my fears and comforts me. I long to kick off my worn shoes, nearly burned through from Roltwart, and let my bare feet sink into the cool relief of soil.

It would be stupid to leave proof of my presence right at the door of this portal, however.

I do my best to avoid leaving a trail of footprints as I hurry to the treehouse. Kaladen's healing seemed to restore more than just my burned skin and seared lungs, also alchemizing my weariness into strength. I take the gift gratefully and climb the staircase into the familiar sight of wood floors and ceiling arranged around the enormous central trunk of the tree. There is the cabinet with an endless supply of food, the bed we shared exhausted naps in, and the ledge where we spoke of days past and kicked our legs over the drop. I can almost believe I'm safe here, that Kaladen and the Wolf will never come for me here, that I can eat, lay down, and rest as I've done so many times before.

My stride is swift as I circle to the back of the treehouse. I open the large cabinet there, and the sight nearly transfixes me as it did once before. Rows and rows of egg-shaped souls radiate with their many colors in a whirling rainbow of dazzling beauty. The one in my pocket thrums in excitement, and I pull it out.

Its violent, angry red seems suddenly like the missing note of an exquisite symphony. I place it in one of the two remaining spots, and it brightens to such a blinding blaze that I shield my face. Then it softens, joining the music of color around it.

It is like an unknown part of me softens with it. This is where this soul belongs. Together, to be one again with the other pieces of the worlds that have been scattered. Balance is not complete, but it is closer than ever before. I feel the physical relief deep in my body.

I peel my eyes away from the souls. There's no time to waste. Where is the Crenfyre mist? Kaladen said it was with the souls. I squat down to the lowest level of the shelf, and sure enough, there is a small vial, the size of my hand, with a long, thin neck, tucked away in the back.

It feels so delicate, so breakable when I lift it out and shut the cabinet door. There is a loop on the lid. I go to fasten it to my sash when the entire portal shutters.

The waterfalls seem to hiccup. The tree shivers. Even the floorboards I walk on stop their creaking.

"Little wife! Oh, little wife! Where are you hiding, my dear?"

Every muscle in my body freezes in horror.

He must have sensed my entry into various portals, and now that the sun is going down, he is determined to collect me. Does he intend to parade me before him through Risya tonight? Or . . . or am I tonight's sacrificial meal? Will he take my blood to seal portals, and then tear into my flesh? What if he never goes to the city—what if Tariq and Kanza and the guards never get a chance to kill the Wolf? What if the Wolf doesn't reseal Crenfyre, and it breaks open tonight?

Blood pounds in my ears. I scramble to the edges of the treehouse, knowing that going down the staircase will be throwing myself into the Wolf's arms. I reach for my rope, only to realize I don't have it. I lost it in the Roltwart Portal.

I try to measure the distance to the ground, but it's impossible; the foliage around me is so thick I cannot even see it. Jumping would be stupid. I'd be just as likely to break my spine on an unexpected branch. I swing myself over the ledge, intending to find some way to climb down.

A meaty, hairy hand clamps hold of my wrist.

I nearly scream from the shock of it. How did he move so fast, so silently?

I grab hold of the edge of the platform, my knuckles going white as he yanks me up. My grip breaks, and he drags me like a doll onto the flooring. I kick and struggle for my weapons—all uselessly. He tosses me against the tree trunk. I hit hard and try to scramble to my feet.

This time, it's Kaladen's grip that pins me.

He is not at his full strength, but the curse of the Wolf's orders seems to give him enough to restrain me. His face is the blankest I've seen, focused and grim. His eyes, however, are a storm. A storm that latches onto me. A thousand words pass between us, fury and hurt and apologies and pain.

The Wolf's distorted face leers before me, his tongue lolling out the side of his mouth as he grins, as he watches me struggle fruitlessly against my husband.

"Take her weapons," the Wolf orders.

Kaladen pins my arms behind me, pressing my face into the ground as he strips me of my knives and my scimitar. I writhe, a violent yell ripping my chest as I fight to not lose the few remnants of my power. His knee sinks into the back of my thigh, preventing my carefully aimed kicks.

The Wolf's grin grows. "Bind her wrists—with a knot she *cannot* untie."

I want to spit, *I can untie anything, you fool.* I did not spend so long as Jabir's slave to come away with knots I am helpless against. Somehow, I manage to avoid letting the words spill from my lips. The last thing I need is to be bound in chains.

I don't make it easy for Kaladen to tie my wrists. I wrestle and writhe. My hair falls in my face, my mouth, my eyes. I put every ounce of my strength into twisting my wrists free.

It's no use. The Wolf watches with great amusement as Kaladen secures a length of rope around my wrists. When he is finished, the Wolf bends down toward me, hooking a claw under my chin and jerking my face up to his.

I lurch forward to bite him. He dodges just beyond the reach of my teeth and laughs. His grip shifts to my jaw, holding me still, squishing my cheeks and angling my head painfully. I meet his gaze, refusing to shirk away.

"Kaladen's little wild thing," the Wolf muses. His other hand comes up to pat my nose and then gives my neck a stroke above my iron collar. "Now *my* little wild thing. I'm sure there is some sweetness beneath the adorable feistiness. You and I will find it together."

So maybe he doesn't intend to eat me tonight. Does that mean he will still go to the city to get his meal? Maybe Tariq's chance isn't lost after all.

"What is this?" The Wolf's tone changes from patronizing humiliation to interest. He ducks closer to me. Kaladen holds me still, not letting me move an inch as the Wolf's hand slides down my waist to my hip—and closes around something attached to my sash.

Everything inside me turns to panic.

"A bottle of mist?" He unhooks it. I try to lunge for the bottle, but Kaladen restrains me. His limbs quake against mine. As though he would choose to die instead of hold me here. "This seals Crenfyre, doesn't it? You were so thoughtful to bring it to me, little pet."

I restrain the biting words I long to hurl at his face.

"This is the last of the mist to seal Crenfyre?" This question is directed at Kaladen. When he doesn't answer, the Wolf snaps: "Answer me, Kaladen Ashrift Felladyr!"

The answer seems torn from deep in Kaladen's throat. "Yes."

The Wolf's maniacal eyes trail from him, down to me, to the bottle he holds in his claws. He tilts his head, his scraggly hair falling to one side as he sniffs the bottle. It looks so breakable in his grasp, so small and delicate.

I dare not even breathe while he holds it.

Neither does Kaladen.

"So much hope for the worlds rests on this mist, doesn't it?" the Wolf muses. "Isn't magic so beautiful? Creation and destruction wrapped together to make a force so powerful, nothing can stand against it. If you don't have this mist, you cannot seal Crenfyre, and we all three know Crenfyre will break open during Lulythinar—if not sooner. And if Crenfyre breaks open with nothing to seal it . . ." He drags a finger across his throat. "Your poor human world. This entire Bridge. The worlds beyond these portals. So . . . *tragic*."

"What do you want from me?" I spit, trying to take his attention away from the mist. "You already have my blood. Surely you haven't run out of what you took—you clearly aren't sealing the portals."

Kaladen's grip tightens on me. I cannot work the ropes yet, not with my bound hands directly in his line of sight. But maybe if I can change the dynamic here, distract the Wolf enough to forget the mist, get myself in a different position where I can work the ropes binding me . . .

Suddenly, the Wolf's face is only inches from mine. Saliva drips from his lips. "I want many things, pet." He strokes a line down my forehead, my nose, my lips, and then grips my chin tight enough to break the bone. I wince. "I want so many things from you. And I will have them."

Then he rises, and before I can scream, before Kaladen can react, before *anything—*

He smashes the vial of mist against the tree trunk.

"No!" I lunge forward.

"Wolf!" Kaladen bellows.

"Silence!" the Wolf whirls on him as the last remnants of mist vaporize into thin air. Broken glass tumbles to the wooden planks, only a few inches from my face.

I stare in stunned shock at that glass, catching the rainforest light. I stare at the place in the air where the mist vanished.

Kaladen trembles. With a plethora of emotions I can only guess at. Rage, despair, hatred. All he has spent his life for, all that Liliana died for, all that I will die for—*gone.* It won't matter if Tariq can kill the Wolf now. We are all going to die.

It doesn't even seem real.

"You," snarls the Wolf, sticking his finger in Kaladen's face. His grins are gone, and all that is left is snarling rage. "Do you think I am stupid? Do you think I haven't surmised what the High King intends to do after Lulythinar? You and your *noble concern* about the worlds and the seals—do you not see how Faradir orchestrated this whole thing?" He spits a thick globule onto the ground near my face and steps over my body. My vision is cut off, but I hear him grab the front of Kaladen's robes and his voice rises to an ear-splitting volume. *"I am not stupid!"*

Searing pain slices across my scalp. I brace myself, tensing against the Wolf's grip in my hair as he drags me away from my husband and deposits me on the ground. His hairy, taloned foot lands on my back, pinning me again. "You don't matter. I don't matter. This Great

Kings-cursed human wench doesn't matter. We are all pawns in the High King's hand and if you haven't realized it yet, you are the greatest fool of us all. No, I will not be sealing the portals this Lulythinar and neither will you."

My entire body throbs from the force of his words.

"The High King used me to enslave you," the Wolf continues, casting his words like blows at Kaladen. "I was foolish enough to let him, thinking I had outsmarted you and I would finally get to see your deserved destruction. But no, the High King *never* intended to make me the Neverseen King. He *never* intended to give me your throne. He used me to enslave you, and now that you're under his command, he will use you to destroy me. You are my slave *only* until Lulythinar, and then you are to return to him after. What do you think he was going to have you do? Did you truly think he was going to finally sever your connection to the Bridge, give me the throne I earned, and keep you his dutiful watchdog? No, he was going to have you kill me. And then he was going to restore you to the role of Neverseen King—his eternal slave, burdened with the weight of the Bridge. He was going to take the power of the Bridge, so you could never overthrow him, and so he could use the Bridge against his enemies. *That* was Faradir's plan."

I twist enough to watch grim understanding dawn in Kaladen's eyes.

The Wolf's grin is bitter. "And I was foolish enough to think he truly intended to make me the Neverseen King. I played right into his hand. Well, no more! If Faradir wants the Bridge, he can have it—in utter, lawless, uncontrollable destruction. I will not make my defeat easy for him. I will make it so the Bridge can *never* be contained."

He wrenches open the cabinet door. My vision swims from compounding horror as the beautiful dance of rainbow glows fills the treehouse.

"Stay where you are," the Wolf growls at Kaladen, just before he grabs a handful of portal souls, radiant in their splendor, and smashes them to the ground.

This time I do scream.

The souls shatter, joining the broken glass on the floor. Their colors vanish with a high-pitched screech into nothing.

"Stop this!" I shriek, getting my feet beneath me now that I'm not pinned. I hurl myself at the Wolf. He smashes more souls on the ground, and I tear with my teeth into his arm. Copper fills my mouth.

He flings me backward. I hit another tree limb hard, but immediately get up again with a scream of rage. Kaladen, bound by magic to be mute and immobile, tries to tell me with his eyes to stop. But I will not stop! How could the Wolf do this? How could he doom us all like this? How could he destroy my world, my people, everything I love? And for what? Because he allied himself with the wrong person?

The screeches of the souls, separated from each other, broken to dust on the ground, pounds against my ears.

"I will kill you!" I aim my knee at his most vulnerable places, trying to break him like he breaks my hope.

"Restrain her!" the Wolf demands.

Kaladen is there the next second, his arms around me, clutching me to his chest. Fury nearly blinds me as I yank at my bonds, as I writhe violently to escape his grip. But he crushes me to himself, not restraining me like a prisoner, but holding me as close as he can and shielding my body with his.

My screams turn to sobs. Each cry of the souls rends my heart deeper. Each one seems to proclaim: *"It is all gone! Eshe is gone. Kaladen is gone. Arbasa is gone. Tariq is gone. Zara and Abbi and all the orphaned children are gone."*

Everything I've done. Everything I've suffered. Everything I've lost.

It was all for nothing.

Kaladen covers my face, turning it against him, but not before the Wolf picks up the pulsing red Roltwart soul and crushes it in his palm.

It goes on forever. There are *so* many souls.

He breaks every single one, until at last everything is quiet.

Breath knifes in and out of my lungs. I can feel the burn of Kaladen's gaze over the top of my head. My wrists chafe from my bonds, my body aching from how the Wolf threw me.

I peer over the confines of Kaladen's arms at the cold eyes of the Wolf as they latch onto mine. I've never hated anyone so much as I've hated Eldreth of the Star City for killing Eshe. Not until now.

"Take her to my bedchamber," the Wolf orders, and the anger in his face clears to triumph. "I must be a good husband to my wife, after all."

CHAPTER 20

NADIRA

EVERY STEP KALADEN drags me is another dull thud resounding through my body. *All is lost. All of this—for nothing.*

It goes so much deeper than everything I did in Valehaven and here at the Bridge. It goes as deep as those dark years as Jabir's slave, all the blood on my hands, the deaths of those dearest to me. I had thought . . . I had believed . . . that if I could save Kaladen, if we could take back the Bridge, if we could save Arbasa from Lulythinar, all of it would have been worth it. All my life spent in the ravages of a bottomless pit would have meant something, if it prepared me for this final stand.

But now I have nothing.

I don't fight as he takes me through the shadow-drenched hallway where he once gave me his name. Even my bonds are not worth struggling against. What use is fighting at this point? We're all going to die. There is no hope anymore, now that Crenfyre cannot be sealed, and we have not the hope of getting its soul to balance the Bridge. The Wolf clearly has no intention of going into Risya tonight, meaning that Tariq's plan will crumble to nothing.

So much fighting. So much struggling. So much bleeding.

And all of it—completely, *utterly* futile.

Shortly, one of the few remaining vestiges of my bodily autonomy will be stripped from me. A numbness creeps over me. Do I even care at this point? I have borne torture of many varieties and severities. What is one more?

I long for the coursing of ice through my veins, something to steel and strengthen myself with. Something that can burn and freeze and make me feel something.

Kaladen's breath is hot on the back of my head, coming in broken pants, as though he fights every moment. I smile ruefully to myself, glad one of us still has the will to fight. I doubt that determination will hold out much longer, however. Kaladen's heart is too soft. The Roltwart portal nearly broke him. This might be the final grain of sand to tip the scale. He will go back to who he was when I first met him: cold, ruthless, torn to pieces, with nothing but his own misery for company.

Night falls around us, biting and threatening. It promises black teeth and hungry monsters. I hate watching the change come over the palace, as though it is as afraid of what it becomes after dark as we are.

The Wolf got ahead of us somehow and is waiting when Kaladen kicks open the door to the chambers that once belonged to him. To *us*.

I can almost see Eshe draped across the comfortable furniture in the main room, stuffing her face with food and teasing me about my new husband. I can almost hear the bubbling of the water in the bathing chamber when the House was angry I left my dirty clothes on the floor. When Kaladen shuts the door and pulls me, as slowly as he dares, to the bedroom, dark save for the light of all those beautiful *lumiral* globes, I can almost feel what it was like to wake up in his arms.

The Wolf shouldn't be here. Grinning and violent in his triumph. Sitting on the bed as if he owns it. As if he owns *me,* and my real husband. This room is sacred to me. But he cannot suffer one special place being spared from desecration.

"Give her to me," orders the Wolf.

My mind abandons the room suddenly. I sit atop a worn wooden beam in the abandoned belltower. I hold my blade to my chest, ready to pierce my heart and end my misery. Hot wind rushes through my tangled hair.

One push is all it takes, I tell myself.

The rusted old bell hangs beneath my feet, ready to proclaim my death with its tinny cry.

My hand was stayed once before. Fear made me stop. But now, nothing will stop me. I draw a deep breath, tightening my grip on Separator. Nothing will stop me. I will push with all my might—

A hand lands on mine. Brown, slender, strong.

My head whips up.

There is Eshe, sitting beside me on the beam. She is cross-legged, while my feet dangle. The wind catches the sun-bleached highlights of her hair, tosses them about the face I have so longed to see.

Then, abruptly, the vision of Eshe is cut off. Hands on my arms quake with strain. It is Kaladen—hesitating. His breathing turns ragged as he struggles to defy the Wolf's command.

I blink, and the bedroom melts away to the belltower, the Wolf's snarl to Eshe's smile. It is a far more welcome sight.

"Eshe!" I gasp.

She tsks her tongue. "Always so dramatic, Nadira." With that, she takes the knife from my hand—I let her—and sets it on the beam between us. Then she sighs, grips the beam, and stares out at the city.

"I've missed you," I whisper, trying not to cry.

She smiles sadly. "I've missed you, too. But you know I don't regret it."

"You regret nothing."

She tilts her head to one side, considering. "Almost nothing. I do not regret why I left, but I do regret that I had to leave you. Why are you giving up?"

"Because we've lost."

"You aren't going to hold out hope that you will be taken into exile where they have good food?"

I draw one knee up to my chest and hook my elbow around it. "I don't think Crenfyre takes prisoners."

"You never know." She shrugs, then peers at me with her bright eyes. "Tell me the real reason you're giving up."

"There is no point in going on. I've been fighting my entire life. Everywhere I go, there is another enemy to face." I drag a hand over my nose and cheeks. "There is always someone hunting me. Always someone trying to hurt me and those I love. At every turn, it is nothing but struggle. I'm *tired* of it all, Eshe. I want to rest and be at peace. Even if those who deserve killing get away without justice. What's the use of endless fighting?"

"I'm afraid you might be one of those unfortunate people who have to suffer more than their fair share so that others can reap the rewards of your efforts. It is a hard reality of our world that some sow, while others reap."

I shake my head. "There will be no reward for my effort. Crenfyre will destroy Arbasa—*all* of the human lands."

She goes quiet for several minutes. She inspects the ends of her hair, picks at them. "So you're giving up?"

There is something in that tone. Something that turns me defensive and ashamed at once. "Why shouldn't I? I'm not interested in the romance and tragedy of fighting losing battles. That was always more your style."

She shakes her head, laughing quietly. "Don't pretend I'm the only dramatic one of the two of us. You were the one who fell in the love with the Neverseen King. You couldn't accept a normal man with a mild temper and hard work ethic. You had to find the most tragic and wounded piece of work that I've ever *not* laid eyes on. The hopeless Bridge, the doomed night of Lulythinar—all of it drew you in like a flour moth to a candleflame. There's something about hopeless causes that calls to you. Why?"

Her mouth does not move, but I can hear her voice in my head. *"Because you always feared that you were a hopeless cause, and you wanted to prove that there was always something worth fighting for."*

"The only thing I can still fight for is the Wolf's destruction," I mutter. "Everything else is useless."

Eshe's eyes spark. "Then why are you letting him do as he pleases?"

"Because I'm weary."

Her mouth turns up in the corner. "Are you truly, Nadira?"

I scowl at her. She laughs.

"The Nadira I know would never roll over, expose her belly, and wait patiently for someone to kill her. How could you, when you are somehow in possession of the softest heart and the grittiest determination I have ever known? You were made to fight, Nadira. You were made to rise up. So few people in this world are strong—but you are. You have known so much defeat, and yet every single time, you have gotten back on your feet and faced your enemy again. You wouldn't be Nadira Ashrift Felladyr if you didn't."

Her use of my full name, the name she never knew, burns my gut and breaks the illusion. For one painful moment, I am still sitting on that beam in the belltower and Eshe's specter is gone. I want to call after her, to demand where she's gone, even though I know she was never truly here.

"Give her to me, Kaladen Ashrift Felladyr!"

The force of that name, snapping across the belltower, rips me back to my body and sends me hurtling toward the Wolf. He grabs me, pulls me back against his chest. The stench of rot and dried blood nearly makes me choke as he caresses one talon-tipped hand down my arm—the arm he once sliced open for my blood.

I go stiff and still.

The Wolf's voice rips me from that place. "Stand there in the doorway, Kaladen Ashrift Felladyr. Do not intervene, except to keep her from escaping."

I look back at Kaladen. He stares at me, and I watch as the fire in his eyes—always crackling, always burning and vicious—fades to nothing. As though he, too, has left this room, despite standing right there. My strong husband has finally broken.

How could it be that in just a few hours, we've lost everything?

No.

Everything inside me suddenly screams that single word of defiance.

No.

Eshe was right. Crenfyre and the Bridge might be hopeless, but if I am going to die, there is one person in this world I am not leaving without destroying first.

"My sweet pet," the Wolf is saying—right before I knee him so hard my bones rattle.

I have half a second of surprise, and I use it to roll and flip myself off the bed. With my hands still bound behind me, I lose my balance and crash against the tapestry on the far wall, the *lumiral* globes bobbing around me in the air as I try to pull myself upright before the Wolf is upon me.

I have no such success. The Wolf pounces on me. His weight is so heavy I can barely dodge the fangs coming for my shoulder. He is so much stronger than me, but in this wild, desperate moment, I don't care.

I will never stop fighting.

I will fight to my very death. I will fight—not to win, but to resist until the last bitter moment.

Some battles are worth losing. And some enemies do not deserve to win without paying a vicious cost.

Lumiral globes flicker, illuminating in stark relief the claw that comes toward me. I cannot dodge it, and it rakes down my side and arm. I hardly feel the pain as my blood goes flying in every direction. What I do feel, however, is that his claw caught on my bonds. He did not cut completely through one section of rope, but frayed it just enough to weaken. I get my legs up and kick hard. I barely miss his nose, but the blow snaps his head back. Kaladen stands beyond him in the doorway, frozen by command, breathing hard. I refuse to let my thoughts follow him now.

The Wolf lunges for me again. I hit the tapestry hard. My collar smashes into a *lumiral* globe.

And just for that one tiny moment, ice surges inside my gut.

It is gone the next moment. I am so stunned the Wolf catches me by the front of my tunic and wheels back his arm to hurl me back to the bed.

"I will break you to pieces!" he screams. "I will take that spirit of yours, and I will crush it!"

"No, you won't!" I scream back. I twist in his grasp, just enough to bang my collar against another globe. Like before, a powerful force builds inside me. The second the Wolf drags me away, it locks down again.

He brings another claw swiping toward me. At the last second, I twist violently. His talon cuts into my back, my wrist, my palm. I feel the pain this time, and it wrenches a guttural cry from my chest that turns into a roar. My mind works ahead of me, scrambling as I juggle my loosened bonds that I work as fast as I can, the realization of the connection between my collar and the *lumiral* globes, and my dire need to fend off the Wolf before he kills me in a bout of rage.

The Wolf's hand comes shooting for my throat. To grab me, to choke the life out of me. I dodge and send my unsteady weight falling toward the tapestry instead of the bed. *Got to stay on this side of the room. Don't let him drag you away.*

"Restrain her!" the Wolf demands.

Kaladen flies across the room. His ironlike grip closes around my upper arm just as I nearly work my bonds free. In a flash, he has me on my knees, staring up at the Wolf.

But he has positioned me in the densest part of the globes.

He realized it too.

My mind skips back to the moment he told me about how I needed a force strong enough to remove the pollution of the spell on my iron collar. It skips back even further to our wedding night, to what Kaladen said then.

"Those lights are magic. We call them lumiral globes. They are much more efficient at lighting spaces than candles—and they have a purifying influence on the air."

The *lumiral* globes counteract my collar. One may not be strong enough, but more . . .

My lungs swell as I pant hard. My wild hair falls into my face as I glare up at the Wolf. He breathes hard, too, and there is no grin on his grisly face as he straightens his shirt and returns my glare. In that moment, I see clearly why the High King never intended to make him the new Neverseen King, why Kaladen beat him time and time again.

Because he doesn't believe he is strong enough to fight his own battles. When he took down Kaladen, he didn't do that himself—he used Eldreth of the Star City and the High King. While here in Arbasa, he made Kaladen fight all his battles. Even his battles against me. And he had no intention of fighting the High King. He intended to make the Bridge fight for him.

Suddenly, the frightening visage before me twists into something utterly wretched and pathetic. His grins and bloodlust and violence are nothing but a front to hide just how weak he truly is.

If he sees my realization in my face, he does not show it.

"I will have you," he snarls, bending down to me, trying to intimidate me with his harsh voice. "I *will* have you. I will bend you and break you and then I will eat you, piece by piece."

I meet his gaze. The gaze of the monster who destroyed my only hope of saving all I love from Lulythinar. I hate him so deeply, and yet a stronger emotion grows inside me: *pity.* He and I are not that different, after all. Two fools trying to run from their own failings, knowing those failings would one day catch up and devour them.

The difference between us is that I learned to fight for the good in this world.

My lips pull back from my teeth. "I have been ruined. I have been shattered. I have been poured out like water on the ground. I have been chained and devoured and destroyed. And I will *not* bend to your will."

I throw myself backward. Kaladen keeps me restrained, but gives me just enough room to slam my collar into several *lumiral* globes. A torrential flow of ice crashes into my belly. The collar fights against the force, trying to lock it down. But I grab hold of that force. The *lumiral* globes shift, allowing the collar more success, yet the Wolf's eyes have already widened. He springs toward me—realizing he doesn't even have time to order Kaladen to drag me away.

I dive into the awareness of that power. That raw, tumultuous energy that so desires to be free, to spill forth in destruction. It is so cold that my gut burns. The iron around my throat surges and fights, the Wolf's spellwork writhing in desperation against the glacial waterfall inside me.

I'm not going to let this collar overcome me again. I cling to the power spinning inside me. Awareness of the room around me, of Kaladen's hands gripping my arms, of the Wolf hurtling toward me—all of it vanishes. It is just me, gripping at the swirling energy inside me, refusing to let it fall back against the thrumming violence of my collar. If I let go, for even a second, the collar will win. My magic will lock. The Wolf will drag me away from the purifying aid of the globes that gives me the barest edge I need.

So I don't let go. I hold it, letting it burn, letting it rage and whorl.

My collar cracks.

The Wolf's hand closes around my throat just as the iron splinters, and shatters. He knocks me onto my back, pinning me to the floor with his massive weight. His breath is rotten on my face, his eyes white-ringed, his bloodied teeth snapping in desperation, diving for my jugular.

I am done waiting for Tariq and Kaladen's aid against the Wolf. I see now with pristine clarity that he was always meant to be my quarry—*my* quarry, if I would stop expecting others to fight my battles for me.

The corner of my mouth lifts.

And then I explode.

CHAPTER 21

KALADEN

I SCREAM HER name as I roll the Wolf's heavy, limp body off her. His blood has already soaked into her clothes, splattered across her face, and stained the floor. But all I can see is that Nadira's eyes are open and alert. They are the large, liquid darkness that could drown me every time I look at them.

She sits up and rubs her head, wincing slightly. Iron shards scatter in every direction. Her throat is now bare, with only the slightest discoloration where the collar once was.

She's fine. She's alive. She's here.

The relief that floods me is more powerful than the ice she just unleashed. I grab her face in my hands, forcing her to look at me. Immediately, her expression softens. She smiles. Then her gaze shifts slightly, looking past me. At the violently sharp protrusions of ice on every surface. Her eyebrows go up. Her voice is dryly amused as she mutters, "I've made such a mess of our room. It's going to be so annoying to clean up."

My throat thickens to the point of pain. The only words that escape me are a desperate, "Oh, you." Then I clutch her to my chest, probably squeezing her too hard. My hand cups the back of her head, my fingers digging into her hair, her scalp. I cannot get close enough to her. I cannot exist with a breath of air between us. I'm not even sure she is real, that this isn't a dream. In a moment, I will wake, and she will slip away with the wind, and I will realize that he killed Nadira when he pounced on her, and that I am still a prisoner of the Wolf.

Moments pass, and I don't wake up. She embraces me in return, her arms wrapped around my neck, her body flush with mine. We breathe the same cold air. It puffs like clouds, then dissipates like mist. Still, this moment doesn't vanish.

Still, I do not wake up.

Beyond our ice-enclosed world is Lulythinar, portals that break open, an unbound Crenfyre, a High King with possession of my name. Enough disaster and tragedy waiting to strip us of our lives and our world and everything else. But right now, in this sacred, liminal space, there is just me and the wife I love with every fiber of my being.

Whole. Unbroken. *Free*.

She tilts her head to my shoulder, looking up at me. I canvas her face. The small, pockmarked scars along her jaw, the fresher one ripping across her cheek, nearly slicing into her eye. The Wolf's blood streaked across her brown skin. The tendrils of hair that have curled from sweat. Every blink of her eyelids, every sweep of her thick, black lashes, is the dearest comfort and reassurance.

"You are pale, Kaladen," she says softly. Her hand reaches up to brush the hair out of my face, then rests her palm against my cheek. I close my eyes and lean into her touch. My insides are so ragged, but that one gesture soothes the ache in my throat. "You looked like . . . like you'd given up. Forever."

A cold, dark cloud sinks over my chest. I don't want those images in my head. I don't want their reaching, haunting fingers scraping at the inside of my mind. I never want to remember what it was like to stand at the door of this room and strain helplessly against the magic that bound me. Forced to watch the person dearest to me in all the world be hurt. Powerless to stop it.

It echoed Liliana's death, of Nadira hanging above an endless chasm.

I will never be free of this fear and this horror. We are on the cusp of Lulythinar. Just because I didn't see Nadira die twice by now does not mean I will not face that blow before tomorrow's dawn, or the next dawn after Lulythinar.

Nadira presses her face to mine and whispers, "We are both still here."

I hold her closer, unable to draw a full breath around the pressure in my lungs. I open my mouth to repeat her words, but my tongue cannot move. I shut my eyes, briefly, and I find my own shaken core of strength. It is cracked inside me, ready to splinter.

No.

I will not break. I will not give up.

Dawn will come again.

I look into my wife's blood-streaked face, her hard gaze softening only for me, and I realize simultaneously the depth of my own need for her—and her need for me. Neither of us can break, and neither of us will break.

We have an impossible task before us. One we will not shirk from. It may destroy us, but it will not defeat us.

Finally, I find my voice. "If we die, we will not do it as slaves."

Not to the Wolf. Not to the High King. Not to the Bridge. Not to the memory of Jabir.

A fiery grin bursts across her features. I think of the fearful, frigid, and solemn assassin I met that fateful night. She is not the same woman who leaps to her feet, a catlike gleam in her eyes. "I need knives. A scimitar, too. And a new rope."

It has been ages since my blood hummed with something other than fear. The heady thrill of battle rushes through me. I give Nadira an answering grin. "As you wish, my queen."

I haul the Wolf's body through the window, into the courtyard. I leave him there. We have no time to clean the blood in the room, or to deal with the excessive amount of ice crystals. That is for another time.

Right now, the palace's defenses are activated. I sense a host of weakening seals. Several have broken open in the time since Nadira closed the others.

Normally, I would deal with them immediately, but we must regroup first. None of these seals have denizens that will get past the House's defenses. So we take this precious opportunity and hurry into Risya.

We find a city wreathed in utter silence. It is the silence that creeps through one's bones, full and waiting to devour. Nadira already informed me of the plan to take down the Wolf. We split up, her taking a route through the mazelike alleys to sneak into the guardhouse, and me through the dream realm.

I find Tariq, belly down on a rooftop, the arrow of his crossbow poised over the edge of the parapet. I slip out of the dream realm right beside him. His only flinch is how fast his eyes shoot to me. The rest of his body braces—likely expecting a killing blow, knowing he cannot fend me off, especially when I've caught him in such a vulnerable position.

"Nadira killed the Wolf," I say.

Tariq's hard, blank face splits into the tiniest of proud smiles. He pushes back from the parapet and withdraws his crossbow, switching the safety on. He puts his fingers into his mouth and whistles a bird call into the silent night.

A shift in the wind makes me glance to my left. A slender, shadowed form leaps from the neighboring roof. She wears a hood, covering most of her face, but I recognize her anyway. Gladness fills me at the sight of her, here and unharmed by my earlier shot at her.

"The Wolf is dead?" she whispers, glancing uneasily between me—mostly concealed in the darkness—and Tariq. "How?"

Tariq's proud smile hasn't gone away. "Nadira."

Kanza's own smile is hesitant, but her jubilation wins out only a moment later and she gives a little hop of excitement and squeezes her fist. "*Yes!*"

Tariq grins at her. I hold up both hands. "It means I won't shoot you again."

She shoves her hands behind her back and rocks on her heels, not quite meeting my gaze even as she tries to get a better look at me. "Thank you for missing."

I nod. "I was loath to do otherwise." To both of them, I say, "Come, we must assemble at the guardhouse. There is much to discuss and very little time. We have control of the Bridge once more, but Lulythinar is tomorrow night—only hours away." I cannot keep the grimness out of my voice. "It will be a difficult battle, but if we all pull together . . . there might be some hope."

Torches illuminate the street below as guards climb down from their posts, following Tariq's signal of victory and safety. Kanza hurries ahead, but Tariq hangs back.

"Some hope?" he asks quietly.

So he did not miss my tone. I wish I could find it in me to lie to him.

Tariq deserves to know the truth.

"The battle we face is impossible," I reply, dropping my voice even quieter than his. "It is not a matter of too few warriors against too many foes, but a truly impossible battle. The most dangerous portal, Crenfyre, will break open during Lulythinar, if not sooner, and when it does, we have no means of sealing it. It is a ravenous mist that devours everything in its path."

"Can it be contained within the palace?"

I shake my head.

He nods, an iron resignation passing over his features. “How long does the city have?”

“Twenty hours at most.”

“We will order an evacuation of all civilians.”

“You should go with them.”

Tariq’s shoulders are braced wide. It reminds me of the steely resolve in Nadira when she went after the Roltwart soul. “My men and I will stay here.”

Admiration rises inside my chest. This is what High King Faradir cannot understand, and why I carry more respect for this race of earthly beings with short lives than I ever will for the likes of Yirmuth, Prince Trenian, and the rest of Valehaven.

They cannot understand what it is to willingly face death.

My voice is nothing but a murmur as we reach the guardhouse. “It will be my honor to fight alongside you.”

CHAPTER 22

NADIRA

THE PLAN IS that Kaladen and I will return to the palace to do whatever we can to forestall disaster. Tariq puts Kanza in charge of evacuating the city, clearly intent on her evacuating with them. She declares that she would like to stay and fight with him and his men against monsters that escape the portals and make it into the city.

Tariq fixes her with that solemn, unbreakable gaze of his and says only, "Evacuation is our most important job. I need someone I trust to handle it."

Her eyes widen slightly, her face coloring—and only partially from the embarrassment of speaking out in a large meeting.

"We must give the evacuees the best chance at survival," Tariq continues. "That is why I ask every man who can, to stay with me as a last line of defense between our people and what might break free of the palace."

I catch Kaladen's gaze. He wears no shadows. Torchlight falls across the filthy strands of his hair, the broad structure of his face, the expanse of his shoulders, and the scars riddling his tented hands. The truth remains unspoken between us. We know what we're walking into. There is no need to say out loud that he and I will be the first to fall on Lulythinar. Tariq clearly knows what he is walking into, and many of his men seem to read the reality of the situation beyond his words. Only Kanza, and the children sleeping a floor above us, don't understand.

Kanza's face contorts in confusion, her brows drawn together. It is like she understands that the situation is dire, but not that everyone in this room realizes that tomorrow is their last day alive. I don't want her to understand it. I would rather she have a chance to cherish her hope for our survival—and her hope for her own survival.

"Does anyone wish to work with Kanza to aid the evacuation?" Tariq asks the room—giving an opportunity of escape to those who are afraid.

That is what makes Kanza's eyes suddenly snap with realization. Tariq looks at her, the line of his mouth deceptively mild. She parts her lips to speak, then closes them. She shoots me a look as if to ask, *"Did you know?"* My answer must be clear in my face because she folds her arms across her chest and scowls.

Tariq studies her for a moment longer, then returns his focus to the room.

Only one man asks to be moved to the evacuation effort. The rest commit themselves to protecting the city.

If only you could see this, Eshe, I think. *You would never believe the city guards would lay down their lives to spare the orphans.*

When groups are organized among the guards and the meeting finished, Kanza springs lightly to her feet and catches Tariq's arm just before he disappears up the stairs to tell the children they are leaving. I hold back, endeavoring to give them privacy, but their quiet conversation still floats to my ears.

"You're going to die," Kanza accuses. "That is why you are sending me away. Because everyone who stays here dies."

"Yes," he replies coolly. "But sending you away does not guarantee your survival, or that of anyone's. The situation is . . . not what I hoped it would be."

She processes this, her throat bobbing. "You think the children and I, and the rest of the evacuees, will eventually be overrun and slaughtered?"

"It is a possibility."

"Then why don't you and the guards come with us? Or why don't we stay here, if we are going to die anyway?"

Tariq sighs. "I am not going to leave those who cannot defend themselves—of which you are not one, lest you think I insult you—in the city like fish in a barrel. Neither are we going to go with you and leave an open trail to you when we could delay pursuit."

"Let me stay. Send that guard who was going to join me. Have him lead the evacuation. Let me stay and fight for this city."

His voice drops slightly. "No. I want it to be you, Kanza."

"Why?" she demands. "If I want to stay and die, why can't I? Don't give me your excuses about needing someone you can trust."

"I am sending you for several reasons. The children like you and feel safe with you. I want a woman to go with them anyway, and a woman trained in combat is an ideal candidate. You survived the Neverseen King's trials, so you are familiar with magical foes—should you encounter them. I trust your skills, your character, and your devotion to the task. It must be you."

She is quiet for a moment, and from here, I can see that her arms are crossed over her chest.

"That is not all, is it?"

Tariq lifts his chin, almost defensively. "No, it is not."

"Tell me."

"The other reason . . . is that I wish to protect you, Kanza. If I can." Tariq's jaw works, his hard gaze flashing. "I do not care if you do not like that. But it is true. If I can buy you time, if I can give you a chance at survival, I will do it."

Surprise flickers across Kanza's face, and instead of being angry like Tariq expected, she instead looks almost *hopeful*. Her voice is quiet. "Why?"

The stair creaks beneath Tariq's weight as he begins climbing, leaving Kanza holding onto the railing at the bottom. "Likely because I have a soft heart, despite my father's best efforts. Anyway, there isn't time to waste. We must get to work."

Kaladen is at my side then, his glittering eyes searching my face. "You are exhausted."

I huff a laugh. "We will all sleep when we are dead."

"No, I want you to rest. Even for a few hours. We have a long day and a long night ahead tomorrow. This is the calmest it will be before Lulythinar."

"But the portals at the palace—"

"Not too much for me to handle."

"Kaladen—"

The barest smirk lifts his severe expression. "I did this without you for nearly a hundred years, remember."

I cock an eyebrow at him. "Very well. Then take my blood with you."

He draws back immediately. "No."

"I know how you feel about it, but we cannot afford scruples at a time like this. I know you don't think of me as a resource to use up. So be practical and take my blood for the seals."

He leans down to my face, a scowl etched into his. Then, to my shock, he grabs the back of my neck and gives me a hard kiss. He doesn't seem to care about the nearby guards who could poke through the doorway and see us. They make me self-conscious, and I flush hot from embarrassment for only one moment—and then Kaladen's kiss makes me forget them, and my skin turns hot for another reason.

He releases me and I blink rapidly, trying to come back to the guardhouse, Lulythinar, and . . . What were we just talking about?

He flashes me the most devilish grin at so thoroughly discombobulating me. That grin is also discombobulating, and if he wanted to, he could simply vanish without my blood, and he would have won our argument.

"This is not fair," I grumble, rolling up my sleeve to expose my left forearm. I point my knife at him. "You will not make me forget the blood. Do you have something to contain it in?"

He smirks with such masculine triumph, I know he intends to kiss me again the first opportunity he has. He holds out his palm beneath my arm and catches my blood. His fist closes over it, and when it disappears into the folds of his cloak, I have no idea what sort of magic he uses to preserve and contain it.

Then he reaches for me.

"No," I say firmly, dancing backward. "I need my brain, thank you very—"

His lips are on mine again, and all protests die as I forget exactly why we cannot stand in this landing forever and kiss until Lulythinar wipes us all away.

He pulls back before I am ready, chucks my chin affectionately, and orders, "Now get some sleep. I will be back at dawn for you. Tariq! Make sure she rests."

Tariq calls back down from the upper level: "I will give her a room, but I'm not going to tie her down, if that's what you're asking."

Kaladen's eyes dance. "I'd enjoy watching you try."

With that, he vanishes. My energy vanishes with him. I catch myself on the rickety banister and suppress a yawn. He was right. I do need rest if I'm going to be at all useful for Lulythinar. I climb the stairs and run into several of the orphan children piling out of their room. Abbi rushes toward me and throws his arms around my legs. I find myself bending down and kissing his curly head.

Tariq gestures up to the next floor. "You'll find a room there to rest."

He, Kanza, and Zara prepare the children to leave, and for a moment I stop. I should help them. I can rest when—

"Off with you," Tariq says. "We have more than enough hands."

I hesitate only a second longer, and then do as he says. I climb the next staircase. At the top, there is only one more staircase leading to the eagle's nest. Instead of taking it, I follow a hallway and push open one of the doors.

Somehow, I know what I will find when the creaking door swings wide. The room is dark, save for one stubby candle in a mostly melted pile of wax on a small table beside a low bed. Spiced perfume tickles my nostrils. It comes from the linen-wrapped body on the bed.

Pressure builds in my throat, behind my eyelids. I close the door behind me, walk across the dusty floorboards, and kneel beside Eshe.

She lies so still. When I lay my hand on her shoulder, it is not warm or cool. It is the same temperature as the bed itself, as the scented air I breathe. No matter how many times I kill, I'm not sure I will ever understand the strangeness of death. If I pull back the linen, it will be Eshe's face I see. And yet, this is not Eshe.

She is not here.

I find the outline of her hand. It is stiff. Still, I clasp it. My voice comes out like a frog's, croaking and unsteady. "I know you don't regret it. But I wish you could have made it. I wish you could be by my side now." I shrug weakly. A few tears run down my cheeks. "Though in truth your death might have been a mercy, if Lulythinar goes as badly as it probably will. At least you died with hope. But I will be selfish and wish that you were here."

There is no silly, quipped response from her. No warm squeeze of her hand in mine.

The lone candle flickers against the darkness, threatening to burn out. Tariq probably intended for me to sleep in a different room, but when I close my eyes, I can almost believe that Eshe sleeps on that bed. There is a strange comfort in what little I have of her presence.

A stack of blankets lay beside the bed. I take two and spread them out on the floor. They smell a bit like dust and man, but it isn't too strong. I lay down and stare at what little I can make of the rafters.

Exhaustion pulls at my limbs, yet my mind races like a herd of wild donkeys.

Crenfyre. Lulythinar. Eshe.

Suddenly, I sit bolt upright. My hand goes to my pocket. I dig around, my heart in my throat. My fingers close around something thin and delicate. I lift it out. A single, wiry strand of hair. It hangs in the darkness, illuminated by the candle, just before the flame burns out completely. The night closes around me with a puff of smoke.

I scramble upright, holding the strand of hair to my chest, and stumble into the next room. Away from Eshe. This room is completely empty, save for the cobwebs illuminated by the light of the full moon coming through the window.

I shut the door, place the strand of hair on the windowsill, draw a knife, and then take a deep breath. I lay my finger on the hair and whisper, "Come to me, Eye of Baltor, and fulfill my bargain."

The Eye did not leave calling instructions, so I hope this is what I'm supposed to do.

I wait, my breath hot in the empty air. There is no flash of light or crackling along my spine. After a moment, however, a prickle of the hairs at the back of my neck makes me turn around.

A hunched form in a tattered cloak and hood stares at me from a few feet away. I nearly leap out of my skin, and get the sense the Eye grins at me beneath its long, hooked nose.

I straighten. Hopefully my fright has not shown across my face. "I am here to call in my bargain."

"So you are. But do not waste either of our times, dearie. If you were about to wish for me to fix Lulythinar and Crenfyre, you severely overestimate my power."

I bite back my curse.

"Nor can I raise your friend back to life."

"Then what are you good for?" I spit, hating the way my stomach drops in severe, ugly disappointment. "How can you do neither of those things, if you could have given Eshe immortality?"

The Eye tsks softly, but its amusement is obvious in the air—thick and putrid and curling my mouth in revulsion. "I do not prefer to allow everyone detailed knowledge of the extents and limits of my power." A chuckle escapes it now. That sound grates along my scalp. "Think of something else, my dear little assassin. I will not give you another hair to call me, so use your favor now or else you must come find me to ask for it later."

Kaladen's nickname, on these weathered, ageless lips, brings my mind back from my discouragement. There *is* something else I want, something I desperately need, something that the Eye should be able to grant—judging by the scene I observed in the High King's throne room in Valehaven.

I draw my shoulders back. "I want you to erase Kaladen's full name from the minds of everyone who knows it, save for him and me."

I can almost make out a pair of thick eyebrows rising in the hood's shadow. My hands are clasped behind my back. I try not to squeeze them too tightly and betray the way I hold my breath for the Eye's answer. This won't likely help us during Lulythinar, but if—*if*—we possibly survived, it would save Kaladen from remaining the High King's slave for the rest of his life. No one could command him save himself.

He would be free.

"I did not expect such a request from you," the Eye rasps finally.

"I do not care what you expected. Honor our bargain."

That invisible grin returns. "You think like a fae. It is an unusual sight to behold in a half-dead human."

I draw my knives. Moonlight flashes off the blades. "Honor. Our. Bargain."

"It is already honored, my sweet. No one knows Kaladen's full name anymore—save you and Kaladen himself."

It is an effort to keep my shoulders from sagging dramatically. I take an aggressive step forward. "You swear this?"

It lifts both knobby-knuckled hands. "It is within my power. I am bound by your bargain to honor what you ask if it is within my power."

"So it is done."

"It is done."

I bare my teeth. "Then go back to Valehaven."

For a split second, the moon catches the light of one large, white eyeball. An eyeball with no iris, and no pupil. Then the vision is gone, and I stare at nothing but a nose protruding from a cloak. "You do not wish to know what your lost surname is?"

"I know my name. I will not bargain with you for it."

The Eye smiles once more. "No bargain. I will give it to you, free of charge."

"Fae don't give gifts."

It chuckles again, that wet, raspy chuckle. "Kaladen has taught you well. You are right, I will be paid for this."

"What will you get?" I demand. "And from whom? I will not play into your games any longer."

"I will get your reaction, my dear."

I draw back one step. My brow is a thick furrow, straining the muscles along my temple. "Go back to Valehaven, Eye of Baltor. I am through with you. Kaladen can take you to the Valehaven Portal if you need it."

I stride past the Eye, intending to stand guard at the door until it disappears and I know it is safe to leave.

"Your lost surname, Queen Nadira of Arbasa, is bint-Kinid."

My steps freeze. My heart stops in my chest. Everything in the world holds still, dust particles suspended in midair.

I can almost hear the silent laughter behind me, but I don't care. It is almost like my mind refuses to comprehend those words, to understand what the Eye even means.

So the Eye adds, "You and your thieving friend were cousins."

My chest is too tight to draw a full breath. My heart kicks back into rhythm, a broken, syncopated rhythm.

"Your fathers were brothers."

Now the Eye's laughter becomes audible, starting at a slight rumble, and increasing to nearly a full cackle. "What a reaction! This is even better than I expected—and all I can see is your back!"

I close my eyes. The storm inside me calms. A dozen, mislabeled pieces shift and find their home, settling into the foundation of my identity. And strangely, it feels like something I have known to be true all along. I recognize the truth of it at once. Like the face of my long-lost mother, like the warmth of my Baba's arms. This truth is my home. Eshe was not just a dear friend. She was my blood. She *is* my blood.

My sister.

A river of inexplicable peace floods every inch of my body and soul.

I turn around. And I smile at the Eye through the tears blurring my vision. "Thank you."

The Eye folds its arms across its chest. "Now you've gone and ruined it. I liked it better when you were shocked."

Somehow, I actually *laugh*.

And that, it seems, is all the motivation the Eye needs to leave. It vanishes without a trace, and I imagine the bargain-infused strand of hair made it so it could leave without using the Valehaven Portal. Which, as it turns out, is very convenient, considering that Kaladen has far too much to do tonight to play escort to a random fae.

My steps are light as I return to Eshe's room. Somehow, the darkness does not feel so oppressive, but more like a thick, warm blanket around my shoulders. Kaladen is free. And Eshe is my cousin.

Bint-Kinid.

I am no longer Nadira al-Risya Ashrift Felladyr, but Nadira bint-Kinid Ashrift Felladyr.

I lay one hand on Eshe's stiff shoulder. "Goodnight, sister," I whisper.

Then I lay down and fall into deep, deep rest.

CHAPTER 23

NADIRA

I WAKE TO a torrent of shouting that smashes through the dirty floorboards and rips me from sleep. I am on my feet a second later, my mind wheeling, my eyes trying to adjust to morning sunlight. *Morning sunlight*. I hadn't meant to sleep so late. What is going on?

I grab the sheathed scimitar I had slid under Eshe's bed last night, cast one last glance at her wrapped, still body, and then hurry down the stairs. I spare a thought for Badh-o, wondering where she is and why I haven't seen her since yesterday.

"You need my help, and you know it," a familiar voice snarls. "This place is going to be destroyed tonight at Lulythinar—but you're not willing to accept my help because I betrayed you? I never thought you to be so shortsighted."

"You will stab me and my wife in the back the moment we trust you," Kaladen roars back. "You've done it once, and you will do it again."

"Ask the human if he wants my help," replies the first voice.

The only thing that punctuates the silence that follows is my hurried footsteps down whining stairs. Then Tariq's cold voice: "I trust Kaladen's decision in this matter."

"Would a bargain help you?" demands the first voice.

"Why do you care what happens at the Bridge?" Kaladen demands. "Why do you care if we all die tonight? I don't trust your motives, Trenian!"

My sleep-fogged brain clears at that name. Prince Trenian! Sands, what is *he* doing here? My hackles rise instinctively as I reach the lowest level of the guardhouse and follow the shouting to an office with a door swinging on its hinges at each of the bellowed words from the room's occupants.

Trenian is the first person I see, sitting on the desk at the center of the room, his long legs braced wide, his hands gripping the edge of the desk, his gold-flecked eyes burning brightly as a lock of his dark hair tumbles over his shoulder. Tariq stands like a pillar beside the door, the shortest in the room and yet no less dignified for that fact, his arms crossed over his chest, his spine straight. He looks a little more haggard, his clothes torn and filthier than they were last night.

Kaladen has thrown his hands wide, droplets running down his temple, his long cloak swishing with each one of his movements. His hair is sweaty, the front wisps curled in unexpected ringlets that shake as he gestures.

Trenian's gaze snaps to mine when I appear in the doorway. A wide and completely untrue smile springs to his lips. "Nadira. Hello. Make your husband see reason."

I cross my arms and lean against the doorframe. Kaladen's head whips my way, and his scowl brightens immediately. It nearly distracts me—just how much my heart flutters that the sight of me could make Kaladen actually happy at a time like this.

I try not to let my thoughts show on my face when I reply coldly, "You know I side with Kaladen on this, too."

"You too?" Trenian presses a hand to his heart, as though I've wounded him gravely. "Such a shame. And I thought we'd gotten along so much better after all our misunderstandings."

"The second I let my guard down, you lied to me." I keep my voice from rising, but inside my gut churns with the sensation I've forgotten—frigid ice, like a waking dragon uncurling its tail. "The High King caught me because of that lie. He got Kaladen's name because of that lie. We are in our current *situation* because—"

"I was not the one who fell to the Wolf's tricks and let him gain control of the Bridge. What he did while he was the Neverseen King can hardly be placed on my shoulders."

I might beg to differ, but pursuing this line of argument will get us nowhere.

"Who sent you?" Kaladen asks.

Trenian smirks. "You don't think I came of my own—"

"Who. Sent. You?"

The prince's mocking expression hardens just a smidge, and I can almost feel Tariq bracing beside me, preparing for blows to fly. He continues to handle otherworldly drama and disaster exceptionally well. I cannot help but wonder if he ever asks himself if he is dreaming or if this truly is reality.

"The High King sent me," Trenian answers.

Kaladen's voice lowers to a growl. "And why, pray, did he send you?"

Trenian tilts his head one way, then the other. "He might have been the slightest bit concerned when his link to you snapped last night. Which, I might add, I also felt."

I cannot help the way my mouth twists. "I'm sure that was very disconcerting for him."

Kaladen's attention whips to me. "What did you do?"

"You didn't feel it? Last night?"

"I felt it. And I would have asked about it, too, but I was just the *slightest bit* occupied. What did you do?"

All eyes in the room fix on me. For a moment, I hesitate to tell them with Trenian present, but Kaladen isn't concerned—and it isn't like he can undo what the Eye did last night. "I called in my bargain with the Eye. I made him remove your name from everyone's memory except for yours and mine."

Kaladen's gaze flashes like fire as he regards me. A proud, glowing fire that looks ready to consume me any second. My face goes hot despite my best intentions, and grows only hotter when Trenian huffs an amused laugh.

"She must have fae blood, Kaladen."

That is enough to bring my husband's attention back to the matter at hand. "So Faradir is angry he no longer controls me. And you are here to . . . what? Collect my name again?"

"He sent me to find out what happened—and to find out what was happening with the Bridge." Trenian turns to Tariq and explains as though they are friends, "The High King can sense when the portals are open, you see."

Tariq does not move or reply.

"My father is concerned about the force of this Lulythinar. He likes being ruler of beautiful, intact worlds." Trenian smirks at me. "He is not fond of ruling ugly, destroyed ones. Oh, and I'm pretty sure he does not want to be eaten by Crenfyre."

"He wants you to help us?" Kaladen asks with a biting amusement.

Trenian gives his head a singular shake. "No, that part is me. Faradir only wants me to report back to him about what is happening here."

"Then why are you offering to help?"

Trenian's bright eyes flick to mine. "I did not want to lie to you."

I stay where I am, leaning against the wall, coolly meeting his gaze and not saying a word.

"I had to get my collateral from Kaladen," the prince continues. "And I was able to offer a bone to Faradir by claiming responsibility for your capture. It should give me enough leeway to offer you what help I can during Lulythinar."

Kaladen grabs a stool from the wall and sinks onto it, his arms still folded across his chest. Every muscle of his body is tight, rigid. "How could you help us?"

Trenian counts on his fingers. "Sealing portals. Containing uninvited *guests*. Entertainment, if we found ourselves getting bored—"

"I don't trust you!" Kaladen throws his hands wide. "It doesn't matter what you—"

"You know when I'm lying. You know when I'm telling the truth."

"If I could even think of what all to ask you that you wouldn't be able to answer by evasion!"

Trenian's brow slants downward. "I am on your side. I would not sabotage you. Or Nadira or this good fellow—or anyone else working with you. If Faerieland falls tonight because of the portals getting out of hand, I lose my future throne. Now that I have my collateral from you—which, keep in mind, I also lose if you and the Bridge fall tonight—I have no reason to deceive you or betray you."

Tariq clears his throat. We all turn to him. He shifts his weight slightly and gives his elbow a rub. "Perhaps one of you can enlighten me on the benefits or risks associated with Prince Trenian joining our efforts. From my vantage point, if we are doomed, we are doomed. One more ally or enemy is not going to change that."

I read behind the tired lines of his eyes the concern for Kanza's fleeing group, mingled with a discouraging realism.

Trenian's mouth slides into a smile that doesn't seem like a smile at all. "I am glad you asked. If I join your efforts, you could gain time. I doubt I could offer much more, but even a little bit of time could be the difference."

"The difference between what?" Kaladen snaps. "If we cannot seal Crenfyre, we cannot seal Crenfyre. That is the end of the matter."

"A previous Neverseen King figured out how to seal Crenfyre. You've been riding on his efforts until now. It can be sealed—and it can be sealed *without* your destroyed jar of mist."

Kaladen's brow lowers. "I know the story of how he sealed it, but there are some glaring gaps to that tale."

"Perhaps my presence would give you time to figure it out," Trenian replies tartly. He returns his attention to Tariq. "The risk of letting me join your efforts would be, of course, that I would steal your queen here, take her to the High King, and let him use her to extract Kaladen's full name from him again, thus returning him to the status of slave once more."

"He could also kill you and your men," Kaladen adds.

"I'm not worried about that," Tariq replies, making Trenian's brows lift in something between amusement and interest. "I consider me and my men already dead." He does not shrink when he speaks. There is no flicker of fear in his expression. Only determined resignation.

I read between his spoken words: *I consider the refugees already dead, too.*

Tariq continues. "If the Bridge falls, does the High King gain anything by enslaving Kaladen again?"

"If the Bridge falls, I won't be useful to the High King," Kaladen says. "But that does not mean he wouldn't enjoy punishing me for my failure by torturing my wife."

I speak up. "It seems like the only thing that could make our situation worse is if the High King took me. And he can do little to us beyond killing us or making us wish he'd killed us. If the Bridge and the human lands are gone, and everything we love is destroyed . . ." I shrug. "I certainly wouldn't choose to be tortured, but by that point, nothing would truly be on the line."

Kaladen's head turns abruptly in the direction of the palace. A new portal must have opened. I do not feel anything, and it makes me wonder if my sensitivity to those things is dulled by my distance from the palace. His jaw flexes as he turns back to the conversation at hand. His eyes turn to me, the scars across his face and neck standing out starker than usual. A subtle war rages in those pinpricks of sapphire. He does not want to do anything to put me at risk. He wants to protect me, but there is nothing he can do to protect me. With the worlds bursting open tonight, there is no place safe where he can stow me until later. There is no safehouse, no land or sea where I could hide from the reaches of Crenfyre.

Trenian has spoken aloud what has hummed in the back of my mind. Crenfyre *can* be sealed. But how to enter it and retrieve mist from near its anchor—that is the impossible feat somehow accomplished ages ago.

Despite my own dislike and distrust of Trenian, I find myself swayed by his arguments. We truly have nothing to lose, and if he can buy us just enough time to figure out how to handle Crenfyre, there just *might* be a chance we could survive this.

Kaladen seems to already have come to this same realization. He pins Trenian in place with a deeply etched scowl. "You will swear not to touch my wife."

Trenian's shoulders rise and fall with a breath. "I won't promise that, because I think you will cleave me in half if I stand by and let her be killed because I cannot *touch* her. But I swear I will not turn her over to the High King or intentionally do anything to jeopardize her safety. I have no plans to harm her or you or any of these humans. Nor do I intend to *make* such plans of harm."

He wants Kaladen to trust him, I realize abruptly. He would never offer so much truth up if he didn't. For a spare moment, I wonder if he is sorry for how he betrayed me, but I dismiss it quickly. He got his favor from Kaladen, and he would do it again if he had the chance.

"Then come," Kaladen says gruffly, getting to his feet. "We've got a long day and a long night ahead."

Trenian's grin makes me want to take back Kaladen's words. He rubs his hands together. "This will be the most fun I've had in ages."

Kaladen rolls his eyes.

"The children? Kanza?" I ask quietly, leaning toward Tariq.

He exhales. "Long gone. Most of the city went with them. A few stragglers are still working to leave, and others insisted on staying."

Kaladen strides over to me. Tariq pointedly turns the other way to give us a moment of privacy as one of Kaladen's large thumbs lands on the apple of my cheek. I look up at him, and the hard look in his expression softens.

Only for me.

"Did you get some rest?"

I nod.

"Breakfast?"

I shake my head.

"Get some. And pack some food for later if you can. We might not be able to come back."

I smile. "We're standing at the end of the worlds, and you want to make sure I have snacks."

"No one is dying today because of a stupid reason like being weak from hunger."

"Yes, Sultani."

That earns me a tiny smirk. I watch the memory of the trick I played on the Eye and the High King pass across his irises and he gives a subtle, almost disbelieving shake of his head. Then he pinches my cheek. "You have more audacity and luck than the feral cats filling this city."

"Ouch," I say, rubbing my cheek as he strides past me.

"Come to the palace when you are ready."

"Yes, Sultani."

He shoots me a glare, and I laugh.

Trenian hops off the desk and strides past us, heading for the door out to the gloomy, overcast city. "I'm off to seal portals, if anyone intends to join me."

I am about to peel off to do as Kaladen said and get some food when his hand lands on my elbow, stopping me just after the guardhouse door slams shut. I glance up at him in surprise, and find all vestiges of merriment wiped clean from his face.

"Watch your back," he growls under his breath. "He will take you to the High King if he gets a chance."

"He said—"

"Prince Trenian is a trickster at his core. His interests might temporarily align with ours, but he will not hesitate to hurt us if he believes it will help him. He is skilled at evasion, skilled at telling lies without telling lies, and I do not trust him. Working with him is a gamble we must take, but—"

"But be careful and don't trust him," I finish for him, and he nods. "I was already planning on it."

"That's my shrewd wife." He kisses my forehead before we split up on our way to the palace.

CHAPTER 24

KALADEN

"NADIRA TOLD ME to give this to you." I force my reluctant hand into motion, holding out my fist toward the prince. We stand in the courtyard by the fountain that burbles cheerily, as if tonight will not spell the end of everything I've ever wanted and worked for. Clouds gather overhead. A peal of thunder rumbles in the distance, soft and threatening. I've been so caught up in Lulythinar I did not notice that Arbasa's monsoon season had arrived with it.

Trenian, who has his hands planted on his hips as he peers through the doors at the palace, turns in surprise. An eyebrow tilts almost suspiciously. Still, he puts out his hand. I open my fist and let the precious stream of crimson blood flow into his palm. He closes his fingers around the blood, not allowing a drop to escape between his fingers, and tucks it into the breast pocket of his long tunic. He smirks. "Allowing me the good stuff, I see."

"Her idea, not mine."

"She is more practical than you are."

"On that, we can agree. How long has it been since you last sealed a portal?" I keep him in my sight at all times—a luxury I can afford at this moment. My skin crawls at how much I will be forced to trust him as the day progresses.

"Oh, not long. Sixty years, perhaps?" That spark never seems to leave his bright eyes, as though he finds everything around him, including the doom of Lulythinar, endlessly amusing.

I force myself not to drag a hand down my face. Nadira's life is in the hands of this idiot. "Do I need to give you a few lessons?"

"Lessons?" He waves flippantly. "I'm a professional. And I've got *the good stuff*." He pats his chest where he tucked away Nadira's blood.

My pulse hums, my mind trying to anticipate what horrible things he could accomplish with the blood I've freely given him. I remind myself that none of his plans will matter if we cannot save the Bridge. Nadira and I are useless without it—except as objects of the High King's wrath.

"Which portals are open?" Trenian asks, turning toward the palace doors once more. A gust of cool wind skates across the courtyard, toying with the tops of palm trees and forming gentle ripples across the surface of the fountain.

"Only Sakatel, but when the goblins were out yesterday, they chewed down many seals. Farboor and Wellmung will open in a matter of minutes."

"And Crenfyre? How long until then?"

I turn my senses inward, to the hundreds of distinct threads that anchor deep inside me. I know Crenfyre's by the weight and weft, the way it tugs and pulls. It frays, not rapidly, but surely. "Maybe hours."

Trenian's brow darkens, even as his smile remains firmly fixed in place. "I will leave you in charge of that one. Now is the time for creative solutions. Are you going to put Nadira in the dream realm or have her stay in her body? Today will not be a good day to have her body lying around the Bridge unguarded."

His observation is one I spent much of the night mulling over. The only reply I give him is a simple, "I have a plan."

Trenian shrugs, his eyes glittering, and then he vanishes as he steps into the dream realm. I step into the dream realm behind him, but while he heads toward Sakatel, I head toward Crenfyre.

The sickly gray door of Crenfyre looms above me. The force behind it pulses like a drum, determined and deadly. I dread this portal with every fiber of my being. It is like an endless, roaring waterfall that drowns anything that comes near it. Now, as I stand here, the magnitude of its energy has a new tone to it. A tone it always has on Lulythinar.

Desperation.

Misty fingers claw down the other side of the door, prying and searching and digging for any weakness in the seal. Normally, I would reinforce it while I was here. I curse the Wolf again—pointlessly. His body still lies outside my quarters. Waiting to be devoured by wild dogs or swept away by the coming storm. What is done is done.

I stare at the cracking wood and the bolted metal reinforcements. My mind turns over the options before me. We cannot seal the portal without entering it. No Neverseen King before me, even the best ones, figured out how to seal a portal without something from the inside. Someone has to go inside. But how—*how*? Even the story of one of the original Neverseen Kings using a string of humans, controlled by faerie fruit to parade inside and pass back a vial of mist in the few seconds they had before they died seems impossible. It seems like what would have actually happened is that each person would have died the moment they set foot inside and they would not have gotten anywhere near the anchor. I also do not know where the anchor is. It might be in an easy, simple spot, or it might require searching.

With Crenfyre, what we don't have is *time*. Time to explore our options with the portal, time to strategize, time to search around inside. The idea of taking a dozen guards of Tariq's, placing them under the influence of faerie fruit, and sending them to their death sits with me wrong. The rational part of me argues that intentionally sacrificing a few people is better than refusing to do anything and letting the entire human world collapse. I would sacrifice more than a dozen men to spare Nadira's life.

But what I cannot do, in good conscience, is to send them to their death if I know a piece is missing. No matter how many men eat faerie fruit and follow my bidding, if they cannot get over the threshold of Crenfyre, it will not matter.

So how can I get them over that threshold? How can I get them to penetrate twelve paces deep into a parasitical portal when the mist crawls along the ground first? Perhaps if they had wings . . .

Suddenly, an idea slams into my consciousness.

I know what we can do. It is tremendously risky, but *theoretically* it could actually work—and that is all I need. The possibility of success.

A thread twinges inside my chest. Not a new portal opening—this is a different thread.

"Nadira!" I call in excitement, even though she's too far away to hear me. "I've got an idea!"

CHAPTER 25

NADIRA

KALADEN APPEARS VERY suddenly as I lay my hand gently on the banister. It purrs at my touch, and beneath that satisfaction, I sense an unusual energy humming. *Are you ready for Lulythinar?* I ask the banister.

It often is afraid—afraid of enemies, of Kaladen, of the Bridge. And yet that humming increases, buzzing into my fingertips and zipping up my arm.

Yes, it replies. The word is a sigh, almost a longing.

It reminds me that Kaladen once said that Lulythinar is a celebration among the fae.

Though after tonight, I think morbidly, it may not continue as a celebration. If we fail.

Those thoughts are wiped from my mind as Kaladen bursts into existence at my side, breathing hard, but not from exertion. There is a light in his brilliant eyes, a light I so rarely have the privilege of witnessing. "Kaladen?"

"I know what we can do!" he gasps. His big hands land on my shoulders, gripping hard. He is almost smiling. Even the weathered lines on his face, weariness and scars, seem to fade and the youthful beauty he once possessed shines through. The sight dazzles me momentarily.

"What?" I demand, regaining possession of my mind.

"Wings—I need wings. Creatures who can fly, with enough sentience to follow orders. And I need a way to control them. Faerie fruit may not be enough, depending on the creature."

"Um—"

"I was *just* telling Trenian that Farboor was about to open. Those denizens have wings. They're frightfully ugly and mean, but if we can get some means of controlling them, we can send them into Crenfyre."

Which would work, because Crenfyre's mist sinks to the ground. So if the door was open, and enough mist released to clear a path, something could fly in *above* the mist. It would be tricky for the creatures to bottle the mist, and we would need more than just one to ensure it happened. Some fae have wings, but finding a way to control them would be impossible—unlike a creature with less will and sentience. This could be a way to get into the portal.

A light blooms in my gut, melting the icy stirrings that are so easy to trigger now with fear and danger around every corner. I look up at Kaladen, and hope morphs my expression into a replica of his.

"I think this can work," I breathe. "We'd have to plan it carefully—and Trenian would have to handle the portals that keep opening. But maybe . . ."

"But maybe," Kaladen repeats firmly. "*Maybe.*"

It is so much more possibility than we've had since the Wolf smashed that vial. So much possibility, so much hope, that I fear it will choke me. I think of the city, Tariq, his men, Kanza, the children and refugees. I even think, just for one moment, of Kaladen and me.

He's thinking the same thing. He clears his throat and points up the staircase. "Farboor is this way. But we need to go to the rainforest portal first so you can join the dream realm."

We do not go around the trunk of the tree to see the broken cabinet, nor all the dead shells of the portal souls like broken glass strewed across the floor. Still, there are a few fragments near the bed. They are grayed, burned, and fogged. I swallow the pained lump in my throat and step past them. All is not lost.

We might seal Crenfyre yet.

But bringing balance to the Bridge . . .

I shove away the thought. No use mourning the loss. We need to get through Lulythinar. Only then will we decide if we are going to start collecting portal souls from scratch.

Kaladen is behind me as I climb into the bed. I lay down and stare up at him. Something unreadable flashes across his face. Then he bends down and places his calloused hand over my face. I'm taken back to that fateful moment in Jabir's cell when he did the same thing to kidnap me. His palm smells of rich, tingly spices. The smell I've come to associate with magic.

"Sleep," he murmurs.

The shift is so fast, so imperceptible, that I always question if it actually happened. I sit upright, opening my mouth to ask, when Kaladen nods. "You're in the dream realm," he says. "We will make sure this portal stays locked so nothing can get in and find your body."

We make our way out of the portal. At once, the familiar sight greets me—of flashing rainbows swirling in the air around each door, the thumbprint seals in various shades of red and brown. Red for strong seals, and brown for those breaking down.

"I forgot how much easier it is to do this in the dream realm," I say with a small chuckle. "You can see the status of the seals so easily." My chuckle dies when I see just how many seals are brown. Only the barest handful are still red. I wonder if those are the ones Kaladen sealed last night and early this morning.

We climb the stairs to the next floor. Kaladen takes me to the Farboor Portal. It is down one long hallway. Its door is a dully reflective slate blue, with feathers etched into the metalwork, arranged like the door is an entire wing. The handle is like a petrified eagle's talon. Like the other doors, it glows—primarily blues that shift subtly as though blown by the wind. The seal is brown and flaking.

"Are we going to let it break open?" I ask.

He nods, surveying it.

A whistle from down the hallway makes both of us turn. Trenian's gait is pure saunter, leisurely and uncaring. Kaladen somehow manages not to move and place himself in front of me, even though I know that is exactly what he wants to do. The prince throws a grin at us. "You should have seen how flawlessly I executed that seal. What are you doing here? I thought you were supposed to fix Crenfyre." He stops suddenly, reading our expressions, and something flashes across his face. I cannot read his emotion, but it is unexpectedly genuine. "Don't tell me you already have a plan."

"Not a fully formed one." Kaladen's attention returns to the door. The engraved feathers seem to shift slightly.

Trenian glances between the door, Kaladen, and me, clearly trying to piece together what this plan could possibly be. It almost makes my mouth twist upward. Then his eyebrows rise. "Surely . . . You're not intending to actually *capture* several skyreavers?" He turns to me. "He doesn't intend to capture skyreavers."

"Is it hard?" I ask.

"You cannot make skyreavers do your bidding," Trenian insists to Kaladen, a wrinkle appearing along his prominent chin.

"I suppose faerie fruit isn't strong enough to control them?" I say.

The prince gives a wry laugh. "Faerie fruit rarely affects anything as much as it affects humans." An evil twinkle comes into his eye. "You should try it some time." When Kaladen shoots him a violent glare, he holds up both hands. "Only when it's safe, of course, and my cousin is the only one who could give you orders in your inebriated state."

"I'm not drugging my wife," Kaladen growls. His shoulder twitches the moment I feel something inside me twang like the string of a crossbow. "Wellmung is open. We don't have much time."

"You will need all three of us to execute your mad plan," says the prince. "So either we leave Wellmung to its business or we wait until it's sealed. Speaking of which, is it just me or is it a little concerning how few portals are open now?"

I look around me. From my limited vantage point, I can only see about a dozen seals. Only one of them is a bright red. The rest are various shades of faded red and brown.

Kaladen does not answer immediately, leaving Trenian to add, "If I didn't know better, I would think they were trying to all break open at once—the moment Lulythinar begins."

"They like doing that," Kaladen mutters. "Some of them cannot wait that long, but they certainly try."

The prince lets out a single huff of air. "Diabolical portals."

The way they speak of portals and magic always feels as though they discuss sentient beings, but Kaladen has told me before that that is not the case. Yet how can portals *like* doing something if they are not sentient? How can doors to other worlds be sentient anyway? Or rather, is it the world itself that is sentient? I did carve out a piece of Roltwart's heart. Hearts imply sentience.

Kaladen's abrupt curse yanks the prince's and my attention to him.

"Another portal?" I purse my lips. "I didn't feel that one."

"You won't feel them all," Kaladen replies. "This is a bad one—I must address it immediately."

Trenian shrugs. "I suppose Nadira and I will capture the skyreavers then."

Kaladen points one long finger at him. "You're not going into that portal until I return. I won't be gone long."

With that, and one cautioning look at me to be safe while alone with the prince, he disappears.

Trenian looks at me. "Don't lie. I know you're thinking of disobeying his orders as much as I am."

Ice burns to life in my belly. I breathe deeply to stop my anger from flaring too brightly. "We cannot go in without a plan."

"Can't we?" Trenian grins. It shifts into something hard-edged only a moment later. "The seal is going to break soon. We might not have a choice."

He's right. The seal is flaking away, piece by piece, as we watch.

"Then we make a plan while we wait for Kaladen," I say, stubbornly, as if he didn't tell the truth about what I had been considering. We're in the dream realm; the portal shouldn't be able to kill me. "Tell me about this portal, and the skyreavers."

Light flashes in the prince's cold eyes. "The world beyond this door is filled with every danger imaginable—"

I blink slowly, my face not moving an inch.

"I've never seen someone so clearly and yet so silently say something with one look," Trenian laughs. "Fine, I'll stop wasting your time. Farboor is vast, like most of the worlds, but if I remember correctly, this portal opens into a cluster of rocky isles in the midst of an ocean. These isles are home to the dreaded skyreavers. Some refer to them as birds, but the similarities end with wings and nests. You won't think they look anything like a bird."

I nod. "Does the portal open onto one of these rocky isles? Or into the ocean?"

"One of the isles, thankfully. It's where they have many nests, so we will be careful. Skyreavers do not have a fondness for trespassers who threaten their hatchlings."

"And how do we capture them?"

The words are hardly out of my mouth before the walls of the palace suddenly crush me together. Or, at least, that is what it feels like. One minute, I'm standing there, talking to Trenian, and the next, I hit the wall next to another door with enough force to stun me for several moments.

I don't even realize what has happened before an echoing rattle fills my awareness, and then a circular . . . *tube* filled with bristles appears out of a fog and launches straight at my face.

I stare at it stupidly for an entire second before my brain catches up to me, telling me that the Farboor Portal just broke open, and that *thing* coming for me has wings with scalelike feathers. It must be a skyreaver. One of the creatures we need to—

A sword appears in midair, with no hand on the handle, and it swings with deadly precision just as I'm forcing my body into a roll. The rattle reaches a crescendo, then abruptly cuts off.

My head whips to the side. There is Trenian, several paces away from me, cutting his hand through air. I look back as the tubular body of the skyreaver is sliced in half and falls to the floor in a heavy, scaly pile.

"Shouldn't we have tried to capture it?" I call over the wind rushing from the open portal. "It cannot kill me while I'm in the dream realm."

Trenian jerks his hand toward his body, and the floating sword rips backward until the hilt lands in his palm. "Technically, yes, but if it had just bitten off your head, we would have had to delay this to get you back to the waking world and then bring you *back* in the dream realm."

I acknowledge the wisdom of his actions with my lack of protest, and he runs to my side. Violent wind tears at our hair and clothes. I wince against the pounding of my head and the bruising of my body. None of my injuries are permanent here in the dream realm. The pain running up and down my spine doesn't seem to agree, however.

Sorry Kaladen, I think with a mixture of grimness and amusement. *We don't have a choice but to go in.*

Not unless he wants the entire city overrun with these creatures.

The world before us is a cast of gray sky. Stone as white as ice extends on the other side of the door—punctuated with black, thorny nests—though it abruptly drops off into a turquoise sea. The sky is full of swarming skyreavers, their large, tubular bodies about four feet long on average, their wings waxy and their eyeless faces nothing but a chasm of bristles that I realize now are teeth.

I spin on the prince. "You did not tell me that these isles were so . . . *high*!"

Trenian peers over the threshold, down into the hundred-foot drop to the sea below. "Must have forgotten."

I step onto the stone and am surprised by the coldness that seeps through my sandals into my feet. "You capture the skyreavers. I'll find the anchor to reseal."

"You do *not* get the easy job while I get the impossible one."

I give him my most patronizing smile. "I'll help you when I've finished."

Trenian steps through the door. "Just for that smugness, I won't tell you how the skyreavers sense your presence since they cannot see. And I shall laugh when you get your head bitten off after all."

My mouth falls open as he lightly runs ahead, plunging toward the swarms of skyreavers and their nest, leaving me behind. At first, I kick myself for being petty and losing valuable information from the only person who can help me—and then I scowl. *He's* the one being petty.

"Anyone else would have been preferred to him," I mutter under my breath.

I glance back at the open door. It is a rectangle of hallway cut straight into the middle of gray sky and white stone. It beckons for all the denizens of this portal to leave and explore worlds beyond their own.

A rattle makes me draw my scimitar in one hand. I start to draw a knife in the other, only to stop myself. I've gotten so used to having my magic bound it's difficult to remember I can use it now. I leave my left hand free, and I don't even have to intentionally stir my ice before it thickens my belly.

A skyreaver dives toward me. On silent feet, I step lightly to one side. It redirects its course, following my movements. *It doesn't see the world through sound, then,* I think. It has some other means of knowing where I am.

Its round mouth constricts slightly, then opens wider as it tucks in its wings and dives toward me at a frightening speed. I should just kill it, but it feels counterproductive when our goal is to *capture* several.

I take my left arm and cut it upward through the air. My renewed control over my magic shudders slightly, but I succeed in erecting a barrier of ice between me and the skyreaver just before it swallows up my head.

The ice cracks from the impact of the skyreaver's hit. Stunned, the creature falls to the ground and twitches.

"I found the anchor!" Trenian calls from ahead.

Apparently, we've accidentally switched tasks. I leap around my ice shield as fast as I can. The creature is so long, its scaled body like a very fat snake's that has been cut in half. Its bristled mouth constricts and expands, as though breathing. Delicate, papery wings shudder and twitch. Those wings look like they could tear at the least provocation. If I damage them, the creatures will be useless for Kaladen's purpose.

But I must restrain them somehow.

I crouch beside the skyreaver and lay down my scimitar. How long until it overcomes its temporary stunning? Maybe only seconds. With two fingers, I pinch the thickened edge of the wings, the part that protrudes from the body, and bend it backward just a little bit. The creature thrashes its tail. Clenching my jaw, I strain against the billowing force of magic inside of me and try to draw only the barest sliver. My entire body goes taut from the effort. *Just the littlest bit,* I tell myself. *Just a tiny bit.*

More than I intend comes flying out of my fingertips. The ice does pin the wing as I'd hoped, but six extra inches of delicate wing are covered with ice.

"Please don't be damaged," I whisper, and tend to the second wing just as it starts flapping.

The skyreaver contorts and whips its body around. It yanks the second wing out of my grip. I only barely remember to release it so I don't tear it, and then I leap out of the way of its snapping mouth that comes for my left arm. It doesn't stop there, though, and the second I'm on my feet, it flops toward me. The pinned wing flaps and tries to break the ice.

"Hold still! You'll hurt yourself!" I cry, trying to find a way to dodge its mouth while still reaching for that stubborn free wing. I slip on the cold stone, nearly end up on my backside, and that gives the creature the chance it needs to flop onto its side and bite at my foot.

I drag myself behind the ice wall fast enough that it only clips the edge of my sandal. Two bristly teeth slice the ends of my toes. Blood wells, spills from the cuts, and stains the white stone.

But the creature doesn't flop after me like I expect. Instead, it whips its mouth around in various directions, and then tries to launch into the sky. It fails, of course, its bound wing flapping uselessly, while its free one tries to compensate. It tosses aside my fallen scimitar in its effort. The long blade slides dangerously near the towering edge of cliff.

It suddenly occurs to me then.

Heat.

The skyreavers can see via *heat*. That's why, when I'm behind this ice wall, it does not know where I am. Quickly, I get to my feet. I run my hand over my clothes. It is fast, clumsy work that results in some neatly frozen patches, and other heavy blocks of ice hanging from my tunic and sirwal. But I count it as a success when I don't accidentally stab myself with my own magic.

Then I bolt out from behind the ice wall. I didn't cover my skin, so the skyreaver will still be able to tell where I am—I'm only hoping that I won't be as much of a beacon this way.

The skyreaver, struggling violently now, nearly pitches itself over the edge of the cliff. My heart twinges in pity. I shove it aside with the reminder that if we cannot figure out how to seal Crenfyre, the parasitical mist might end up in this portal too and kill *all* of the skyreavers.

That does not make it easier to imprison a sacrificial tribute to the cause.

I creep up behind the frantic skyreaver and grab hold of its free wing before it realizes I've come. The thrash it gives me nearly sends me flying. I cling tightly and send ice into my palm. I successfully coat its scales with ice and miss the wing entirely. I throw my body across the winding, struggling length of scales, straddling it and clinging for dear life as I reach for that stupid wing.

"Why don't you coat the whole thing in ice?" a drawling voice interrupts my struggle.

"You could help!" I growl between clenched teeth as I clench my knees tightly around sharp scales that cut through my sirwal and into my skin. "And I don't want to hurt it!"

"You seem like you're doing just fine without my help," Trenian replies, and in the corner of my eye—when I'm not nearly being thrown to my death—I find him leaning casually against my wall of ice with crossed ankles. "My intervention might only make things worse."

The skyreaver nearly bucks me off. I grab hold of the wing in desperation. Ice follows at the contact. *Too much ice, too much ice!* I think desperately.

The wing goes still. The body still writhes and wriggles, but when I peel open my wincing eyes, its second wing is almost completely coated in ice.

"Sands," I curse, climbing off the creature. Its struggles are much less productive, so I step back and breathe hard as its movements slow down. Then I shift my glare to the prince. "Did you get what we needed to seal the portal?"

He holds up a single gray-blue scale with a grin, then slips it into the front pocket of his long tunic and pats it. "Acquired and secured."

"Well," I pant, splitting my attention between him and the half-frozen skyreaver. "Care to help me get two more? I don't know how Kaladen is planning to control them, but—"

Trenian's eyes suddenly double in size. He lunges toward me.

I throw myself to the ground.

But not fast enough.

Something clamps down on the back of my tunic. A rip fills my ears. *My tunic,* I think at first, in the second before the pain thunders through my back. Then I'm lifted straight off my feet. Trenian grabs my foot, and I suddenly feel as though I am being torn in two. A scream rips from my throat. He lets go. The world grows smaller in a second.

Trenian's blazing sword shoots from the ground, past me. The rattle against my skin pierces my entire body.

And then I'm falling.

I've never fallen like this before. I want my rational brain to catch up, to think, to try to save myself. Instead, I wheel my arms and legs uselessly as I plunge straight to the glasslike surface of the ocean below me.

Abruptly, I crash sideways into a cliff. My fall stops.

My limbs don't stop moving. My legs are trying to run, my arms flailing, my scream locked behind my terror.

"Hold still!" Trenian's voice booms from far away. It sounds strained. "Don't move, or it'll rip!"

The panic is too all-consuming. I want to obey—I really do—but the drop below me is so far, and I don't even know what pins me to the side of the cliff. I'm hanging from my tunic. I cannot twist to see what it is. I cannot even grab on to something.

"Stop moving!" Trenian's scream is almost frantic. I cannot see where he is, but he sounds far away. The rattle of skyreavers fills my ears. When I look up, several circle just above. Ready to dive and rip me to pieces.

I've got to do something. I'm going to die.

Not die, I remind myself. *You're in the dream realm. You* mostly *cannot die.*

But I'm not sure I believe myself. This body feels very real. The hot blood dripping down my back is as real as anything I've seen or felt or tasted.

A skyreaver dives for me.

Kaladen would lose his mind if he saw how things were going here, I think hysterically.

A crash and light explodes above me. Then another, and another. Scales and ripped wings fall around me and continue falling to the roiling ocean below.

"Almost there!" Trenian yells, just before another explosion happens.

I get one hand out, fingernails digging for purchase in the solid rock of the cliff face. I turn my head just enough to see a glowing blade lodged deep into the cliff.

I'm hanging from Trenian's blade.

You can't die. Dream realm. Dream realm. It is a chant repeating through my head as I hang there, my tunic biting into my ribs and underarms.

Then his voice is above me. Strained and frantic. "Nadira!"

My position feels far too precarious to shout back.

"Where is your rope?"

My rope. I have new rope. It's on my belt. My hand shakes as I reach for it. I unhook its end, my sweaty palm clinging to it like a lifeline. The moment I go to throw it, however, my shirt catches the edge of Trenian's blade and slices. I freeze.

"Use your ice!" Trenian calls down. "Make a foothold!"

I'm more likely to create a bed of sharp icicles to impale myself upon when I fall. Still, trembling violently, I aim my hand at the cliff and unleash the power of my own fear.

Then I'm falling again.

My feet catch on slippery ice. I slam my palms into the side of the cliff. My heart leaps completely out of my body. My mouth is open, my breathing a jagged rhythm. Somehow, my icy hands stall my fall, and I cling to the cliff like a barnacle. When I look down, blood stains the bumpy, icy ledge I stand on.

Spots erupt across my vision.

"No," I snarl, sucking in cold air and strands of my own hair. "You are *not* passing out. That's not what you do anymore. You're in the dream realm! You cannot die!"

I peer below me again. I see the blood, the drop. I close my eyes and scream.

"I need the rope!" Trenian yells. "Throw me the rope!"

"I can't!" I scream back. My hands are pinned to the cliffside.

"Fine! But then you need to hang on *really well*!"

I try to look up, to understand what he means. Then an explosion rocks the cliff. Rocks come tumbling down toward me. I pull close to the cliff and bury my face in my own ice. Rattles fill the sky, like a chorus of angry birds. Another explosion, and another. Rocks and debris fly in every direction, raining down on me like tiny, sharp knives.

Trenian's voice is suddenly much closer. "Give me your hand!"

I look up. And there he is—dark hair wild about his face, his bright eyes flashing with the light of danger, his mouth set in strain. He crouches on a blackened ledge that wasn't there before. I think he might have just . . . *carved* that ledge out of those blasts of light and magic the fae love so much.

"I can't," I cry. My hands are practically glued to the cliffside. If I force the magic to retreat, I'll fall.

Trenian's angular face is hard. "Yes, you can. You can, and you will. Give. Me. Your. Hand."

The black spots return.

I am sick of this! Sick of hanging off a cliff, sick of inopportune fainting, sick of all we have had to do to prevent Crenfyre and

Lulythinar from destroying us. And I'm sick of thinking I'm going to die right now when I'm *not going to die*.

My right palm squeezes into a fist. The ice cracks around it. With a burst of determination, I throw that hand toward Trenian. He catches me around the wrist. We lock grips, and then we lock eyes.

He could have left me here. Maybe he wanted this to happen all along so he could capture me and take me to the High King.

But it is not a scheme or mere self-preservation searing across the gold-flecked eyes boring into mine. Trenian does care. About many things—and far more than he ever wants anyone to believe.

He pulls me up with strength well beyond a human's. I land on flat, blackened stone on my hands and knees. I stay there for a moment, gasping hard, staring at the ground. I drag my gaze upward, toward Trenian's, and his wild glance around us at the swarming skyreavers is the last thing I see.

CHAPTER 26

NADIRA

MY EYES PEEL open to gray sky, a cacophony of rattles, and a sharp grunt of pain from Trenian. Everything hurts. I guess I haven't woken up in my normal body yet. We're still in this stars-cursed portal. Part of me had hoped that I would wake in the rainforest treehouse bed, calm and still. But it's almost Lulythinar. Nothing is calm and still.

I push up on my elbows, my face contorting from the pain in my back. When I look around, I find that I'm positioned behind the ice wall I created.

Trenian ducks behind it as I'm struggling to sit up. He breathes hard, his shirt torn at the shoulder, blood seeping out. He offers me a distracted smirk. "You're up! Just in time. I need you to—"

Smash!

The ice fractures from the force of the blow on the opposite side. We both tumble forward. Trenian springs to his feet, grabbing me by the forearm. "Freeze the wings! That was very effective."

He drags me out, and I nearly tumble back into unconsciousness, but let the force inside my belly steady me. A skyreaver lies stunned, just like the first. I coax my shaking limbs into motion and freeze its wings fast enough that it doesn't have a chance to recover before it is effectively bound.

"That's all we need!" Trenian declares, whipping out a rope—*my* rope. He must have pilfered it while I was unconscious. Its end is already binding one unfrozen skyreaver that tries to thrash. With quick hands, the prince binds the two frozen skyreavers to the rope in a line and then wraps the loose end around his palm several times. He grins at me. "How unfortunate that we must leave already. Cheers, Farboor!"

Then we're diving toward the open door, dodging the nests that will make the circling skyreavers even angrier at our presence, while Trenian drags our captives.

I stumble out of the portal. The hand that I press to the doorway is soaked in blood. I grit my teeth and look away. I've gotten so much better about not passing out . . . *generally*. My huff is dry and pained. Trenian is right behind me, the muscles of his shoulders and back straining as he pulls the three heavy bodies from the portal. I move before he is finished, slipping my hand into the pocket of his tunic and yanking out the scale he collected. I yank the door shut, press the scale to the seal, and print my bloody thumb against it.

The seal flares a bright red.

I sag in relief. Trenian lets out his own sigh of relief as he lets the rope drop. The pile of skyreavers wiggle uselessly in the middle of the palace hallway. I try not to feel guilty again for their fate.

"That rope is *excellent*," Trenian gasps as he collapses against the wall. "I never knew humans made such good rope. It *is* human make?"

I laugh quietly. "Human make. It's the only rope I use. It's called *jurbah*."

"I will need to get some before I return to Valehaven."

My laughter fades as I look at the skyreavers. "We *were* supposed to bring them out into the dream realm, right? Or were we supposed to bring them into the waking world? Can we even bring them to the waking world now?"

Trenian's brows come together. "Kaladen did not say anything about bringing them into the waking world. My guess would be that it doesn't matter, since Crenfyre can kill and be sealed in either realm. But *you* do need to get to the waking world."

I glance back at the seal and a quiet cry leaps to my lips. "It's already brown!"

Trenian's mouth draws into a long, thin line.

"We *just* sealed this." I gesture wildly at the browning seal. "And we sealed it with *my* blood. How is this possible?" I look around at the whole hallway of brown seals. My stomach drops inch by inch.

"This is Lulythinar for you," the prince says grimly. "This is Kings-cursed Lulythinar for—"

A shiver runs the length of my entire body. Trenian's head whips up, darkness burning across his face as he abruptly stops talking.

We're not alone.

I glance up and down the length of the hallway, but aside from the imprisoned skyreavers, there is no one else. I might have assumed it was Kaladen, were we not already in the dream realm and if this premonition were not so . . . *chilling*.

I catch the prince's eye, wordlessly asking what is happening. He gives me a look that indicates something is wrong, but he does not know what. *Great*. Even the heir to the High Throne of Faerie does not know what is in this hallway with us. Whatever it is, it's in the dream realm too.

Even the skyreavers have gone still.

My hand goes to my weapons. I cast a frantic look to Trenian and hiss, "My scimitar! I left it—"

He presses one finger to his lips and shakes his head. *You don't need a scimitar,* that look seems to say. Tight concern passes over his features as he regards the blood staining the back of my ripped tunic and the unsteady way I move. Not concern for my life, but for my ability to fight in this state. I need to return to the waking world before I am nothing more than a useless, bloody pulp.

Trenian points to himself and the hallway to our left, then to me and the stretch to our right. I nod and straighten. We put our backs to each other and begin creeping down the hall in opposite directions.

My senses are sharp, yet there is nothing tangible for any of those senses to grab hold of. Muted daylight streams overhead, the shadows growing longer and longer as clouds thicken and the day progresses toward evening. Strange doors, with their otherworldly designs, vibrant glows, and flaking seals flank me on every side. Hungry, waiting, threatening, watching—and yet they are not the presence I feel stronger with every step.

I slow my progress, raising both of my hands in front of me. My ice twists and burns in my gut. I breathe carefully, intent on keeping my magic on the thinnest leash I can, ready to snap it any second.

The hallway splits ahead. I approach that blind corner. My heart roars in my ears.

Suddenly, the air ripples at the hallway split. I stop moving.

The ripple goes high toward the ceiling and takes up almost the entire breadth of the hallway. It is like the air folds and bends around . . . *something*.

Something very large.

I open my mouth to call to Trenian.

Then, abruptly, I blink, and my vision is completely different.

I stand on the opposite side of the hallway, facing the way I've just come. The ground is far, far away. A few paces away from me is a mortal woman, dressed in filthy, torn, bloodied clothes, her hands outstretched toward me. Her hair is wild about her face, her dark eyes violent and just a little bit afraid.

I love that fear. I breathe in the smell of it. It is rich, intoxicating. I want to be drunk on that scent. I need to get closer.

I move forward, toward the woman. With each prowling step, the scent of her fear grows stronger. I fill my vast, billowing lungs with it. *Ahh.* The sweetest smell. I must have more. More. *More.*

She stands rooted to the spot, her hands outstretched but shaking. I have not known pleasure like this in ages. I bend down toward her. I reach out. My talon catches her hair, and she catches her breath. A brighter, headier thread of fear floods my nose.

Oh yes.

I can make this mortal so, *so* much more afraid.

There is nothing like this in my world, nothing like the fear of a mortal. I long to bottle it, to—

Pain erupts across my limb.

And then my vision flips once more. I stand on my feet, low to the ground once more, facing the rippling air beyond me. Trenian's hand is like iron on my shoulder as he drags me backward so violently he practically throws me to the ground. I land, catching myself with my palms against the floor, breathing hard. My mind reels. Not a shred of understanding swirls in my brain—only confusion and questions.

"It's a *bhogra*!" Trenian cries. "You have to keep your dista—"

He goes still. His head tilts up toward the shifting air that disguises such a large, frightening creature. *Bhogra*. I don't know what that is, but whatever just happened to me must have also happened to the prince. Those ancient, rumbling thoughts that were in my head . . . were *not* my thoughts. And they're in Trenian's now.

I do the only thing I can do.

Which is throw my hands above the prince's head and blast as much ice as I can.

There is no cry of pain indicating that I hit my mark or successfully hurt the *bhogra*, but Trenian snaps to one side and scrambles backward toward me, eyes wide.

"That is not an experience I recommend," he gasps, failing to produce his usual mocking grin. "Kaladen wasn't joking when he said the open portals were bad ones."

We run down the hallway, putting distance between us and the invisible monster, but it floats after us, undeterred by pain.

"What do we do?" I hiss. "How do you kill these things?"

Trenian winces. "I'm not entirely sure you *can*. We're in the dream realm, remember. One of the portals must have broken open here instead of in the normal world." Then, as if the words are sour on his tongue, mutters, "Kaladen would know better."

My husband's name is on my lips, ready to call for him to help us, but I stop myself. If he isn't here, then he is handling something more important. Like closing the *bhogra's* portal so more do not escape.

The skyreavers lay helplessly, encased in ice and rope. They shiver as the *bhogra* approaches. Their fear might be stronger even than ours. Together, the five of us are irresistible.

"We cannot let it hurt the skyreavers," I whisper, keeping my eye on the rippling reality before me. "Is there some place we can put them?"

"Where is your body?" Trenian asks. His hand flexes on the hilt of his glowing sword. Before I answer, he sends it hurtling toward the *bhogra*. It pauses for one singular moment, then continues.

"Rainforest portal."

Trenian's blade returns to his grip. "If we can put the skyreavers there, they should be safe. You could return to your body so you're not so wounded."

"But I cannot get back into the dream realm without Kaladen!"

The prince shrugs one tight shoulder, then grabs the end of the rope tied to the skyreavers and hands it to me. "We'll have to deal with that later. You haul. I distract."

I pull on the rope, leaning my weight backward as leverage. The heavy pile barely moves. I grit my teeth, my weakened muscles shaking, and pull harder. I swear under my breath. The *bhogra* approaches faster.

"You distract. I haul," Trenian amends with a humorless laugh. He grabs the rope from me, and it makes me feel a little better when his face contorts in strain as he uses all of his fae strength to get the pile of monster birds moving down the hallway.

I get between them and the *bhogra* and release another torrent of ice. Instead of sending them like spears into the creature, I swipe my hands upward in a harsh motion, like I did in the Farboor Portal, and create an icy barrier that stretches from floor to ceiling. The effort leaves me even weaker than before. I scramble backward, not wanting to get close enough for the *bhogra* to steal my awareness again.

"Please work," I mutter under my breath. When I glance over my shoulder, Trenian is almost to the staircase.

I turn back to my ice wall, only to see the entire thing ripple. A violent curse springs to my lips. There's nothing I can do to slow it down! Except let myself fall into its thrall again. I whimper at the thought—and I can almost feel the way the *bhogra* ducks closer to me as though to drink the fear rising inside of me.

Trenian reaches the stairs and with a last look at me, disappears down it. The skyreavers thump down each step after him.

I can almost feel the *bhogra* looking past me at the knot of bound skyreavers. Their fear must be stronger than mine, a deeper, more intoxicating brew of terror. To my horror, the ripple begins . . . *sinking*. My eyes widen with realization. The *bhogra* is not bound to space like I am, as demonstrated by how ineffective my ice wall was. It is leaving this floor, sinking to the lower level to ambush Trenian and his captives.

Ice floods me, but it's useless. I nearly tear out my hair in desperate helplessness as I watch the folds of reality sinking.

The bhogra cannot kill me, I think to myself, racking my brain. Not unless Kaladen forgot to mention it as one of the few things that could kill me in the dream realm. I'm already desperately weakened. The only way I can keep it occupied is to offer it myself.

I grit my teeth and run straight toward the warping edges of reality.

The change hits me like a blow. One minute, I am running toward it, and the next, I'm watching from above, a cruel, coiling delight filling my body. *Ahh, a mortal's sweet, sweet fear.* There is nothing more beautiful, more gleeful than fear. I want to make her more afraid—so *very* afraid of me. I come close enough to touch her. She has gone still, standing exactly where I want her. This is a delicate dance; an exquisite equation to perfectly calibrate her fear to its most potent measures. Her heady scent feeds my excitement. So much desperation. *Yes.*

The closer I get to her, the more aware she becomes of my presence swirling around her on all sides, the deeper her fear. The slightest touch on her neck makes her stiffen. A longer, sharper touch on the back of her calves sends her fear rushing toward me. I might lose my head if I'm not careful. Oh, how *long* it has been since I—

A wordless roar cuts my thoughts in half.

The next moment, I am pressed against a wall, a large body wrapped around mine. I look up, breathing hard, to see Kaladen's face turned in a vicious snarl toward the *bhogra*, his shoulders and back angled to shield me. I could melt from the relief of his presence.

He gives me a single, quicker-than-lightning glance and then pushes me behind him as he faces the towering, rippling folds of reality. Something scurries around my foot, and I jerk away, only to look down and recognize Badh-o. She has wrapped her tail around my ankle and pulls fruitlessly with all her might. I allow her to pull me further away from the scene.

Kaladen shouts something in a language I've never heard. It is low, rasping, and throaty. He blocks the hallway, and not one inch of his body quivers—despite how close he is to the *bhogra*. Close enough for it to steal his awareness.

I wonder, perhaps a little smugly, if the *bhogra* doesn't find the scent of anger quite as alluring.

The rippling air surges at Kaladen. My smugness is gone in an instant. But Kaladen does not move. Instead, he holds up both hands and repeats the strange language in a roar. The air buckles backward. It tries to launch itself forward again, but this time I notice that it has shrunk. Not just in height, but also in breadth.

Kaladen advances sharply, repeating the same phrase with each step. The *bhogra* lashes, struggling as it folds and bends smaller and smaller.

I watch, my mouth hanging open, as Kaladen takes the invisible creature between his hands, and with one last pronouncement of that phrase, crushes it into nothing.

When he turns around to face me, towering in height, his eyes like twin flames, I am rendered speechless. This is not just Kaladen, not just my husband.

This is the Neverseen King.

This is what the High King has feared from the beginning. This is why he used the Wolf, why he used Yirmuth and Eldreth and Trenian and *me* to take him down. Because, as glorious and supreme as Faradir is, the Neverseen King has something he could never dream of: the power to bend worlds to his dominion.

If Kaladen survives Lulythinar, if he ever figured out how to control the Bridge, the High King could never touch him again. No one could.

"Why did he leave you to be ensnared by the *bhogra*?" Kaladen demands furiously, striding toward me in a rage-fueled march. "Where is that snake? Why are you bleeding so much?" He has me by the shoulders the next moment, turning me so he can see my back. "Nadira! Did Trenian do this to you?"

I shake my head, a delirious laugh bubbling up on my lips. "No, no, he saved me, but we had to split up so one of us could take the skyreavers to the rainforest—"

"You went into Farboor?"

I push his hand away and arch one eyebrow. "We didn't have a choice. It broke open. We got three skyreavers for you, and Trenian was the only one who could carry their weight. He took them to safety while I distracted the *bhogra*."

His brows come together in a hard line. "You are going to be the death of me, woman."

The next thing I know, I'm waking up in the rainforest bed. Kaladen bends over me. One of his calloused hands pulls me upright and then runs down my back. I nearly sag in relief of the constant, dizzying pain that followed me since the Farboor Portal.

"Better?" he asks.

"*Much*," a bright voice replies from only a few feet away.

I grab Kaladen's forearm before he can whirl and begin shouting a harsh tirade at the prince.

"Thank you," I whisper.

Kaladen cools slightly before he turns. Trenian sits on the floor against the wood planked wall, knees up. The hilt of his sword, sans the blue glow and the blade, hangs from his belt. To his right is a large pile of incapacitated skyreavers.

"I am going to wring your neck for what you've put her through!" Kaladen growls. Badh-o slips from his ankle and slides into my lap. I stroke her spine enough to earn a small bloom from her flower.

"This was *your* harebrained idea."

"I told you not to enter that portal without me!"

Trenian's face contorts into its most bullheaded arrangement. "It broke open, you imbecile!"

"Who is that?" I interrupt, pointing at another vine coiled like a snake in the corner by the cabinet.

Kaladen glances over impatiently. "It's Badh-a. Now Trenian, you did *not* have to get the skyreavers while I was busy! You could have just sealed the—"

"That's the one that was mean to me?" I ask, glaring at the vine. "The one that helped Safya *cheat* in the maze you gave us? And unfairly strung me up in the courtyard?"

The vine pulls back its head and then lets out a loud spit.

"The same," Kaladen answers distractedly.

"Then what's it doing here? Is she going to open Crenfyre to finish me off?"

Badh-a comes shooting across the room like a slingshot. Badh-o screeches in my lap and dives for cover. Kaladen catches the angry vine in his fist before she makes it to me.

"Behave," he tells her sternly, and to me: "Stop provoking her. She's always grumpy and you're only making it worse. She is very loyal to me. Her actions during the trials came from that loyalty." He turns to the hissing vine in his hand and says, "We have been over this. Nadira is my wife, whether you like it or not, so if you want to help me, you'll help her. In return, she will not say any more mean things about you."

Then he lets Badh-a down on the bed. She tilts her bud toward me, regarding me like a suspicious cat might sniff a potential meal offering. Badh-o peers over the edge of the bed and glances between the two of us as if we might explode into fighting at any moment.

"Truce?" I say, offering a hand toward Badh-a.

She slides her bud from peering at my hand slowly upward to my face. And then stays there. Staring pointedly.

Trenian snorts from the floor. Kaladen sighs. I shrug and withdraw my hand.

"What do we do next?" I ask, nodding my head to our captives as Badh-a slides silently back to her spot, curls up in a ball, and returns to watching us.

A muscle flexes in Kaladen's sharp jaw. "We wait until Crenfyre opens."

"We need a way to control them," says Trenian.

"I think I have a spell that will work," replies Kaladen.

"A spell? You found a compulsion spell that works on skyreavers while sealing the *bhogra's* world?" The prince's surprise is palpable. "Do enlighten me!"

He might not mock if he'd seen what Kaladen just accomplished.

"It is not a proper compulsion spell. Skyreavers stay in swarms. They are always communicating to each other." Kaladen folds his arms across his chest. The subtle scratch of his elbow gives away his uncertainty. "I think I can use one of their calls, mixed with a compulsion, to make it work."

Trenian shuts his mouth, tilting his head to one side as he considers this. Then he gives a small huff and shakes his head. "Your creative use of magic theory astounds me sometimes."

Kaladen stiffens at the compliment, as though he hasn't a clue what to do with praise from his double-crossing cousin. "We should get back to sealing portals so nothing gets into the city. It is not long before Lulythinar, and we don't have much time before Crenfyre opens."

The unspoken words hover in the air. We can reseal portals until dawn, but the moment Crenfyre opens, we either will succeed in Kaladen's plan, or we will fail. And if we fail, there is nothing else to be done.

None of us move.

I stay where I am on the bed, Kaladen doesn't move from his post beside me, and Trenian stays on the floor, staring at the rough panels between his feet. Despite the still, half-frozen skyreavers lying there silently, despite the hopes of our plans, it is like we all know it won't work in the end. It's like we all know this *is* the end. Maybe not for Trenian—he will leave before Crenfyre can kill him in this world, at least. But for the rest of us. Even for Kaladen.

For this small pocket in time, this rainforest treehouse is still safe. We are still alive. There is still hope for Crenfyre's binding. There is still time before Lulythinar. Not much time—but *some*.

Once we leave this room, however, we leave it for forever. We walk to our deaths. We hand over the last vestiges of our hope. We face the end of the worlds.

So none of us move. We will. But not yet.

I imagine Tariq lying in wait with his men, ready to die stopping any monsters that break free of the palace. I think of Kanza and Zara, fleeing the city as quickly as they can with the rest of the townspeople, Abbi and all the children hurrying on aching feet in hopes of saving their own lives. I don't want to imagine monsters slaughtering Tariq and the guards, finding their way to Eshe's body and destroying it. I don't want to imagine them catching up to Kanza's group of refugees. I don't want to think of the fear, the pain, the blood.

But that is what is before us tonight. So I think of it. I let my imagination turn down dark paths full of inky blackness and despair.

I let the melancholy wash over me. When I look up, I see the same thoughts floating like storm clouds across Kaladen and Trenian's expressions. Kaladen looks at me, and I know the haunting visions he sees are of my death. I cannot guess precisely what haunts Trenian, but he has the look of a man with almost as much at stake as the rest of us.

He is the one who lets out a deep sigh and gets lightly to his feet. "More portals, then. Off we go!"

I swing my legs over the side of the bed. Kaladen stops me with a hand on my shoulder.

"Back to the dream realm," he says. "You're not going out there in your physical body."

I'd already forgotten. Trenian has stepped out of the treehouse, leaving the skyreavers behind, when Kaladen pulls me to his chest and clutches me tightly to himself. I wrap my arms around him and squeeze as close to him as I can. It is only for a moment; we both know the longer we linger, the harder it will be to leave.

A fine, misty sheen dulls the blue of Kaladen's eyes when he pulls away. He blinks hard and clears his throat. Then he covers my face with his hand, and we enter the dream realm.

CHAPTER 27

NADIRA

TIME MOVES LIKE a stranger, simultaneously fast and slow. We work hard for the rest of the day. The only breaks we take are to eat and re-enter the dream realm when the wounds get to be too much.

It is a fog to me. I watch the shadows shift as the afternoon lengthens and the sun descends toward the horizon. One of the few times I go into the courtyard to chase down a stray creature making a dash for the city, I find myself pausing after dealing with the threat. Something feels wrong. It isn't the clouds thickening and darkening overhead, or the cold splatters of fat raindrops. It isn't the rumbling of thunder growing louder. What is it? It is not the sense of being watched; I know that too well. This is something else. Something—

The fountain has stopped.

There are no birds chirping.

The courtyard is completely still, completely silent. I check the angle of the sun, visible through a break in the clouds. We still have two hours before dusk. Two hours before Lulythinar begins.

A rush of air pebbles the skin of my arms. I draw in a deep breath.

Then I return to work.

CHAPTER 28

NADIRA

JUST BEFORE DUSK, the portals stop opening. One minute, we're scrambling to seal and reseal, and fight off various bloodthirsty monsters. The next, everything goes deathly still.

I look at Kaladen in question. He nods and beckons that Trenian and I follow him to the courtyard. We step outside under a covered portico, followed by Badh-o and Badh-a. It is darker than dusk usually is, the sky filled with thunderclouds and flashes of lightning.

"It is always quiet like this, just before Lulythinar," Kaladen says softly.

The scattered raindrops from this afternoon coalesce into sheets, and before either of us can answer him, we stand in the midst of a heavy downpour. The air turns cold and windy, splattering droplets where we stand beneath the portico. The fountain overflows. I could almost believe it was running again, and that perhaps Lulythinar just wouldn't happen this year.

For a moment, the clouds on the horizon part. Sunlight cuts through the storm, turning raindrops into gleaming, golden diamonds. The yellow disk is already halfway below the horizon. The three of us stand there, watching it descend. King, prince, assassin. And two vines.

Then the sun vanishes. The rain turns torrential.

Night descends hard and heavy.

An unearthly scream echoes from the palace behind us, cutting through the thunder and sending chills straight to my bones.

Lulythinar has arrived.

Kaladen looks at me. There is a world of emotion in that single glance. My mind flashes to the night we met. I think of waking in his arms as he kidnapped me, his rumbling voice terrifying the sense out of me. I think of the trials I endured with Eshe and the other women. The night I nearly left my room and died, only for him to appear out of nowhere and stop me. The notes we exchanged as we began to understand each other. The times he made me breathe when I lost myself to panic. The slow, gentle way he touched me. The dance we shared in the dark, firefly-lit ballroom. The sun-kissed portico before our wedding when he gave me his name. I think of all that followed: what it was like to wake up in his arms, to shatter to a thousand pieces with him in the dark, to fight and struggle and forge something unbreakable in the midst of it.

I draw a knife in one hand, my other braced to use my ice. My voice is much stronger than I feel. "Dawn will be here before we know it."

Kaladen's attention shifts to Trenian. Their gazes meet. Kaladen hesitates. As though he debates whether he should say something. In the end, he remains silent. Not that it matters—the hesitation was telling enough.

"On to death and glory!" Trenian cries, throwing his arms wide at the palace.

My mouth curves up just slightly, my blood humming with the headiness of battle. Badh-o slides onto my ankle while Badh-a follows at a dignified distance. "On to death and glory."

CHAPTER 29

NADIRA

THE HOUSE IS vibrantly alive in a way I've never seen before. I expect hordes of strange and terrifying monsters. Instead, I find nothing but rows upon rows of peacefully open portals—their seals completely disintegrated, their doors swung wide open. I purse my lips grimly. The dream realm is deceptively calm, but if I returned to the waking world, the chaos I would find would be unimaginable. Despite the stillness, the House hums and vibrates beneath my feet, its color-filled hallways almost blinding in their intensity, and when I touch the wall, a doorframe, anything at all, that same hum fills my hand all the way to my heart. It is like everything I touch is the banister. Alive, vivid, potent. There is none of the usual dread I encountered when night fell before. An energy fills this place.

Excitement fills the House.

Excitement for what?

Shadows move strangely, short and erratic, long and undulating. I keep thinking something is behind me casting those shadows onto the flooding light of the open portals, but when I turn, there is nothing.

Kaladen sent the vines to the rainforest portal—claiming he needed them to guard the skyreavers. Truly, he wanted to make sure they stayed safe.

"I hope the palace's defenses are doing all our work for us," Trenian says glibly as he grabs the open handle of one portal to enter and reseal it.

"They aren't," Kaladen replies, reappearing after a momentary disappearance. "In about a minute, the city will be under attack."

My jaw falls open, my blood quickening in my veins. How could it possibly happen this fast?

In an instant, I realize what the strange shadows are. They are glimpses of the waking world—glimpses of the monsters ransacking the House. As I watch, one of those shadows coalesces into a seven-foot-tall centaur lifting a cudgel high into the air. Another shadow morphs into a great dragon, just like the one that tried to eat Eshe, Safya, and me once upon a time. It opens its mouth, and a stream of fire billows out. The shadows continue morphing around us, telling tales of strange and terrifying violence.

"We have to split up," I gasp. "One of us should leave the dream realm to kill what we can before the city is overwhelmed."

Kaladen's face is as hard as granite. "Tariq will handle it."

I knew this would happen. I knew it, and yet air rushes from my lungs, and panic fills my limbs. The force of my own fear shocks me. "He will *die*. All of them will die!"

"Which is why we must seal what we can," Trenian says, just before he disappears into a portal.

Kaladen locks eyes with me, and no part of him softens. "Dawn will be here before we know it."

Then he, too, vanishes into a portal.

I stay where I am, immobilized by the dozens upon dozens of open portals I can see before me. There are hundreds on all the floors of the palace. Seeing them now, wide open, watching the glimpses of the waking world play around me like a vicious puppet show, I don't know what to do. I know that I need to seal portals. I know that every moment I hesitate is precious. I know this is the best way I can help Tariq, his men, Kanza, Zara, and the rest.

If I knew more portals, I would head to the most dangerous ones first to shut them before too many creatures escaped into the city. But I don't know.

So I force my feet forward to the one right in front of me.

Commotion rips my attention to the left just as Trenian barrels out of his portal, breathing hard, a long gash across the front of his chest. He slams the door shut, presses a small bundle of what looks like puffy fabric against the seal, and extracts a drop of my blood from his person so fast I don't even know how he does it.

At least my once-sworn enemy is being productive while I'm petrified for no good reason. A shadow looms above the prince, and a massive pair of jaws opens wide, then dives forward as though to swallow Trenian whole. I could have screamed, except that the shadow vanishes only a second later.

Trenian spits a dark curse just before I enter the portal. I stop and lean out. "Trenian?"

He lifts a stricken gaze to me. "Look."

I hurry to his side. I'm just in time to watch the fresh red seal turn brown and crumble. The portal bursts back open with a scream of violet.

"Did you use my blood?" I demand, slicing open my finger even before I finish speaking. I grab the small puffy thing from the prince and smear my blood across it again.

"Of course I used your blood," Trenian snaps.

The seal flares again. We wait, breathless, as macabre shadows remind us of everything we are losing by the second.

It turns brown.

"It's stronger with your fresher blood," Trenian growls. "But not much stronger."

Kaladen is there a moment later. He spews a string of curses, stronger and blacker than the prince's as he tries—and fails—to seal his portal.

"How long do you think the seal will last with my fresh blood?" I demand frantically.

Trenian's face has turned the color of the thundering night around us. "Five minutes, at best."

I rush to Kaladen's side, smearing my blood across his seal. It holds—but barely.

"I have to seal everything." My voice rises to a fever pitch. "And even then—"

"This is *not* how Lulythinar goes," Kaladen bellows, grabbing at his hair and tearing at the roots. Shadows move faster behind him. They rush across the ceiling, the walls, the floors. They dance in what is visible of the wet courtyard through the windows. "It never stops sealing! Why won't they hold? *Why won't they hold?*"

He pulls an entire handful of blood from inside his tunic and throws it at the browning seal. It doesn't react the slightest. Trenian has disappeared into the next portal, the one I was about to seal, but the last I see of his expression is one of utter futility.

A rock falls heavy into the pit of my stomach. My voice is dead. "We cannot seal the portals."

"We *can*, it's just—" Kaladen cuts himself off. His eyes are wild, his hair standing in every direction, and then abruptly, his shoulders sag. "No, we cannot seal the portals."

Trenian reappears, faster than I expect, and I hurry to smear my fresh blood across the seal. The first one we sealed together is already flaking. This is a game we can play all night. If we are lucky, we might be able to keep ten portals sealed at a time before we have to start over.

"Crenfyre?" I ask Kaladen.

"Not open yet," he says, raking one hand furiously against his scalp. "But we don't have long."

The prince is about to throw himself into another portal, but Kaladen grabs him by the shoulder and drags him back.

"We can't give up!" Trenian shouts, yanking free. "This isn't over yet!"

"It's *no use*!" Kaladen shouts back. "The portals are open. This Lulythinar is too strong. We cannot close any until it passes."

Trenian throws his hands wide. "That is *hours* away. The human lands won't survive. Valehaven won't survive! The Small Cities won't survive. My staff, Edvear, Rahk—they'll all die. How am I supposed to fix everything my father has broken if there isn't even a Valehaven left to fix? How can I protect *my people* if we cannot seal any of the portals?" The last words come out as though they dragged knives up his throat and across his tongue. I don't know half of who he refers to, but I don't need to.

"We can go to the waking world and kill everything we can before they destroy too much of the human lands and Valehaven—and the rest," I say. The offering feels pathetic even to me. My ice, usually activated by fear, fades away as cold helplessness fills me.

"We would die without the protection of the dream realm," Kaladen growls, pained. "The three of us cannot hold that much back until dawn."

"We're going to die anyway," I remind him.

"But we have to stay alive long enough to attempt to seal Crenfyre," says Trenian.

"We. Cannot. Seal. Crenfyre," Kaladen grits out.

Trenian and I both start to blurt, "But the skyreavers!" only to stop at the same time. Trenian hangs his head. Monster shadows turn his dark hair black as obsidian.

We would go to all that effort, risking our lives, killing the skyreavers—for nothing but five minutes of closure before it broke open again.

Trenian turns to Kaladen. "You have to survive the night."

Kaladen stiffens, but doesn't reply beyond a desperate glance at me.

"If there is to be any curb on Crenfyre's appetite, any way to seal it, it must be done *after* Lulythinar. Crenfyre will sweep the worlds for the night, but someone must seal it at dawn. You are the Neverseen King. You must stay alive to do that—to spare whatever is left of the worlds from utter destruction."

Kaladen's throat bobs as he swallows hard. He knows Trenian is right.

"You need to protect the rainforest portal to keep the skyreavers alive until you can use them tomorrow. Nadira and I will protect our worlds as long as we can."

I offer a rueful smile at Kaladen's stricken expression. "It's better than waiting for Crenfyre to come for us in the dream realm."

The prince gives one sharp wave. Then he's gone. Slipped into the waking world.

It hits me with finality. I won't see him again.

I pull my rattled composure together and turn to my husband. "Will you help me wake up?"

Kaladen doesn't reply; he just disappears like Trenian. I stand by myself in that long hallway, surrounded by nightmarish shadows and the blinding glows of open portals. I watch the portals we managed to reseal break open once more. A weight settles across my shoulders.

Then I blink awake in the rainforest portal.

The haven I've known for so long shudders, wind stirring the thick foliage of the forest. I throw my legs over the edge of the bed. The two vines watch the skyreavers where we left them, though the monsters' icy bonds have started melting. I reinforce those quickly before turning to the tall, broad back set against me.

Kaladen's hands are clenched into fists at his sides. His chest shudders with each breath.

"Is this portal open?" I ask quietly, slipping to his side and wrapping my arms around one of his.

He shakes his head wordlessly.

But it will be soon. He will have to stand at the open door and kill anything that tries to pass, and he will not be able to leave it. Not if there is to be any hope for anyone.

"It would be easier," he begins, each word shaking, "if I did not know that you are afraid."

My chest caves as though a knife has sliced into it. "Kaladen."

"I know you do not want to die. I've seen you broken and terrified, and the thought of you having to go out there by yourself, and face the darkest, most brutal of fates, *alone* . . . If you must die, I would have it be in my arms. So I could hold you. So you would not be alone again. So you could feel safe as you passed from this life to the next."

Tears fill my eyes until I cannot see anything except the blurry green of the world around us, and the black outline of his cloak. I press my head against his shoulder and cling to his arm.

He threads his other hand into my hair to press me close. "I know I cannot save you. But I do not want you to die alone."

"I will not be alone," I grit out fiercely between my own shuddering breaths. Wet tears slide down my cheeks. "I've never been alone—not since I married you. Remember the ties that bind us? Yes, I am more frightened than I wish I was. I also wish it did not have to end this way. But you must know that I would not change anything. I would still marry you over again. I would marry you a hundred times over and die this death a thousand times over, just to finally know again what it meant to . . ." I trail off, struggling to find the right word. *Loved* is not right—Mama and Baba loved me. I remember that. But there was something I found with Kaladen, something else. At last, I clear my throat and finish. ". . . be safe."

He looks down at me. I could drown in the ocean depths of his eyes. His voice is a whisper. "I would do it again too. *All* of it."

I smile at him through my tears. "So, you see, it is fine that we are scared."

His nails dig into my scalp as he presses me closer. Then he rips his arm out of my grip, pulls me to his chest, and kisses me. One last time. I let myself melt into him, refusing to let the state of the world take this moment away from us. When I die, this is the moment I will return to. His lips on mine, his warmth surrounding me.

He pulls away enough to breathe against my face: "Dawn will come again."

"Dawn will come again," I say back.

He gently pushes me away, devastation fighting his thinly propped courage. He rasps, "You must leave now. Before I break down and lock you in here with the skyreavers and the vines."

There is a slight lilt at the end of that statement—as if he quietly offers this option to me. *Stay here, and let me protect you. Maybe you can survive this with me.*

The temptation is there. Part of me longs to value my life above all others this way. But I cannot stay in hiding while everyone else I love is in danger, and Kaladen knows it.

So I refuse to throw myself into his arms once more. I hurry down the stairs instead, jog through the path leading to the portal's door, and then, with a flood of wild energy like the House's constant hum, I grit my teeth and throw myself into the death trap waiting beyond the door.

CHAPTER 30

NADIRA

THE FIRST THINGS I notice—probably because they are familiar to me—are the many, round-bellied blue goblins running in every direction.

"I just cannot be rid of you, can I?" I mutter, just before throwing myself back against the shut door as something swoops low through the hallway and nearly impales me in the process.

The second thing I notice is the sound. Layers upon layers of the strangest cries, screams, calls, and roars fill the walled space. They hammer against my skull and beat down my spine. It takes me several moments to realize many of them are cries of pain, and another moment to register where it comes from.

A thick stripe of violet fire stretches down the hallway, almost completely covering the floor. It dances, flickers, and burns everything that touches it. The tips of my sandals are only inches from the blaze.

I swipe my hair out of my face just in time to see a blade come plunging for my chest.

I twist, drop, roll. My shoulder hits the floor with a crack. The blade slices only air. I look up, and my breath catches.

It's not a person. It's a suit of armor, hollow inside, but moving like it remembers being worn. Pale smoke seeps from the gaps in the joints, and it turns back toward me with creaking menace, its sword dragging a thin screech against the wall. A second one lumbers forward behind it. Neither of them care about the fire licking up the side of their armored calves.

I throw one hand toward them. I try to restrain how much power I release at once, lest I drain myself dry too early in the fight.

Thin spikes of ice form midair and lodge at the joint of the suit of armor's knee. It hits with a crack; the leg buckles, metal groaning. But the armor still moves, dragging itself toward me and swinging its heavy sword with eerie determination.

My second hand joins the first. I blast an entire wall straight across the width of the hallway, cutting it in half. The armor clangs on the other side, but the ice holds. For now.

So much for not using too much of my power at once.

I've got to get to the courtyard. That is my only chance at effective work instead of being cut down immediately. I throw a thin sheet of ice across the fire so I can cross the hallway. It melts almost instantly, but I make it before the fire burns through my sandals.

Something long and sinewy lashes down from the ceiling and wraps around the leg of a goblin, yanking it into the air with a gurgled shriek.

I don't stop to see what devours it.

The hallway ahead erupts.

A door bursts off its hinges as a dozen squawking, half-melted crow-creatures swarm out, wings made of blistered parchment and molten wax, eyes like dripping candles. One swoops for my face. A strangled cry escapes me as I fling both hands forward.

Twin blasts of ice streak from my palms, colliding midair into a jagged wall. The crow-thing smacks into it and shatters into pieces that fall to the fiery floor. The rest screech and scatter. One tangles in my hair before I freeze it solid and smash it against the wall with a grunt. I stumble into the flames by accident and scream as pain sears across my awareness. I drag myself against the wall and blast the floor with enough ice to give refuge to my burns.

Get to the courtyard.

Get out of here.

Loud, angry chitters surge behind me. I glance over my shoulder.

A swarm of small, furry creatures like rats, but with limbs twice as long, multi-jointed, and twisting, floods toward me along the wall, teeth gnashing like chattering stones. I blast the wall at their feet, sending half skidding and tumbling into the violet blaze. I shoot another stream up the wall—slicking it—then snap my palm sideways. A blade of ice peels outward, slicing across them like a scythe. Screeches echo as they collapse.

There is a break in the stream of monsters. I seize it and run forward as fast as I can. I make it past the fiery floor onto the blessedly cool stone floor of the entryway. I grab hold of the banister, and a loud, powerful voice fills my mind.

Crenfyre! Crenfyre! Crenfyre!

It is so jarring I release the banister and fall onto the steps. But there is no time to wonder what is happening. From an archway before me bursts a creature of carved wood and cracked alabaster, its limbs jerking like a broken puppet's. Taut and trembling strings make for its ribs, and each halting motion plucks a discordant note.

Two more just like it flank its progress toward me.

Above me, a web of thick, wiry spider silk quivers as a great, bulbous . . . *thing* with innumerable legs descends toward me. And behind me, something like an enormous centipede crawls down the stairs. I startle when its face is a mirror of my own, filthy, sporting a thin slice along the cheekbone, and a focused, wide-eyed expression.

They close in on me on all sides.

I've just got to get through those doors blocked by the wood-and-alabaster creatures.

I drop into a crouch, dodging the sharp spinneret stabbing toward me from above, and blast a sheet of ice horizontally at the three creatures before me. Dozens of small icicles impale their chests, but they keep moving. They're like the cursed suit of arms! One lifts its cracked arm and swings it with shocking force at my head. I twist and roll, and from the ground I blast ice upward at it again—this time intent on dislodging its balance. The first one's torso cracks, and then tumbles clean off the legs while the legs keep moving. I blast the other two, the force of my blow sending me sliding backward until my back hits the wall.

For a moment, there is only the rush of blood in my ears and the fading crackle of magic—but then I hear it. A whispery, featherlight rustle. The sound of dry leaves shifting on marble. I glance down.

They're already crawling toward me.

Tiny, glimmering dots—no larger than beetles—flutter along the floor. They look like scraps of silver parchment, folded into crooked shapes with too many angles, skittering on invisible legs.

One leaps and lands on my ankle, searing heat through the fabric of my pants. I shriek and stumble, smacking it off. It vanishes in a puff of burnt air, but others follow, digging into my skin with tiny barbs.

It's only a few feet to the door. I ignore the rest of the creatures crawling up my legs, refusing to look back at how close the centipede has gotten, and ram my way to the doors. I fling them wide and throw myself into the courtyard.

The courtyard is full of strange creatures too, but it is not as crammed as the hallways. I scrape the rest of the tiny creatures off my legs, kicking the few that try to climb back on, and finally, they scatter. I gasp, heart pounding. Blood beads where they bit. The wounds are shallow, but they sting badly. I ignore them, leaping to my feet. Rain drenches me the second I leave the covering and run as fast as I can to the gate of the palace. If I didn't know this courtyard well—and if the creatures weren't distracted by the open gate—I would be dead in an instant. Instead, I'm able to remain relatively unscathed as I cut a path to the gate and use my rope to haul myself onto the slippery roof of the structure nearest to the gate. I wish I had a crossbow to pick off monsters from here. I stare for a moment at the stream of otherworldly creatures leaving the gates. I glance toward the city. The sound of fighting, of blades, and roars float toward me, only drowned out momentarily by cracks of thunder overhead.

I need to cut off their escape route. Or what I can of it. It will accelerate my death, but I might be able to slow down the influx to the city.

My body shakes from the rush of fighting and the pain of the injuries I've already accumulated. My leg is bleeding, and I don't have the faintest clue what from. It is not bad enough to kill me. I lift my trembling arms and reach into my cold gut for ice. A curse passes my lips. My belly feels almost empty. There is more to draw from, but now that I've stopped to feel it, there is a weakness rushing through my limbs. If I drain my stores, I will probably pass out—and if I pass out, I'm dead. Water pours down my face, stinging my eyes, getting in my mouth, plastering my hair to my scalp.

A tiny squeak has me whirling, my knives flashing.

"Badh-o!" I cry, barely stopping myself before I slice her in half. "You scared me! Are you alright? You should still be in the rainforest portal!"

She whimpers slightly and holds up one leaf with a small bite taken out of it.

"I'm sorry." I stroke her stem gently. "You are very brave for coming here instead of hiding."

She nuzzles my foot. I take one extra moment, a moment I don't have, and give her another stroke of reassurance. I look up and find, a few feet beyond her, another coiled vine. This one is silent as she watches me.

"You are brave too, Badh-a," I whisper. I hope the vine does not find that condescending.

She does not reply.

"I'll be right back," I tell them both, hoping it's true, and then swing off the rope. This must be fast if I am to have any hope of getting back to my temporary safe spot before I pass out. Or before I get eaten.

I run on unsteady legs along slippery flagstone to the gate, fling up my hands, and drain the last reserves of my power across the iron grate. The stream of monsters is cut clean in half as I grit my teeth, focusing my energy on pulling every last scrap of ice from inside me, forming a wall even higher than the gate itself. Cold sweat breaks out on my forehead. Ice pulses through my veins and turns my entire body frigid. Something slams into the wall I've erected, but it holds. I close up the last section.

The torrential rain stops briefly, darkness falling over me. I look up just in time to watch an enormous dragon fly above the gate. Straight into the city. Many of the creatures duck into hiding, and I take the blessed reprieve and rush back to my hanging rope. My head spins, and the world tilts on its axis. I grab hold of the rope after two tries. As fast as I can manage, I pull myself up.

A humanoid creature awaits me as I climb onto the roof. With my vertigo, I can see little more than a swaying form with a large grin beneath a cloak. My ice is gone, but my fury is not. I have my knives out the next instant, and I throw myself across the space with a roar. Somehow, my blades find their mark. The grin disappears. I yank out my knives and kick the chest, shoving it off the roof to the flagstone below.

Then I stumble against the parapets. Everything swims. My head bows as I grab hold of my knee in one hand, the stone parapet in the other. Badh-o chirps something to me, but she cannot stay in focus.

I hope my ice wall did something to slow down the crush of monsters into the city.

My shoulder hits the edge of the roof and everything turns to blackness.

I peel open my eyes to the frantic movements and screeches of Badh-o. My mind trips over itself, trying to reorient. "What's wrong?" I ask as I roll to my side and push upright. I'm soaked through. My wet clothes cling to my body as rain pelts my skin. My body nearly gives out again, but I grit my teeth and pull myself up so I can peer over the edge of the roof. With the clouds filling the sky, blocking the moon and the stars, I haven't the faintest idea how long I've been out.

But Badh-o and even Badh-a move erratically, dragging my focus toward the palace. A cry echoes from the gate below us. The ice wall has had a hole blown through it, but most of it still holds. It slows down the flood of creatures, though not by much. Several centaurs leap ridiculously high into the air to get over it. They yell a war cry as they go that I hear with more than just my ears: *Take the green grass of the mortal lands!*

That is not what my two vines are afraid of, however.

When I look toward the palace itself, something billows out of the doorways and each window. My blood freezes inside me. That is when I feel the difference inside me—the alarm bells screaming as a very strong thread pulls at my core.

"Crenfyre," I gasp. "It's open."

CHAPTER 31

NADIRA

I WATCH, PARALYZED, as mist floods the courtyard, devouring screaming creatures as it goes. It does not matter whether the creatures are great or small, violent or confused, physical or made of shadow. When Crenfyre's fingers reach it, they go pale and drop to the ground. The plants wither to dust. The overflowing fountain is sucked dry. The raindrops on the ground are absorbed. Even the flagstone itself cracks.

I've only seen Crenfyre free once before, and it moved slowly, creeping along the ground and crawling up surfaces in search of any speck of life.

Now it rushes like a torrential flood, swallowing everything in its wake.

Badh-o trembles on my arm, hiding her bud in my torn sleeve. Even Badh-a has situated herself partially behind me as she watches what unfolds below us.

At first, I think in relief that I have more time before Crenfyre comes for me from my high location. Then, I remember the city. *Tariq.*

It will decimate the entire place in minutes.

How long until it catches up to Kanza's group of refugees?

The House's voice tears through my memory: *Crenfyre! Crenfyre! Crenfyre!*

The cacophony around me goes still. The rain halts in its descent. The screams, the thunder, and even the softest cries of death turn silent. I stand where I am, on the rooftop parapet near the gate, surveying the palace complex as hundreds of monsters meet their grim end below me. The more sentient creatures realize the threat and try to escape it. Some take to the air, some climb to higher places like me, and others renew their effort to get over my ice wall.

Crenfyre will come for them all.

Nothing will escape its hunger.

Certainty builds inside of me. Trenian's golden voice arguing with Kaladen's roughened one returns. They remind me of everything I know.

The portals cannot be sealed until Lulythinar is over.

We have a very slim chance of binding Crenfyre . . . *after* the sun rises. *After* it has destroyed everything. Even then, it is most likely to fail.

It is Kaladen's job to stay alive until then, no matter what. It is the rest of our jobs to die.

Crenfyre! Crenfyre! Crenfyre! the House screams across my memory again.

An image flashes across my mind's eye: a storybook illustration of Crenfyre's sealed door, cracked in two.

"No," I whisper aloud.

Badh-o and Badh-a both turn to me with twin non-expressions of surprise.

My voice builds in strength. Instead of ice, it is fire building inside me. And a wild, cataclysmic determination. "*No.*"

There is a piece missing here.

I am going to find out what it is. And there is only one place to find this missing piece.

I bend down to the two vines. "Badh-a. Badh-o. I am going on a mission. I'm not waiting for Crenfyre to come for me. I'm going to save this place, or I'm going to die trying. You can come with me, or you can find a place to hide."

They both stare at me. Badh-a is steady, while Badh-o trembles.

"You will probably die if you come with me," I say, softening my voice. "I would rather you stayed safe as long as you can."

Badh-o rushes forward and wraps herself around my calf in a hug. I lay my hand on her and give her a stroke. "Don't be afraid, little one."

Badh-a does not touch me, but she gives a firm nod.

"You're coming with me?"

She nods again. I purse my lips in grim respect. Then I turn down to Badh-o.

"You don't have to come," I whisper.

She clings tighter. I don't know how to interpret that response, whether it means she won't leave me or she regrets that she will. I stroke her again.

"Are you coming, Badh-o?"

She squeezes my calf. Then she nods.

I pat her bud. "You are a brave vine, Badh-o. The two of you have all my respect. Climb onto my shoulders instead of my ankles. If Crenfyre gets me, you might have a chance to be spared."

They do as I say. I wind up my rope, hook it on my belt, and then I'm in motion.

The years I spent navigating the rooftops of Risya equip me now as I leap between buildings or use my rope to bridge the distance. The courtyard is almost completely full of Crenfyre's mist and the bodies of its prey now.

Only a very few monsters remain, trying their best to escape the death sweeping toward them. The few that have found refuge on the roofs and parapets do not pursue me.

I make it back to the palace quickly, with the only added injuries of a few scraped palms and knees. I find a good perch atop a portico to survey my options.

Crenfyre still pours out of every window. My chest clenches tight. Is Trenian already dead? What about Kaladen?

No.

Kaladen is not dead. I know that. I feel the bond linking our hearts. It hasn't broken yet.

But Trenian might be dead, and I would have no way of knowing.

I steel my spine. My only concern right now is getting into the palace, onto the second floor, and to Crenfyre's door without being drained by its mist.

As I watch, the flow of the mist starts thinning out. The initial flood seems to have worked its way through most of the palace and now hunts through the courtyard. It starts climbing walls, pillars, and the ice-coated gate itself. From my perch, I can make out the pale, milky-white fingers climbing to the parapet I used as a temporary refuge.

Nowhere is safe now.

But it does seem like I have a chance of getting through one of those second-floor windows now that the surge has calmed. I climb higher onto the roof, putting more distance between me and the mist that comes for the portico's covering. The rain makes my steps slick. I fight to keep my balance, and once I nearly slip. Badh-a grabs hold of a spire and anchors me with all the strength in her little body just enough for me to regain my balance.

We work our way across the roof until I crouch above the last window on this section. Crenfyre should be on the opposite hallway just inside. I need to get through the room and into the hallway. Without being killed.

I pull out my rope. My fingers work fast at a knot.

"I'm going to lower to the second-story window," I tell the two vines on my shoulders. "The goal is to keep my feet above the mist coming from the room, but if it gets me, you two need to get to safety before it gets you too. Understood?"

Badh-o nods. Badh-a only lifts her bud.

Energy courses through my veins, fueled by my iron determination. If I die before I get to Crenfyre, it will be so stupid I could never forgive myself.

I fasten the end of the rope to another spire. I hate having to use up my rope this way, but if I need it when I get to the room, I'll pull myself back up it again and see if I can think of another method to avoid leaving the rope behind.

For now, I don't have time.

I tie my wet hair into a tight knot at the base of my neck so it doesn't hang, then lower myself to the window, staying above the trickle of mist coming out of the room. Tightening my core, I slowly rotate myself upside down so I can see into the room without getting too close to the mist.

It is a nicely furnished guest chamber, full of dust.

Mist does not cover every surface, but snakes through the opening beneath the door and heads straight for the window. It looks like Crenfyre already searched this room and found almost nothing worth its time.

"We're going in," I tell my passengers, before swinging right side up and leaping through the upper part of the open window.

I land on my feet, dangerously close to that snaking line of mist. I scramble away, my hand going protectively to Badh-o and Badh-a on my shoulder. My back hits an empty wardrobe. I throw my hands wide, bracing myself. The mist, as though sensing my presence, sends a small tendril toward me. I scoot along the wall, putting distance between it and myself as I circle to the closed door.

My vision flashes back to being trapped in a room like this with Safya, Eshe, and Gaya. I still remember the way Gaya fell. I shove aside the instinctive sickness that curls inside me and make it to the door.

A new problem faces me. Is the hallway full of mist? How do I open it without letting in another deadly flood?

I leap over the mist to the opposite side of the room. Badh-o squeaks in terror. I go to the hinges of the door and eye the handle. Then I look up. There is a high enough sconce. They have held my weight before. I jump, get my hand around the flat bar base connecting the candle holder to the wall. I hang about a foot off the ground. I pull my legs up, get my sandals planted firmly against the wall, and steady myself.

"Can you two make yourself into a rope I could . . . you know, toss at the doorknob?" I ask my vines. When they look at me blankly, I breathe through the mounting tension in the arm I'm hanging from and add: "I need you to open the door so we can let out any extra mist before we try going into the hallway."

Badh-a moves into action first. She grabs Badh-o, knots her tail to Badh-o's stem, and stretches out her leaves like fingers. But before I can toss them, they get ahold of the wall and carefully work their way to the door. Badh-a wraps her leaves around the handle, gives a squeak of exertion, and then pulls. It unlatches.

"Get back!" I cry.

They move too slowly. Mist rushes in.

I grab Badh-o's tail and yank the two of them back as hard as I can. They hit my chest with a thunk. But just as quickly, they're moving, sliding back to my shoulders. I sigh with relief.

Mist pours through the wider opening. It fills the floor. I pull myself higher, walking my feet up the wall to stay above the mist line. Badh-o lets out a high-pitched sound. I glance down, and then go white with fear when I see the mist is only a few inches below me.

I put all my faith in this single sconce and pull myself higher, breathing hard, every muscle in my body straining.

This is as high as I can get.

"Tell me when it clears out of the window," I gasp to my vines. Any second, I'll suddenly feel the life drain out of me. The mist will reach me and suck out my soul. Or the sconce will break, and I will fall into Crenfyre's embrace. I squeeze my eyes shut.

I don't know how long we wait. It feels like hours, but it is probably less than twenty minutes.

At last, Badh-o squeaks. A happy sound. I twist—and sure enough, the mist has receded to the point that I can step back to the floor. I let out the deep breath I was holding, even though we are far from done here.

"Nadira!"

That is Kaladen's voice.

"What are you doing here?"

He is somewhere in the hallway.

"Kaladen!" I call. "Are you safe?"

"Enough!" he shouts back. "But you?"

"I'm fine!" I reply.

He appears beside me, stepping out of the dream realm very, very close to me. He grabs my wet shoulders to steady himself as he quickly surveys the room for Crenfyre.

"What are you doing here?" I ask in a breathless whisper. "You're supposed to be at the rainforest portal. And how are you moving through the dream realm with Crenfyre filling it up?"

"Dangerously," he replies with a dry, unamused curl of his lip. "Stepping between the realms is not safe. Crenfyre moves differently in each." His eyes scour me for sign of injury. When he kneels to the gash on my leg, I yank it away.

"Don't you dare weaken yourself to heal me," I hiss. At his tortured look, I add, "Not yet."

His voice drops as he releases me and stands. "I didn't think I would see you again."

He isn't answering my questions. My lungs seize. "Kaladen. What happened at the rainforest portal?"

His eyes meet mine, then check the progress of Crenfyre. It leaves us this pocket, staying in its steady stream toward the window. At any moment, however, it might sense our presence. I can barely draw a full breath.

Kaladen sighs. It is a dead, resigned sound. "I kept it safe until Crenfyre. But Crenfyre's break was too strong. I couldn't keep it out. I had to escape. As far as I know, it devoured everything inside."

My mouth falls open. The entire portal—destroyed? Our sacred haven? The only place where time stopped, where we could rest, where we had all those beautiful memories? "The skyreavers?"

"Gone."

I turn my head away. That nagging inside me grows stronger.

There is another way. There is a missing piece. Something we don't understand about Crenfyre.

"I need to get into the hallway," I say. "I need to get to Crenfyre."

His face darkens. "Why?"

The mist on the floor suddenly turns toward us. I curse. Kaladen grabs me and the two vines in a flash and drags us aside as the mist surges toward our corner. It finds nothing and circles toward us, forcing us to take the risky leap across the stream in the center of the room to the far side.

"Get me out of this room," I gasp. "Get me to Crenfyre."

"I will get you out of this room," Kaladen growls in reply.

I lower my brow. "Get. Me. To. Crenfyre."

He matches my stubbornness inch for inch. "Why?"

"I'm going inside."

His sudden grip on my shoulders is excruciating. "You cannot enter Crenfyre. No one can."

"You thought the skyreavers could! And you clearly were in this hallway because you were trying to think of something to do!"

"You don't have wings!"

"But I can climb. I can swing from rope. I have my ice magic. I can get above the mist."

His face is a twisted mask of fury. "I know I cannot keep you from dying tonight, but—"

"So let me die this way, Kaladen. Let me choose it. Don't make me spend all night running from the mist until I'm so exhausted I'm glad when it finally devours me! One of us has to go into Crenfyre. We've both known it, but none of us have admitted it. Mindless skyreavers couldn't save us. One of us has to figure out how to get into Crenfyre, and it cannot be you."

Once upon a time, I could not fathom willingly walking to my own death. I could not take my life no matter how hard I tried.

But there are things I love now more than my own life. I will gladly lay it down.

"Why can't it be me?" Kaladen demands. "I'm the Neverseen King. If someone enters it, it *must* be me."

"Because if you fall, we all fall!" I hiss. "No one else can control the Bridge. We need you to survive the night if there is to be *any* hope for *any* world to be salvaged. You're too valuable."

He cups my face with gentleness that rattles through my anger. "There is nothing more valuable to me than you."

Tears well up and spill over my cheeks. I reach up and touch the rough edges of his jaw. "But that doesn't matter now, does it, husband?"

He curses. Then we're moving again, dodging the reaching fingers of Crenfyre. I realize belatedly that it is tracking the rainwater dripping off my clothes. There's nothing I can do about that—it will follow me until it catches me and devours me.

But it is Kaladen who catches me the next moment in a bruising kiss. It lasts only a second, and then he pulls away.

"Let's get you to Crenfyre," he rasps.

CHAPTER 32

KALADEN

IT TAKES CAREFUL, meticulous work to get out of the room and into the hallway. Nadira is thrilled when I pull out one of her same *jurbah* ropes and we use that to swing across mist paths as opportunity presents itself. I rack my brain every second as we puzzle through our options, using weapons stabbed into the wall as ways to stay above the mist's reaches. It does not fill every inch of the hallway, but it fills enough to make it nearly impossible to cross.

If only there was some other way!

How can I stand by and let her walk into that death trap? Every instinct begs me to do the opposite. We're both still alive—it's truly a miracle. I could not believe it when I caught her scent so close. I could not believe she was in this palace and *alive*. Even now, I keep looking at her, soaking in every detail of her scarred, scratched face, her soaked clothes that stick to her skin, her strong hands that work so hard. I spent so long waiting for the snap of the bond between us. The loss of her heartbeat. I didn't think I would see her again, but here she is.

And now I'm helping her get to Crenfyre.

We reach the portal itself.

There is a small patch of ground we tentatively hold beside the opening, watching the mist move around us, slithering and searching dangerously close. The cracked, gray wood of the portal's doors are flung wide, its rusted hinges broken open. The world beyond is white, and all we can see is mist pouring out. An endless appetite searching and searching and searching. Mist swirls around the engraved skeletons on the door.

"Go with him," Nadira says, peeling her two vines off her shoulder and handing them to me. Badh-a comes quickly, but Badh-o lets out a wail and clings. "Don't be silly," she says, tears choking her voice. "I'll be back soon."

The lie has no scent, not like fae lies, and yet it stings me as if it does.

"Take her," Nadira hisses as I pry the crying Badh-o away. She glances down at our feet to see just how close the mist comes to her ankle. We're too deep into this—even if she changed her mind and decided not to enter Crenfyre, she could never make it back out of this palace. Not even with my help.

I might not be able to make it out myself.

Don't let her do this, my heart pleads. *Don't let her die. You cannot let her die.*

But I must let her die. I must let her do this. Though I hate it with every fiber of my being. I always knew any second wife I took would die tonight, just as my first died last Lulythinar.

Lulythinar will always take everything from me.

I remember those cold, dark ninety-nine years after Liliana's death. If I survive this night while Nadira dies, there will be more cold, dark years ahead. Years where I will be gutted and broken and alone. Years I will long for my wife to return to me. Years where I will mourn that I lost not just her soul, but her body too, so I couldn't bury her in the stars as I wished. Years where I will wish for even a glimpse of her face, a note of her laughter, or a single word from her mouth.

It will ruin me.

And yet, somehow, I will survive this. I survived Liliana's loss when I thought such a thing was impossible. Nadira made me see that life can continue. I cannot believe it now, but I know it is true. The only way it won't be true is if I give up on life and give up on happiness.

Nadira has fashioned several steps out of ice, putting her almost above the line of the mist. When she looks back at me, I memorize every line of her face, the way her black eyes pierce straight through to my soul.

And then, just as I finally truly let Liliana go, I let Nadira go.

"I love you," I say.

She smiles at me. "You are the best thing that ever happened to me, Kaladen."

Then she uses her ice to make one more step, and she is above the line of the mist. She takes the rope, makes a loop at the end, and tosses it inside the portal—high. Somehow, it catches on something. She pulls it tight. My heart pounds straight out of my chest. Thousands of knives seem to pierce every inch of my skin.

Nadira wraps the rope around her hand, gives one last glance at me, and then swings into the portal. The mist swallows her whole.

A moment later, an empty rope swings back out.

CHAPTER 33

NADIRA

AT FIRST, THE world is blindingly white.

I fly through the air, my hold on the rope gone. I wonder if I'm already dead, and death is white.

Then I hit the ground with an impact that jars through my body. I roll to minimize the impact, and when I get my feet under me, the whiteness clears.

A bleak tableau appears before me. The ground is dried, cracked clay, leached of its vibrant orange until it is a dull gray. The sky is . . . nothing. White stretches as far as I can see. It is nothing but endless sky and the cracking ground.

Mist swirls along the ground. It rushes past me toward the door, too hungry for the world beyond to waste its time with the meager offering of me.

Except that does not feel quite right.

If I didn't know better, I would think Crenfyre watched me and intentionally kept me alive. But that cannot be right. Even when I took part of the heart from Roltwart, I never had this sense of being watched like I have now. Portals are not sentient. Not . . . *truly*.

"Find the anchor," I murmur to myself, trying to focus the unease rattling inside of me. There must be an anchor. And perhaps instead of capturing mist, I could grab a handful of cracked clay. That would be easier to transport.

I turn in circles, but there is nothing as far as I can see. It is so . . . *empty*.

Awareness follows each of my steps as I mark twelve paces and begin making my circle around the portal's door. That awareness crawls up my spine, my neck, spreading its attention like fingers into my hair. The mist swirls close to me, but doesn't touch.

Suddenly, I stop.

I turn around and tilt my head back. "You want something from me, Crenfyre. Show me what it is."

There is no denying it. A sentience beyond anything I've ever experienced in another world follows me, listens to me. It doesn't seem possible that Crenfyre, the mindless killing parasite, would be the one with true sentience. But I cannot deny it any longer. There is more here than magic simply seeking balance.

As long as it thinks I'm useful, it won't devour me.

I wait. No reply comes. The mist stirs stronger, fanning across the cracked ground.

Something catches my eye. Is that . . . color?

It is just the faintest dot, like a tiny smear of paint across a blank canvas. I quicken my step. The mist grows faster, more agitated. Still, it does not touch me. I keep walking until I get close enough to see what this is.

The mist rushes forward, wrapping around the small thing so completely that it blocks my view.

"I need to understand," I tell Crenfyre. "I won't touch it."

The mist churns, as though conflicted. It rushes toward me—to devour me. My heart leaps to my throat, but I manage to hold my ground.

The mist careens to a halt in front of my toes.

I let out my breath. Then I say again, "Help me understand. Please."

The mist stays where it is. It thrums in the air, along the ground.

Then, at last, it parts.

My lips part.

There, in the center of a ring of protective mist, is the tiniest green sapling. It is two inches high, with one single curled leaf.

And suddenly, it makes sense.

"You aren't trying to devour the worlds," I whisper, stunned. "You never were. You only wanted to keep this sapling alive. So you fought to break out of your prison. You consumed all the life you could find—for this."

The mist rises and swirls like a storm around me. Wind pulls my hair and clothes in every direction. But *still*, the mist doesn't touch me. I can feel its anger, its pain, its deep, deep hurt. It rises up from the ground, sinks down from the sky.

I remember the storybook portal again. The illustration of the Great Kings. The fissure down the center of Crenfyre's door. What am I still not seeing? What am I missing?

Slowly, I lower to my knees before the sapling. The mist turns to a howling rage as I reach out one hand. I pause, letting it rage, waiting. And when I feel its eyes upon me again, I touch the sapling's single leaf.

The mist vanishes into nothing. As if it never existed.

The leaf is soft, almost velvet-like. I stroke it gently, as I stroked Badh-o.

Then, without realizing it, I place my other hand on the cracked clay. A voice fills my head.

I won't let him sand you.

Every thought, every feeling careens to a halt inside me.

I won't let him sand you, the voice repeats. Then, slightly more tentatively: *Hello, my friend.*

I am gasping, air ripping in and out of my lungs. *House?* I ask. My palm shakes against the cracked clay. *Is that you?*

Is that you? it replies. Then: *My friend.*

"What are you doing here?" I choke, planting both hands on the ground. *Why are you here?*

I'll be back later.

"No, no," I growl in desperate frustration. The House's phrases are so limited, we can hardly communicate. I draw a deep breath and exhale. I try again, giving it things to say back to me. *I am alright. I am not alright.*

I am . . . It trails off, as though it does not know which answer it should pick.

I am trapped in Crenfyre. I am not trapped in Crenfyre, I offer it.

Still, it does not respond, as though neither option is true. I take another fortifying inhale. I shut my eyes. I see the illustration of the cracked door again. *I am Crenfyre. I am not Crenfyre.*

This time, it responds quickly.

I am Crenfyre.

My breath whooshes out of me. I sit there, hands planted on the ground, too stunned to move. To even form thoughts.

My friend?

My friend, I assure back.

My friend.

I look at that sapling before me. My brain isn't connecting these pieces. It is all here. I just need to somehow make them fit together—

"Oh." I stop. The word slips between my lips again. "*Oh.*"

Then I'm pressing my palms into the ground, not caring about the sharp edges. My words are spewing out, too fast. *You are the House. The home of the Bridge. But you are also Crenfyre . . . because the Great Kings split you in half. They took your portal and cut you in half. They took your life and they left your death. They used your life to power the Bridge. They took just enough destruction to make the House's defenses. And they left just enough life behind for this sapling. Yes? No?*

Yes.

My heart is raging inside my chest. The mist may be gone, but the storm has come to life inside me. *You didn't always look like this, did you? You were green once. Beautiful, once.*

Yes.

You just want to reunite with yourself. Sweat drips down my face, even though I am not hot. *You want to be whole again.*

Yes.

That was why the House was acting so strange, so *excited* as Lulythinar drew closer. It wanted to reunite. It wanted to go home.

My ribs ache from the pressure cracking me open from the inside. Tears are streaming down my face even before I realize it. I know what it means to want to be whole. To want to go home. To not be a monster.

You want me to help you.

Yes.

I rake a dirty hand through my damp hair and blow a stray strand out of my face. *I don't know how to help you. This is so much bigger than I could have imagined. Assuming I* could *reintegrate the two parts of yourself, how would the Bridge stay intact? What about the other portals? How do we keep them from breaking open?*

No, my friend!

No? I ask, looking up. I try to puzzle through what I just said and what it is that Crenfyre is objecting to. *Are you saying . . . the other portals wouldn't break open?*

Yes.

And then it suddenly makes sense. *The House breaks down the portals! Because it is trying to get back to you!*

Yes, my friend.

But if we reunite you, what will hold the Bridge together?

No.

The Bridge will fall.

Yes.

I sit back on my heels. *I will think of how to fix this. But I need you to withdraw* all *of your mist from the worlds. Right now.*

No, my friend.

Yes, I say forcefully. *You are killing everything. You must stop. If you want me to try to save you, then you must stop killing everything. Pull the mist back. Don't take any more life.*

My friend.

Do it, Crenfyre! Don't fight with me. You are my friend, but I will not let you kill everyone I love. If you don't stop, you will not be my friend. You will be my enemy.

Mist rises from the ground. A threat to me.

I clench my jaw and glare at that mist. *Pull your mist back. Now.*

A gust of wind, like a sigh, rushes across my face. *Yes, my friend.*

I sag in relief, and then the wind becomes a tornado. I twist to look over my shoulder at the door. Mist rushes back inside as fast as it went out, pooling across the ground and sinking into the clay. My relief is quickly followed by dread that I didn't move fast enough, that even this won't be enough. And what will happen when I cannot fix Crenfyre? It will think I'm a traitor, and it will destroy everything it can in revenge.

When the last of the mist returns, I swallow hard. I place my hand back on the ground. *Thank you, my friend. Will you let me bring Kaladen inside? Will you let him live?*

The mist rises as the voice fills me. *Enemy. Enemy. Enemy.*

Friend, not enemy, I tell it.

Enemy. Sand you.

I smile despite myself. *He will never sand me. He loves me. He is my friend, and he is the only one with the power enough to help you. I will ask him to help you. Will you let him come? Will you promise not to kill him?*

Enemy, it replies stubbornly.

Promise?

Promise, it growls at last.

I get up, dust off my sirwal, and march to the portal's door. I throw it open. "Kaladen Ashrift Felladyr! You are needed!"

CHAPTER 34

NADIRA

KALADEN IS WAITING just outside the portal, and his eyes nearly fall out of his head when I emerge. "Nadira!"

I hold up one hand before he can wrap me up in his crushing embrace. "You've got to hurry. Crenfyre agreed to let you enter the portal, but it doesn't like you, so be on your best behavior. Now come!"

He must be far too stunned to resist, because I grab his forearm and yank him into the portal without much resistance. He freezes on the threshold, mouth open, whites ringing his irises, staring at the bleak landscape and the mist that swirls along the ground and climbs into tall pillars as though to intimidate him with their height. "Crenfyre," he breathes.

Quickly, I tell him everything I've just learned and show him the sapling. He listens intently, the line deepening between his brows the longer I speak. The mist makes it very clear it doesn't like him, and slithers like a snake close to his feet.

"I don't know how long we have before Crenfyre releases its mist again," I finish. "It was *very* unhappy with my request. What can we do? I don't know enough about magic, but there must be some way we can fix it."

Kaladen is quiet for several long moments. Then he lifts his head. "I have a solution. But Crenfyre won't like it."

"It has to be something Crenfyre likes."

"No," he corrects, "it must be something Crenfyre *agrees* to."

I cross my arms over my chest. "Then . . . what do you suggest?"

When I carefully lay Kaladen's plan before Crenfyre, my palm on the dirt, the mist nearly explodes in rage. It spins around us like a whirlpool, ready to close in and devour us. I keep my voice steady as I say inside my mind, *I won't let him sand you, my friend. I promise. If you hate this, we will put everything back the way it was. We will only keep it this way if you agree to it.*

A sense of agitation curls into my arm. Crenfyre is trying to reply, but it does not have the words. I try to think of what it might want to say.

You fear I will betray you.

Betray, it immediately replies. *Yes, betray.*

I will not betray you, I promise, *but you have every right to be afraid of it.*

Betray! Betray! Betray!

I look at Kaladen. He won't like this. *I will stay here, inside your world, as your prisoner, as long as you feel that you are treated unfairly. Will you allow it then? Will you let Kaladen try his plan?*

There is a long hesitation. I wait. And wait. And wait.

Kaladen grows impatient beside me, shifting his weight between his feet, but I refuse to rush this.

I will be your hostage. You can use me as leverage against Kaladen, I tell it. *Will you let him try?*

Yes.

I sag in relief, a grin breaking out across my face. I turn to Kaladen. "You can commence. I will stay until Crenfyre approves."

Suspicion flashes across his features. "Stay? Did . . . Did you just offer yourself as a hostage?"

"Just be glad I'm not dead!" I cry. "Hurry—this is our only chance!"

The mist swirls around us, uncertain, afraid, tentatively hopeful, and I feel every one of its conflicting emotions through my palm as Kaladen approaches the sapling. He kneels beside it, gently touches its stem to calm Crenfyre, and then he pulls out a knife.

Crenfyre! Crenfyre! the ageless voice in my head cries as Kaladen digs up the sapling. Its pain spreads through me with an intensity that goes beyond my mortal perception, until I'm shaking from the force of it, my eyes rattling in their sockets, my gut clenching with the need to vomit.

No! No! it screams as Kaladen scoops under the clay and lifts the sapling out of the ground.

I would try to soothe it, but the force of its emotions batters me so soundly I can do nothing but remain on my knees, my lips firmly sealed against my moans, and tremble as the waves roll through me.

With one last glance at me, Kaladen takes the sapling and leaves the portal.

CHAPTER 35

KALADEN

I WORK FAST. The hallways are eerily clear, and though the swarms of Lulythinar magic fill the air, nothing stops me as I cradle Crenfyre's sapling to my chest and run to the banister. Badh-o and Badh-a are gone, having fled after I threatened to eat them if they didn't get out of this palace the second the mist returned to the portal.

When I reach my destination, I gingerly set the sapling down on the bottom step. Immediately, the thrumming energy in the house stills. The energy inside me, however, only billows stronger to life.

I choose a spot in the middle of the entryway. I summon as much magic as I can, close my eyes, and slam that ball of light into the ground. I do it two more times before I have a nicely sized hole. Getting down on my hands and knees, I frantically pull aside the broken bits of tile until I get to the packed ground beneath it. I dig with my fingernails until I'm satisfied.

Then I take the sapling as carefully as I can and plant it in the hole, covering up the delicate roots with soil. The rain has not stopped pouring, so I rush out into the courtyard, scoop up the accumulated rainwater in the broken fountain, and carry it back to the sapling. I water it gently, patting the earth around it.

As a last step, I take the broken tile and rip flagstones from the courtyard and assemble it around the sapling as a protective barrier.

I step back.

I can almost feel the House bending closer to look at it. Curious, tentative.

There is one more thing I must do before I can get my wife back.

I need to destroy the House's defenses.

CHAPTER 36

NADIRA

I FEEL THE difference in Crenfyre when Kaladen returns. The portal's ache became too much, and I collapsed to the ground. Lying with my whole body pressed against the dried clay, I can sense every subtle shift in the portal's demeanor. There is no warmth in it now. The sapling is gone. The last bit of goodness is gone. Crenfyre is nothing but destruction and death now. That deeper severance could slice me clean in half.

Crenfyre surges suddenly, and I know Kaladen is back.

But I haven't the strength to get up. I need to send my voice into the ground and make sure Crenfyre will let Kaladen enter without killing him. I don't have strength for that either.

I lie there, full of nothing but the depths of Crenfyre's pain at its loss over the centuries, and its sharper loss from moments ago when Kaladen took its sapling.

The door opens.

The mist surges. Pure hatred and destruction leaps forward.

It's going to kill him, I realize with a sharp thump of my heart. *It's going to kill him and I cannot get up.*

"I will not seal you tonight, Crenfyre!" Kaladen's shout hits me like a blow. "Let me take my wife and leave. Then you can have the Bridge. All of it. Until Lulythinar is over."

Crenfyre pauses.

"This is the deal I make with you," my husband calls. "I offer the part of you that was stolen to make the House's defenses."

I cannot open my eyes, but I sense when he places something on the ground. It pulses and beats. *My heart.* Not *mine*, I correct myself, but Crenfyre's. And only a piece of its violent, destructive half, but the possessiveness that flares in the ground is followed by temporary satisfaction.

"I offer you this part of your heart, as I took the sapling from you and united it with the House. You are now fully severed—but not forever. I offer you this deal, Crenfyre. For a hundred years, you remain severed. Your destruction, and your creation split in half. But every Lulythinar, from dusk to dawn, you will be fully reunited with the House. The entire Bridge will be yours. You will be whole again every hundred years."

Whole again, Crenfyre aches into my body. *Whole again.*

"In exchange, I want my wife back. Alive. Will you accept this deal, Crenfyre?"

A resounding pulse rises from the ground. *Yes.*

Then, suddenly, the pain leaves me. The ache is gone. I gasp, breathing hard, and I roll onto my back.

"Crenfyre says yes," I croak.

The next instant, Kaladen is scooping me up into his arms. I expect him to kiss me, to hold me, to rejoice with me. But his face is wreathed in panic. He clutches me to his chest and races out of Crenfyre. He doesn't run down the hallway, but crosses into the spare room, climbs into the windowsill, and leaps to the ground below.

"Kaladen!" I cry, terrified as weightlessness envelopes me, and then we're hitting the ground, his body shielding mine as we roll.

He's up the next instant, still holding me close, and runs faster than humanly possible through the courtyard and out to the palace gates. We careen through the gate and then he unceremoniously dumps me on the ground before wheeling around and slamming the ice-crusted gate shut. He squeezes his eyes shut, places his palms on the gate, and murmurs a spell.

I don't know what the spell is, nor can I even make out the words he speaks, but the force of it billows out from him, rising with each syllable, building and building and building.

Then a glow of light coming from the palace drags my attention away from him. My lips part, a question on my tongue—

The light grows.

And then the entire palace explodes.

CHAPTER 37

NADIRA

KALADEN STAGGERS AWAY from the gate—something I hear, rather than see. My eyes are open, but I'm met only with darkness.

"It's done," Kaladen gasps. The words are utter disbelief. "It's done."

I blink rapidly. Slowly, the blackness clears. I'm lying on wet sand, several feet from Kaladen. Both of us—alive, whole. I can hardly believe it. The rain has stopped, and only distant thunder rumbles.

Kaladen isn't looking at me. He's looking at the palace.

I follow his gaze. Did the explosion mean that the Bridge . . . *broke*? What happened to all those worlds? Can they survive the leveling and burning of the palace?

I blink again.

The palace isn't leveled.

It stands as tall and strong as I've ever seen it. And it is awash in blinding color.

Every color of the rainbow dances together, shooting from the windows, the doors, even the crevices between the stones. I stare in stunned awe.

"What happened?" I breathe.

"Crenfyre reunited with the House," Kaladen says, his voice equally awed. "It will stay like this until morning. I sealed the gates so it doesn't seep out by accident."

"And then?"

"And then it will return to its portal until the next Lulythinar."

"But the other portals—"

"They won't break open." His shoulders tremble, but not from fear—from a profound weight lifted. The light from the palace plays across the weathered, yet beautiful lines of his dear face. "We fixed the balance on two levels. Crenfyre was split, but it had *just enough* life to make it unstable, and the House likewise had *just enough* death to make *it* unstable. Now the split is final, fully stable. And the reunion every Lulythinar made the two halves whole again."

"So . . . moving forward?" I ask. "What does this mean?"

Now Kaladen truly smiles. He turns that smile on me. The vibrancy of it stills everything inside me. "It means the seals will never break down again. It means Crenfyre and the House won't be constantly wearing down the Bridge to reunite. It means I can open and close the portals at will. And it means the Bridge will never collapse at Lulythinar again."

It's so much. Too much. Far more than I could have imagined.

I lick my lips and get to my feet, sidling up to Kaladen. "Then you're saying . . . my blood is useless, and you don't need me anymore."

"Great Kings confound you, woman!" Kaladen cries, and then kisses me with all the force radiating from the united Bridge.

CHAPTER 38

NADIRA

"YOU SHOULD HAVE warned me about the change of plans," comes a rasping, drawling voice from behind us.

Kaladen and I whirl. There is Trenian, barely on his feet, staggering at the edge of Risya, bleeding from wounds on his chest, his shoulder, leg, and side.

"I only just so *happened* to not be inside the gates when . . . whatever just happened, happened. And both of you are looking remarkably unscathed."

"You survived!" I cry. I break out of Kaladen's arms and practically tackle the prince with a hug. "I was worried about you!"

The prince goes stiff at my embrace and for a moment, doesn't embrace me back. "Um . . . I'm Trenian. From Valehaven."

"Yes, I was worried about you, you idiot. Despite my better judgment, of course."

The last comment earns me a smirk of amusement and a one-armed squeeze. "That's more like it. Now release me. I'm not the hugging sort, especially with abdominal injuries. Kaladen, old boy, could I trouble you for just a little bit of that healing magic? So I can ascend to my throne some day and wreak havoc on your life?"

Kaladen shakes his head as he strides over and places one hand on the worst wound.

"Ah, careful!" Trenian spits.

Kaladen presses harder. "Don't be a baby. And I'm not giving you much."

Trenian winces but lifts his eyes past Kaladen, past me, to the glowing palace. For a moment, the pain washes away from the beautiful lines of his face, as though he looks upon a most spectacular vision. "I pity all the fools who will die in the outpouring of my father's wrath when he hears of this."

"Will you be one of them?" I ask.

"Not yet." The prince flashes white teeth. "He still needs me to produce an heir. He'll find some other way to punish me for my part in this. But it won't matter." His grin turns wicked. "I bested him in this round, and I got exactly what I needed: the Neverseen King's favor—worth more now than any of us could have imagined with *this* development." He waves a hand at the palace. Then he meets Kaladen's glower with the sunniest of expressions. "I will take down the High King, and you are going to help me when the time comes. Don't give me that face. I know you regret owing me, but look how hale and whole your queen is. You would do it again in a heartbeat."

I walk past them before a fight breaks out and they tear each other to pieces. "I'm going to see the city."

Kaladen shoots me a look—a look warning me to be prepared for anything. I firm my spine and hurry into the slick, muddy streets. Lightning flashes overhead, but the rain does not begin again. I go straight to the guardhouse.

"Tariq!" I call desperately. "Tariq!"

Everywhere I turn are bodies. Bodies of all kinds, but the most frightening are the number of guard bodies I find. Men burned by fire, torn to pieces, impaled and lying in their own blood.

My throat aches as I scream, "*Tariq!*"

An audible gasp makes me whirl. I search the bodies on the ground desperately, calling for my friend. "Tariq! Tariq!"

The croak is almost inaudible. "Here."

I spot him at last. He lies in the street beside the massive, gleaming body of a dead dragon. He has two deep puncture wounds in his gut that bleed hard and fast. He is on his back, struggling to breathe as I fall to my knees beside him. His clothes are wet and torn, his blood pooling on the wet paving stones, his scimitar fallen out of reach of his hand. His hair is burned, along with parts of his face.

"Kaladen Ashrift Felladyr!" I call harshly under my breath. I take Tariq's hand in both of mine. "Hold on a moment longer. Kaladen is coming. He will heal you."

My mind flashes back to Eshe's death. Part of me writhes and shrieks with desperation that this is about to end the exact same way it did last time. Kaladen won't come, and Tariq will die. I squeeze my eyes shut and tell myself *no*.

"Are you alright?" Tariq asks haltingly. "The palace?"

"We won," I tell him with a smile through the emotion clogging my throat. "We fixed everything. This will never happen again."

Tariq answers my smile with a bloody one of his own. "Good." He lifts one weak hand and points at the scales shining at each bolt of lightning across the sky. "I killed a dragon." His smile turns a little rueful. "I also got bit by one."

I squeeze his hand. "Your grandchildren won't believe the stories you tell them."

He gives a small laugh, then winces from the pain.

And then Kaladen is there.

My shoulders sag in relief as his hands cover the gaping wounds quickly. Tariq sucks in a sharp breath, but after a few moments, the tension begins to leak from his body as the wound slowly knits together.

"Need to send for Kanza," Tariq gasps mid-healing. "I need to know if they made it. I need to know if my men . . . if their deaths were . . ."

"We will send someone. Hold still," I tell him, squeezing his hand. "I promise you that no one's death was in vain."

He relaxes at that, his head falling back against the cobblestones as Kaladen continues his work.

"You killed a dragon, eh?" Kaladen says, jerking his head toward the beast. "Nadira couldn't kill one of those."

My jaw falls open as Kaladen's mouth curls upward at my outrage.

Another moan drags my attention away from his playful jab. I let go of Tariq's hand and get to my feet. "I need to collect the injured. We need to see who we can save. And I'll send someone for Kanza." I shoot a stern look at Kaladen. "Please don't overextend yourself. We might need more of your healing."

He smiles at me. "I know."

I take off running, searching for the moan I just heard and signs of life. The work is grim, heavy. Sorting through bodies, checking for pulses, searching through streets and alleyways and in buildings, calling for anyone to respond if they can hear me. I find a young guard alive and unscathed—only terrified. He is the one I send after Kanza. The other able-bodied survivors join me in the efforts. Trenian helps for several hours before he has to return to Valehaven to finish recovering from his wounds.

Despite the heaviness, there is no crushing pressure on my lungs. The night is thick around us, and my exhaustion catches up to me. The minor wounds I've sustained begin to bother me more. For the first time in hours, I notice that I'm hungry.

But none of this matters.

We survived. We did it. Somehow, despite everything, the Bridge still stands. Arbasa, though cut and bruised, still stands. The human and fae worlds will go on.

I had hoped for a chance to halt the impending destruction. It feels far too abundant that any of us would have made it out alive. I have my life, Kaladen's life, and the lives of many others. It is so much more than I could have hoped or dreamed.

At one point, I climb the stairs of the guardhouse all the way to the top floor. I push open the first door, my heart pounding for fear at what I might find.

But there is Eshe's body. Untouched. Just as I left it. Beautiful. Peaceful.

We work all night. The scout returns on horseback in the early watches of the morning to report that not a single life was lost in Kanza's group. Tariq nearly collapses again after barely regaining his strength. Kaladen does his best to measure his healing so he can bring as many injured men back from the brink as he can. He still passes out—but only after tending the last person.

I force him awake with a splash of water across his face an hour later. He is about to growl some curse at me when I hand him another full bucket of water.

"You'll need to dump this on me in a few minutes," I say, swaying from exhaustion. "But first, there's something you need to see."

We leave the guardhouse and step into the streets of Risya as the sky turns pink. The clouds have cleared, and a bright dawn blooms on the horizon. The vivid light of the palace dims from the brilliance of the rising sun.

I take his hand and we lean against each other. "Dawn came again."

EPILOGUE

NADIRA

THE WEDDING BETWEEN Tariq and Kanza a year later surprised no one, nor did their adoption of every orphan they could fit in their new home. They worked with me and Kaladen to ensure the rest were well taken care of in every capacity. The event was the first grand celebration since Lulythinar. Kaladen, with his expert taste in fashion, selected the clothes for everyone involved. I hosted the foreign dignitaries who came as guests—despite the fact that neither bride nor groom were royalty—and cut several excellent trading deals to bring even more prosperity to the kingdom Kaladen and I toiled to rebuild from the dust. Tariq was far too anxious about leaving the guardhouse, but Kaladen told him if he did not take his new bride to the ocean and celebrate their marriage, he would dismiss him entirely from the post. Kanza was radiantly happy during the procession down the full, bustling streets of Risya, and radiantly beautiful in the most lavish turquoise gown. She asked me in her shy way to be her handmaiden for the day—and then quickly asked if it was inappropriate for a queen to have such a role. I told her that perhaps it was inappropriate for a queen, but never for a friend. She liked that. And I liked being at her side throughout the extravagant celebrations.

These days, Badh-o and Badh-a rarely give me any time alone. They follow at my heels and want to participate in everything I'm doing. Badh-o with sweet enthusiasm, and Badh-a always pretending she only *happened* to be going the same direction as me.

Tonight, Kaladen works late with his new steward and Zara, who has become the steward's apprentice. I wait for him in the room he furnished for me in our quarters. The décor is earth-toned and understated, with small details of beauty. He fashioned quartz into replicas of my ice magic as holders for the *lumiral* globes. I have a vast desk with a very comfortable chair to work on whatever I please—which usually involves running figures for new trade agreements and researching enterprises to invest in. Bookshelves, full of Emin's notes, line one wall, and a beautiful painting hangs on the opposite wall. The painting is of the waterfall in the rainforest portal. A place that will never be the same again after Crenfyre's destruction, but I love to look at the vibrant green and remember the special memories Kaladen and I shared there.

As the sun descends, casting slanted, golden shadows across my room, I decide I'm done waiting. I get up, draw a linen robe around my shoulders, and venture out of our quarters. The hallways are peaceful. Quiet. Still.

Dying sunlight cuts through latticework into the portico where the Neverseen King gave me his name for the first time. The name that no one else has but me and him. My breath moves deeply through my body as I walk and bask in the last light of day. I reach the entryway. A tree rises from the center of the room, just beside the banister. It is nearly as tall as the ceiling now. It has started spreading its branches wide instead of high to keep growing. I smile at the sight of it. Kaladen keeps saying he is going to cut a hole through the top of the palace so the tree can keep growing forever and ever, but I do like to think there is a limit to its height.

When I place my hand on the banister, a soft, content voice spills into my consciousness. *My friend.*

My friend, I reply.

"Taking an evening stroll?"

I turn. My husband strides down the corridor toward me. He stopped wearing shadows when the Wolf came, and he never donned them again. I am glad for it. I love seeing his face. I love the peace in his eyes now. I love seeing the upright way he holds himself—never again burdened with a load he cannot carry.

He is still the Neverseen King, but to me, he is just Kaladen.

"I got tired of waiting for you," I say cheekily as he reaches my side.

He bends down and kisses me. "My everlasting apologies, Queen Nadira. As penance, may I join you?"

I laugh and hook my arm in his. The sun has completely set down, darkness fallen across the palace. A soft breeze caresses my hair, catches the edge of my robe. The House remains still and quiet. There is no rush to get to our rooms before the sun goes down. Never again.

We step out into the courtyard. The fountain burbles happily. The new palm trees are still rather small and stubby, but one day they will be grand and glorious like their predecessors.

There is no moon tonight. I am glad for it.

Kaladen wraps his arms around me, pulling my body backward against his, tucking my head beneath his chin. We look up at the starry sky. Emin's constellation winks at us. My eyes settle on a different constellation, however. This one has several stars in a flowing line, like a wild lock of hair, and another arrangement in a profile I know so well. It is a constellation that never sets with the seasons. I take great comfort from its constant presence.

"I wish Eshe could have seen all of this," I whisper. "How far we came."

Kaladen smiles against my hair. "I think she knew all along this was how things would end. We were the blind fools with no hope. That was not Eshe."

I let out a soft laugh and turn, just enough to glimpse the darkness where the sun waits to rise. "I think you're right. She always was smarter than us."

Kaladen's chuckle is as warm as the squeeze of his arms around me.

BONUS MATERIAL

Want to see exclusive artwork of the Neverseen King?
Download it here:

AnastasisBlythe.com/Kaladen

PRINCE TRENIAN'S STORY CONTINUES IN

A shy, dutiful human princess.
A cunning, vengeful Fae prince.
Will their arranged marriage cost them their hearts . . .
or their lives?

Princess Isabelle Louise was raised for one thing: to secure a marriage alliance for the good of her people. All her hopes for a kind husband are dashed when the dark and dangerous Prince Trenian of the Fae comes seeking a human princess for his bride.

Suddenly married and thrust into a world of vicious magic and lethal bargains, Isabelle discovers too late the secret her bridegroom concealed from her: that she is the key to his plan to usurp the throne.And now she is the object of the High King's wrath.

Is any chance at trust and affection gone before their marriage has even begun? Or will she even survive her first night as the bride of the Fae Prince?

MORE FROM ANASTASIS BLYTHE

THE ZHENINGHAI CHRONICLES

Maiden of Candlelight and Lotuses
Guardian of Talons and Snares
Warrior of Blade and Dusk
Princess of Shadows and Starlight
Captive of Twilight and Treachery
Daughter of Darkness and Dreams

THE KING AND THE ASSASSIN

The Assassin Bride
The Neverseen King
The Nightmare Queen

BRIDES OF THE FAE

Bride of the Fae Prince
Bride of the Midnight Prince
(more to come)

ABOUT THE AUTHOR

Anastasis Blythe makes her home in central Texas with her family. When she's not writing, she gardens, accompanies local bands and choirs on piano, rescues feral cats, and tries to keep up with the laundry. She loves exploring the world through reading, walks in nature, and thoughtful conversations.

To stay connected with her, be sure to sign up for her newsletter at AnastasisBlythe.com/Nadira.

Connect with Anastasis online at:
Website - AnastasisBlythe.com
Instagram - @AnastasisBlythe
Facebook - Anastasis Blythe
Goodreads - Anastasis Blythe

www.ingramcontent.com/pod-product-compliance
Lightning Source LLC
Chambersburg PA
CBHW020336310726
48979CB00015B/2388/J

* 9 7 8 1 9 6 0 6 0 6 1 4 3 *